From the best s
Brenda Youngerman

Public Lies

Outskirts Press, Inc.
Denver, Colorado

The opinions expressed in this manuscript are solely the opinions of the author and do not represent the opinions or thoughts of the publisher. The author represents and warrants that s/he either owns or has the legal right to publish all material in this book.

Public Lies

All Rights Reserved.
Copyright © 2007 Brenda Youngerman
V2.0

Cover Photo © 2007 JupiterImages Corporation. All rights reserved - used with permission.

This book may not be reproduced, transmitted, or stored in whole or in part by any means, including graphic, electronic, or mechanical without the express written consent of the publisher except in the case of brief quotations embodied in critical articles and reviews.

Outskirts Press, Inc.
http://www.outskirtspress.com

ISBN: 978-1-4327-1296-9

Outskirts Press and the "OP" logo are trademarks belonging to Outskirts Press, Inc.

PRINTED IN THE UNITED STATES OF AMERICA

For my three;
You are the moon, the stars and the rainbows;
the place where angels are born and wishes come true

I love you more.

Prologue

She drove through the darkness. Every hair stood at full attention, from the top of her head all the way down her spine. Her muscles, thick as cords of rope and twisting taut to the breaking point, were tightly wound in her neck. Her fingers twitched on the steering wheel. Her eyes darted between the rearview mirror, the side mirrors, and the front window.

Driving usually calmed her down. Not tonight …Not now … Not this time.

She was running from the horror, the evil, the unimaginable.

I'm being followed. I know I am. He's watching every move I make. There is no way I'm going to escape without his knowing. He'll find me.

With every sound, her body jerked. Her tension exaggerated each bump in the road. Every car that passed was an enemy to be dealt with. The two children, fast asleep in the backseat, were unaware of their mother's apprehension. They didn't know their futures were about to be irreversibly altered.

She had given up all hope. This was her only way out.

Chapter One

If Vince Cooper wanted something, he didn't give up, no matter what the cost, who got in the way, or who he had to hurt in his quest. When he discovered Nancy, his wife of six years, had left him, he was seething with anger. Fury and betrayal dominated his core. Nobody crossed Vince without paying the price. She was going to pay for ruining his life! Not only had she left him, she had stolen his children as well.

He barely woke up on Monday, August 22. His cocaine hangover had left him in a daze. He thought Nancy was at work and their two children, four-and-a-half-year-old Frank, and two-and-a-half-year-old Lilly, were at day care.

He tossed and turned the entire day away in bed. He hadn't even bothered to get up for dinner. He slept through it. The realization that something was wrong hit him when he went searching for his wife and kids the next morning.

Groggily, he started in the children's bedroom. He noticed the closet door was open a crack. He peered inside to discover it was empty. Yanking the sliding door off their rollers, he became frantic.

Where the hell are the clothes?

He turned and pulled the top drawer off the dresser so hard that it tumbled to the floor. It was empty. Eyes wild with rage, he scanned the room and noticed all the stuffed animals were missing as well. He returned his attention to the drawers. He moved slowly at first, but his actions became quicker as he discovered that each one held only emptiness. Vince tried hard to keep the bile from coming up as a wave of nausea hit him. The room began to spin. His whole world was gone. He had to get his family back.

Vince and Nancy Cooper lived in a two-bedroom home in Vista Oaks, a small seaside community south of Los Angeles. They owned a small auto parts store that they ran together. Nancy had been raised in the sleepy community of Greenbriar, 150 miles north of Vista Oaks. Her parents, Phillip and Emily Lewiston, and her older sister, Olivia Howard, still lived there. Without thinking about the consequences, Vince got in his truck and drove to Greenbriar. He first headed toward his in-laws' house.

Where else would Nancy go? She has no other friends.

Driving frantically, getting more enraged as he drove, he pulled in front of his in-laws' two-story house, but he didn't see his wife's car. He only got madder.

Where the fuck is that bitch?

Standing six foot tall and weighing 250 pounds, Vince Cooper wasn't a man who would be easily lost in a crowd. That day, he drove through Greenbriar, hoping to find the woman who had stolen his family. Vince had never been very patient. Today wasn't going to be an exception. He saw Nancy's car in Olivia's driveway. He knew she was there. Vince lumbered up to Olivia's front door with sweat pouring from his brow. He demanded to speak with Nancy. He didn't have any idea why everyone was so hostile toward him. He only wanted to talk to his wife.

He never even got the chance. Her uppity asshole father, dressed in his shirt and tie, told him to get lost. Matt, her older brother, a pretentious, big-time lawyer, practically shoved him away.

No one pushes me around like that and gets away with it. I'll make certain of that.

Fuming with rage, he drove back to Vista Oaks.

I'll get even with the entire fucking family. Those lousy Lewistons with their holier-than-thou attitudes. They have everything—money, success, and houses. They're always looking down their noses at me. To hell with them. I don't need them anyway. I'll show them who's boss. I'll tell them a thing or two. First, I need to get my family back.

Vince called Nancy daily, begging her to come back. Five days after she left him, Olivia told him she was gone. Vince didn't believe her. He drove back to Greenbriar to check for himself. Pounding on Olivia's door, he demanded an explanation.

"I don't know, Vince," Olivia tried reasoning with him. A small woman, she barely stood five foot tall and weighed a mere ninety-two pounds. Compared to her, Vince's stature was foreboding. Olivia had to look upward at Vince as she spoke. She wedged herself between the door and the frame as she continued her explanation. "I woke up, and they were gone. She didn't say anything to me after she got off the phone with you yesterday. She was really pale. Whatever you said scared the hell out of her. She just walked into the spare bedroom and closed the door. When I knocked on the door later and asked her if she was all right, she just asked me to leave her alone. She seemed better by dinner. We ate, and she gave the kids a bath and put them to bed."

"Let me see!" he commanded, trying to shove his way

past Olivia.

Her attitude had been kind and gentle throughout the explanation. When he tried to physically remove her, Bryce, Olivia's husband, stopped him.

"No, Vince, you may not just barge into my home like you are God and think you can have your way. If Olivia said she doesn't know where Nancy is, then she doesn't know where Nancy is. Period. End of discussion. Nancy is gone, and we don't know where. If we hear from her, we'll let you know. Good-bye, Vince," Bryce said, slamming his front door in Vince's face.

Bryce engulfed his sobbing wife into his arms as she collapsed.

Vince was livid. His tires squealed as he pulled out of the driveway, leaving marks behind. He didn't have any idea where he was going. He was fuming with rage as he wildly drove away.

How dare Bryce and Olivia Howard treat me that way! I'm Vince Cooper. I will not stand for that! I'll show them who's boss! I'll show everyone!

He didn't believe that Olivia was in the dark about where Nancy had gone. He was absolutely positive that Nancy, Olivia, and Matt were all involved in this together.

There's no way Nancy has enough brains to carry out this plan by herself. She's way too stupid to pull anything off alone! I'll just have to outsmart the whole family if I'm going to get my kids back.

Vince knew he needed to make a serious change if he had any chance of getting his family back. But first, he had to find them. He was fairly certain that Olivia and Matt knew where Nancy went. By the time that Vince discovered Nancy was gone, Matt had gone back home to Connecticut. He was worthless to Vince. His only lead was Olivia, and she wasn't talking to him. Vince had to hire a professional, and that would require money.

During their marriage, Nancy's biggest complaint was Vince's drug use. It ate up most of their money and caused friction in every area of their relationship.

I know she blames me for that, but she used them too! If I could quit using the drugs and start selling them, I could make a lot of money. Then hire a professional investigator to find my family, and she'll come running back to me. That's exactly what I'll do ... starting tomorrow.

Chapter Two

Six years earlier, Nancy Suzanne Lewiston married her Prince Charming, or so she thought, in the backyard of her parents' home. Her sparkling, aqua-blue eyes, vibrant smile, glowing skin, and silky blonde hair could fill a crowded room with warmth. Her effervescent personality, wit, and charm surrounded her with a loving family and abundant friends. That was until she was married. Everything changed after that.

On Saturday, August 20, Nancy called her sister and simply asked, "Oli, can I bring the kids and stay with you for a while?"

Oli was the name Nancy had always called her big sister. They had been very close growing up. They were best friends as well as sisters.

Olivia didn't hesitate, "Of course, why would you even think you had to ask?"

"Because …" Nancy started to cry.

"Nance, is everything all right?"

"No," she answered as she sniffled. "I'm so tired. I'm so tired of being tired. I'm tired of being scared all the time. I just need to leave, and I'm scared to leave. He'll never let me leave."

"Slow down. I don't know what you're talking about." Olivia tried calming her sister down.

"I just needed to make sure that I could go to you if I left. That's all," Nancy said in a hushed tone.

"You can come here, Nancy. Any time. Any day."

Two days later, a bedraggled Nancy arrived at Olivia's door with her two children. As Olivia opened her front door, she couldn't help but notice how fragile her sister looked. The once-bright eyes now had dark circles under them, creating a hollow, sunken look. The sparkling, aqua-blue color had turned into a lusterless shade of gray. Her cheeks were drawn. The long, silken locks of blonde hair were now dull and dry. Nancy looked like a strong wind would blow her over.

"Hi, Frank! Hi, Lilly!" Olivia said to the children, trying to maintain her composure. "Remember me? I'm Aunt Olivia. Would you like something to eat?" Frank and Lilly both clung tightly to their mother for comfort, unsure of where they were, or who their Aunt Olivia was. Part of the control Vince had wielded over Nancy included secluding her from her family.

Nancy looked at her children and said, "How about *Sesame Street*?"

Both children smiled and nodded agreement. After Nancy managed to settle Frank and Lilly in front of a television set, she went in search of her sister.

"Nancy, you look awful! What's going on?" Olivia demanded.

Nancy immediately broke down into tears.

"Oli, I've made a major mess out of my life. I married a drug addict, and I didn't even know it."

Olivia was speechless.

"To make matters worse," Nancy sobbed, "he's

managed to take everything away from me. I was arrested a couple months ago after I bought his drugs. He convinced the court that the drugs were for me."

"Oh, Nancy, why didn't you tell me?" Olivia held her sister.

"I thought you wouldn't believe me."

"I'm so sorry. I wish I had known."

"Vince is two different people. The world sees the nice Vince, the one he wants people to see. I see the mean, controlling, jealous, possessive Vince. If I'm out of his sight, he needs to know who I'm with. Even then, he never believes anything I say. It doesn't matter what I do. It's never good enough. The dinner isn't right. There's never enough sex. The house isn't clean enough. The clothes aren't folded right. It just doesn't matter."

Nancy paused for a moment.

"He kept telling me I was stupid and ugly. No one would want to have anything to do with me, and I believed him. He drinks all the time and does cocaine. The only time I can have any kind of a 'normal' conversation with him is when I'm high, too. He threatened that he'd take the kids away from me if I ever left him. I don't know what to do anymore. I can't stand being around him. I'm afraid of him. I'm afraid of what he might do."

"Does he know where you are?"

"I don't even think he knows I've left."

"Why wouldn't he know?" Olivia asked.

"He was high all weekend, and I snuck out of the house early this morning while he was asleep. If I know him, he'll be in bed all day. He'll think I'm at work and the kids are at day care. He probably won't think anything about it until tonight."

Olivia said, "I'm going to call Matt. I think we need his help."

Matt was their older brother and, as the tallest member of the family, he always seemed to be larger than life. His self-assured, poised attitude had enabled him to get through Harvard Law School and attain a high position in a prestigious law firm in Connecticut. The three siblings had been close while growing up. Matt had taken his position as the older brother very seriously.

Matt arrived in Greenbriar on the morning of August 23. Nancy repeated her story to her brother. She'd told their parents the previous evening. They were coming over to Olivia's house shortly after Matt's arrival.

Mid-morning on August 23, the entire Lewiston family heard, firsthand, the venom that Vince spewed. Later that day, Vince arrived to speak to Nancy. Olivia answered the door and was taken aback to see her brother-in-law so soon.

"Hello, Olivia. I'd like to talk to my wife."

"She doesn't want to talk to you," Olivia replied.

"The hell she doesn't!" Vince pushed past Olivia, giving her a hard shove in the process. "Where the fuck is she?" Vince yelled as he stormed into the house.

Matt and Phillip both came running from the kitchen.

"Whoa! Hey, Vince," Matt said, trying to physically block Vince from going any farther. "What's going on here?"

"What's going on here?" Vince echoed. "I'll tell you what the fuck's going on here. My fucking cunt of a wife just up and left me. Took my kids in the middle of the night. No reason. Nothing. Now I see my goddamn car in the driveway of this house. I want to talk to my fucking wife. Now!"

"Calm down, Vince," Phillip said, not believing the words he'd just heard from his son-in-law's mouth. "Let's see if we can just calm down a little bit here."

"Calm down? Fuck you, Phillip. This has nothing to do

with you. I like you. I really do. But stay the fuck out of my business. I want to talk to that bitch of mine. I want to talk to her now! I want to talk to Nancy. She's coming back home with me now!"

"No, Vince. She isn't," Matt said matter-of-factly. "And you're not welcome here. Now good-bye."

Nancy retreated within herself after the confrontation between Vince and her family, concentrating on caring for her children and resting. Vince's deluge of calls went unanswered until she finally relented and spoke with him on Friday, August 26.

"Hello, Vince. How are you?" she asked, as noncommittally as possible.

"Like you really care. I only wanted to talk to you to tell you one thing, and you better listen good! I'm not taking this lying down. I've hired a lawyer. I'm coming after you, you fucking cunt. I'm taking those kids away from you. I'm telling the whole world what a lousy mother you are. You're a drug addict and a whore. You've kidnapped our children. You've abandoned your husband. I'm suing you for every penny your family has. I will see you rot in hell. You fucking cunt, you've stolen everything from me. I'll get you for this! I swear I will get you for this. I will take everything you hold dear from you and rip your fucking heart out. I'll take those children so far away that you'll never see them again. Not as long as you live!"

Nancy went ashen as the phone receiver slipped from her hand. Matt, who had been listening on an extension, ran into the room, quickly hung up the phone, and embraced her. He had expected this to happen.

"Don't talk to anybody but Trent Brown," Matt said. "He'll be expecting you. He's arranged a room for you at the Ramada Inn until you can find a house to rent. Don't make any phone calls, especially not to Olivia, Mom, Dad, or me. You can't call us for a while. I'll check in with Trent and see how you're doing. If you need anything, tell him. I'll make sure you get it. Are you sure you're okay doing this? It's not too late to back out."

"I don't really want to do any of this. But who knows what he's capable of? He can lie to social services and convince them that I'm a drug addict. He'll convince them that he never did drugs." Nancy sadly told her brother, her stomach churning. "Right now, he's threatening to tell the court that I'm an unfit mother. He's already convinced a court that I'm a drug addict. He's lied to social workers, our neighbors, and anyone who'll listen. He could actually get legal custody of my kids, and I wouldn't be able to see them again. I couldn't live with that."

She hugged herself. She was trying to keep warm, even though it was over eighty degrees.

"I don't really see where I have any other choice. He's a pathological liar."

She swatted away her tears as if they were a sign of weakness.

"He convinces everyone around him what a good person he is and what a bitch I am. You have no idea what it's like to live with him. He's the devil incarnate. If you don't do exactly what he wants and when he wants, there's hell to pay. He takes it out of your hide, one way or the other. I'm not going to let my children live like that anymore. I can't! I have to do this. I don't have any other choice."

Gently but firmly, Matt said, "Here are the directions to Trent's office. Remember, no phone calls to this house, Mom's house, my house, or my office. You got that?"

Nodding, she said, "I got it."

The tears steadily streamed down her face. Matt gave his baby sister a hug and held her.

"Be safe, Sis. I love you."

Chapter Three

Vince's plan had one major flaw. In theory, dealing drugs was ideal. But he was, by nature, an addict. It was impossible for him to have drugs of any kind in his possession and not have a taste. And one taste always led to more. Before he knew it, Vince had consumed any profit he might have made. To make real money, a true dealer never dipped into his own stash. That was how the real money was made. After six months of dealing, Vince was no further ahead than when he started. Sure, he wasn't paying for any of his drugs, but he didn't have any money to hire a private investigator either.

He'd given up the two-bedroom house that he and Nancy had rented in Vista Oaks. He moved into a one-bedroom apartment instead. He and Nancy had opened the auto parts store with money from her parents. He had convinced everyone that it would work—and it would have, if he had done the actual labor. But he didn't. He hired all the help because he was either too stoned, or too hung-over, to work it himself.

Consumed with rage, he insisted on revenge, but he didn't have enough self-control to do anything about it. By the March following Nancy's disappearance, Vince was a spiteful, hateful, angry, ugly human being.

He finally made the commitment to get even with Nancy if it was the last thing on earth that he did. He quit…cold turkey. No more alcohol, drugs, or cigarettes. His new addiction was revenge and his new vice was vengeance.

He went to work every day. He fired all but one of his employees. He started to save all the money he could. He dealt drugs and consumed none of them himself. He was determined to see through his reign of rage. If he got a craving for the drugs, he took out Nancy's picture and renewed his vow.

His goal was to find Nancy, win her back, show her he had changed, and then destroy her. No, he wanted to annihilate her. He would decimate every fiber in her being, every thread in her soul, and every twine in her essence. Vince's anger ran through each vein that pumped blood to his heart.

Within six months of starting to save money, Vince had $8,000. That was enough for a retainer of $5,000 to pay a private investigator, Charles P. Murphy. After a year of plotting and fuming, Vince had the opportunity to unload his version of the story to Murphy and send out the bloodhounds.

"Now, Mr. Cooper," Charles warned, "I don't want you to expect any miracles. After all, the trail has been cold for a year now. I'll start with the last place your family was seen. I'll see what I can find out, but please don't get your hopes of quick results up too high."

"Mr. Murphy," Vince condescendingly replied, "I've been patient this long. I don't see what a little bit longer will hurt. Right now, my main concern is the safety and well-being of my wife and children. I'm just worried that something has happened to them. As I told you, they disappeared in the middle of the night over a silly misunderstanding. I didn't mean to scare my wife. I never got the chance to explain to her that I was only kidding about taking our children away from her. I just want to make things right by her. I want to put our family back together. They mean more to me than anything. I haven't had a decent night's sleep since they've been gone."

Vince had always been a convincing liar. This latest fib made Charles a believer.

"Her family has it in for me. They only heard Nancy's side of the story," he continued. "They never really liked me anyway, so you can't ask them any questions. They can't find out that I'm looking for her. We have to make sure that they don't know. I know for a fact that they know where she is. Her sister Olivia said she didn't know, but I'm positive she was lying to me."

"Fair enough. I'll start by keeping an eye on the sister. I'll see if I can pick up a trail from there. If she's had any contact with Nancy, I'll find out," Charles assured Vince. "You'll be hearing from me as soon as I find out anything."

Charles was true to his word. Within six months, he found a pattern of calls from Olivia to Castle City. When he traced the calls, he discovered they were to a single woman with two children. They matched the approximate ages and vague descriptions that Vince had given of his family, but they weren't identical. When Charles gave Vince this news, he was ecstatic.

"It must be them! It has to be them!" Vince exclaimed, hardly able to control himself. "I'm going to go to Castle City and bring them back!"

"Not so fast, Mr. Cooper," Charles stepped in. "I'm not sure that she's your wife. We have to be absolutely positive. I need more time to make sure. It might just be a coincidence. Then you could be in all sorts of legal hot water if you approach the wrong lady and say, 'Hey, Nancy, I missed you. Come back home with me!'" He started to chuckle.

Vince didn't find anything humorous about this conversation. In fact, he was incensed. It added to his fury.

"You know what, Mr. Murphy? You're fired! I don't need you or your services! I'll find her myself! Thanks a lot for nothing!"

Vince stood and headed for the door.

"Wait just a minute, Mr. Cooper," Charles said. "We still need to discuss your bill."

Vince looked back over his shoulder and said, "Yeah, since you did such a hell of a great job, I don't really plan on paying you another fucking dime!"

Vince slammed the door and left Charles' office. He didn't have any idea who Charles had found or exactly where she was, but he could do the exact same thing. And it wouldn't cost him any more money.

The little bitch thinks she can just run off to Castle City, wherever the hell that is. Well, two people can play this game.

The next day, Vince put a "for sale" sign in the store window and prepared to relocate to Castle City. He hadn't expected it to take six months to get everything organized and ready to move out of Vista Oaks.

By the time he moved, nearly two years had passed since Nancy had walked out of his world. He left Vista Oaks and went to Castle City to find his family.

I'll win them back. Then I'll destroy the bitch!

On the day that Nancy had left, Vince was hung-over, overweight, disheveled, and slovenly. That man no longer existed. He had been clean and sober for more than a year and had rebuilt his body. Vengeance was a powerful fuel.

Vince weighed 175 pounds of pure muscle. He looked good, and he knew it. Determination and drive pressed him forward in his quest to destroy the woman who had taken everything from him.

Castle City was a much larger town than Vince expected. As he crossed the city limit line, he read the sign, "Welcome to Castle City, Population 75,642 ... and growing."

Because he fired Charles before he got accurate information on the mystery woman's location and never paid his final bill, Vince didn't have any way of getting that information now.

How hard can it be to find one woman and two children? Why should I have to pay for that information when I can do it myself?

Vince rented a one-bedroom apartment in the first apartment complex he found. It was an older, two-story, horseshoe-shaped building that overlooked a kidney-shaped swimming pool. All the doors of the apartments opened on the swimming pool side of the building. Stairs with black, wrought iron banisters were on either end of the building. The railing ran along the entire length of the upper floor as well.

He struggled to get his belongings upstairs, but he managed to unload everything he owned onto the faded green carpeting. He had a dilapidated recliner he had kept from the house he shared with Nancy, a dresser, an end table, two chairs, and a kitchen table. He had either dumped or sold everything else before he left Vista Oaks. He figured he could pick up a cheap bed somewhere or just camp on the floor for a while. He really didn't anticipate being here that long.

Vince had to come up with a game plan.

Frank was going to be five the March after she left,

which means he'll be seven this March. That means he has to be in school this September, probably second grade.

He found an old phone book and went through the yellow pages looking for schools. After fifteen minutes, he was irate.

"She's gonna pay for this," he said out loud to no one in particular.

He turned to the white pages and looked up all the Coopers he could find. He couldn't find her. He tried Lewiston next, thinking she might have gone back to her maiden name. He had even less luck.

An excellent auto mechanic, Vince didn't have any problems finding a job. He found a position close to his apartment. He made himself familiar with the neighborhood and surrounding area. He lived in the southeastern-most section of the city.

Castle City was a medium-sized city, approximately ten square miles and almost perfectly square. Four main streets ran east to west and six ran north to south. As long as you used the main streets for guidance, it was difficult to get lost.

Vince decided to sit outside a different elementary school each month to see if he could find Frank. His routine varied. He sometimes went in the morning. He occasionally went in the afternoon.

He was also looking for Nancy's car, a white Volvo station wagon. She had driven away in that car, and he was fairly certain she was still driving it.

By mid-March, he had already gone through six schools unsuccessfully. He'd had a few close calls. A couple times, he thought he saw boys who might be Frank.

He even went up to one of the boys and yelled, "Hey, Frank! Come over here, buddy!"

The boy just gave him a blank stare as he got into the

car with his father. Vince pretended to be talking to someone else.

Another time, he saw a white Volvo wagon and followed it. He was sure it had to be Nancy. He trailed behind, making sure not to be seen. He tagged along after it for what seemed like an eternity. He turned on unfamiliar roads. He went into areas of Castle City that he didn't even know existed until the car finally pulled into a driveway. The house was a dilapidated shanty in desperate need of paint. The lawn hadn't been mowed in weeks. The grass was higher than the tires of the car.

Just as Vince was about to get out and confront the woman, an overweight girl with stringy red hair exited the driver's side of the car. She gave him a curious look as he sped away.

Chapter Four

"**M**ommy! Mommy! They're here! They're here!" Russ Keller yelled as he ran into the house. "Brandon, Tristan, Billy, and Kyle! They all came at the same time! Mommy, they're here! Come on! Hurry up!"

Suzanne lovingly looked at her son.

"Russ, I'm going as fast as I can. I'll be there when I finish Angela's hair."

"She has to finish my hair. Then we'll be there," Angela piped in. "Stop being so bossy. I don't want to miss your party!" Turning toward her mother, she whined, "Mommy, I don't want to miss his party."

"Ange, no one's going to miss the party. We're all going to do this together. Remember … together … forever. The three of us." Suzanne comforted her five-year-old.

"I 'member, Mommy. I 'member," Angela said, wrapping her tiny arms around her mother's neck.

Suzanne swooped her daughter off the counter and placed her on the floor. They joined Russ outside on this beautiful March afternoon to greet parents as boys were being dropped off for the highly anticipated birthday party. Russ raced ahead as Suzanne humorously watched.

Her son had grown up quite a bit in the past two-and-a-half years. They all had. Today was a special day for Russ. It was his seventh birthday. Because dinosaurs fascinated him, she drew footprints up the tiny driveway of their rented house to the little backyard where the party was being held. The night before, she had stayed up late cutting and taping dinosaur pictures around the yard. She put dinosaurs on cupcakes and goody bags. She wanted this to be a happy memory for her son. She wanted him to remember this day forever.

At seven years old, Russ Keller was the tallest boy in his class and a bundle of energy. His wavy, blond hair was cut just above his shoulders. It constantly fell into his twinkling, aqua-blue eyes. His eyes sparkled when he laughed. He had his mother's freckles and long eyelashes.

Russ was normally an easygoing kid who laughed a lot and joked around. He was easy to be with. Friends surrounded him. School seemed to come naturally to him, and he enjoyed himself. However, Russ was just plain mean sometimes. These times would come without warning. He had gotten into trouble at school several times for starting fights and then lying about it. Suzanne had caught him hitting his sister twice. Concerned, she was thinking about seeking professional advice. Never far from her thoughts was his father's violent behavior. She didn't want her son to emulate his actions.

Today, she wouldn't think about that. It was his day to have fun and be with his friends. She walked down the two steps of her front porch.

"Hello, I'm so glad you could join us. Would you like to come in? The party's in the backyard," she said, greeting the mothers as they brought their sons for the party.

"Hi, Suzanne. I love the dinosaur feet," Brandon's mom, Christina, said. "They're adorable!"

"Me, too!" chimed in Liz, Tristan's mom, "I can never think of creative things to do for his parties. You'll have to come over and help me next time."

"You could make a whole new career for yourself, Suzanne," Kyle's mother, Jill piped in. "Decorating for kids' parties. I know other mothers who would hire you. You should seriously think about it."

"Really?" Suzanne asked. "I've never given it much thought. I just do whatever comes naturally. A couple weeks ago for Angela's birthday, we wore Barney masks when we woke her up. It was hilarious. I never really thought that I did anything different than anyone else."

"Suzanne, most people aren't this creative!" Christina scoffed.

Two more cars pulled up in front of the house. One held Justin and Jacob, the twins from Russ' class. The other had Jessica and Susie, the only girls he'd invited to the party. Russ ran out on the front lawn to where the cars were. He was so excited that he started jumping around.

"Russ, stop acting like a silly goose!" Angela yelled.

"Shh, Ange. It's his day. Let him be," Suzanne said. She didn't want to embarrass Russ.

"Mommy, he's showing off, and he looks so silly," Angela said.

"I know, but we know that's the way he is when he gets really excited. He's happy and excited that all of his friends are here."

"Today," Suzanne leaned over and whispered to her daughter, "I need you to be my special helper. Okay?"

"Okay, Mommy. I will," Angela replied.

Angela had just turned five. She was her mother's shadow. Standing not much more than four feet tall, her unruly head of brown, curly hair seemed to have a mind of its own. A barrette never seemed to be enough to keep it in place. Long, thick eyelashes and a perfectly turned-up nose surrounded the green eyes that were evenly placed on her oval-shaped face. Her front teeth were uneven from sucking her thumb, a habit she still reverted to when she was very tired.

Russ leapt from each dinosaur footprint to the next as he led everyone to the backyard for the party games, cake, and ice cream.

Before they knew it, the party was over. After Suzanne finished cleaning everything up, the three of them sat alone in the tiny living room.

Russ surprised his mother, "Mommy, tell me again. How come Daddy isn't here?"

"Russ," Suzanne said, scratching her son's head and twisting his hair between her fingers, "Daddy isn't here because Mommy and Daddy don't live together anymore."

"Why?" Russ insisted.

Suzanne was exhausted from the long day. She didn't really want to enlighten a seven-year-old, but she had promised her children on that long drive away from Vince:

From this day forth, I devote my life to you. I will live each day on this Earth as if it were my last. I will show you both how important you are to me. The little things in life are really what are important. I will not be too busy to stop and smell the roses. I will never be too busy to stop and listen to whatever you need to tell me. I will do everything in my power to raise you to be strong, healthy, responsible, caring human beings who treat other people with respect above all else.

In keeping true to that promise, she felt she needed to

give her son an explanation of some sort.

"Russ, your daddy did some hurtful things to me, and we had to move away from him. I was afraid he was going to hurt you and your sister. Do you understand that?"

"Yes," Russ said, "but did he ever hurt me?"

"No, not really you," Suzanne said. "But he was doing things that I didn't want you and your sister to see. He was treating me in a way that was not the right way for a man to treat a woman. I didn't want you and Angela to think that was okay. That doesn't mean that your daddy doesn't love you. He loves you very much."

"When do I get to see him?" Russ asked.

"I don't know."

"What if I want to see him?" he asked. "Can I?"

"Not right now. Maybe when you're a little bit older. Not right now," Suzanne said. "Right now, it's time for you guys to take a bath and get ready for bed."

"Mommy," Angela said, climbing into Suzanne's lap at the same time, "did Daddy hurt you?"

"Not really badly," Suzanne answered as she picked up Angela and headed down the hall toward the bathroom. "Who's ready for a bubble bath?"

"I don't wanna take a bubble bath!" Russ hollered, standing up on the couch and stomping his feet. "I don't even wanna take a bath! Only babies take baths. I'm seven years old. I'm not a baby, and I'm tired of being treated like a baby."

Suzanne stopped in her tracks, remained calm, turned toward her son, and spoke slowly and meticulously, "Excuse me, young man. If there's something you'd like to say about baths or showers, I believe there's a different way to approach the subject. Don't you?"

"Yes," Russ said, hanging his head. He knew he was wrong.

"What is it that you'd like to say?" Suzanne asked.

"Can I take a shower instead of a bath, Mommy?" Russ asked, getting off the couch and looking his mother straight in the eye.

"Yes, you may. You'll have to wait until after I'm done giving your sister a bath. Then you can take a shower."

"Okay, can I watch TV now?"

"Yes," Suzanne said, glad to be off the subject of his father.

Frank and Lilly had become Russ and Angela as Nancy had become Suzanne. She had regained her foothold on life. Starting over wasn't as easy as she had hoped, but she had done it. With assistance from her parents, Olivia, and Matt, Suzanne Keller began life in Castle City with her two children, Russ and Angela. They had new names, a new home, new chances, and new lives. With everything in front of them, they left the horror behind them.

The children didn't take long to adapt to their new names. She had turned it into a game of pretend.

"Frank, pretend your name is Russ. Pretend your sister's name is Angela."

After a couple weeks, the pretend became real. Frank really did become Russ; Lilly really did become Angela. It was much more difficult for Nancy to think of herself as Suzanne. For self-preservation, she convinced herself that it was necessary.

The only people who knew that Suzanne, Russ, and Angela Keller were really Nancy, Frank, and Lilly Cooper were her parents, Matt, Olivia, and Trent Brown, the police captain in Castle City. These five were the only people who knew how to find them. They had helped Nancy, Frank, and Lilly escape from a nightmare that was all too real—a nightmare named Vincent Cooper.

That was almost three years ago. Hardly a day went by that Suzanne's heart didn't sink as she remembered the last thing Vince said to her and his threat to take everything she held dear away from her. She believed every word he said, and she left.

She changed her identity and looks. Her long, flowing blonde hair was now short and brown. Although she was thin to start with, she was even thinner now. Her contact lenses and makeup were replaced with glasses and no makeup. She favored loose-fitting clothing. It would be very difficult for anyone to see Suzanne Keller and recognize her as Nancy Cooper.

Suzanne had worked hard to make a good life for her children. She sacrificed everything for them. They had gone to day care until they were old enough to go to a private elementary school. Angela had just started at the elementary school this past September, where Russ was already in second grade. The school provided afternoon day care until Suzanne could pick them up after work.

She was an office manager in a veterinarian's office two miles from home and one mile from the kid's school. It was close in case there was an emergency. She had learned to be frugal. She had made a comfortable home for herself and her children.

Castle City was 150 miles due east of Greenbriar, where her parents and sister lived. It was chosen as the perfect location to make a new home. It was large enough to get lost in, but it was small enough to be safe. Matt knew the police captain and called in a favor.

Trent Brown had helped Nancy get settled into his town. He made sure she had protection, whether she wanted it or not. He had arranged new identification for her. He had found her the house to rent as well as her job. Trent's son, Brandon, was Russ' best friend.

Trent and his wife, Christina, often had the Keller family to their home for gatherings. Trent became Uncle Trent; Christina became Aunt Christina. Christina didn't have any idea that Suzanne wasn't who she pretended to be. Suzanne wanted it kept that way. In fact, she insisted upon it.

Suzanne had rented a small house with two bedrooms and a tiny kitchen. The three of them often frequented the little living room and play area. It was small, but cozy. Her limited budget made decorating slow. She decorated each room individually. Using the Disney characters in the children's bedroom for a design, Minnie Mouse on Angela's half and Mickey Mouse on Russ's half, Suzanne created stencils. She outlined characters on the walls and ceiling. She also made matching curtains and comforters.

Decorating the living area was next. She furnished it with things she picked up at garage sales. If they were torn or stained, Suzanne bought inexpensive fabric and created furniture covers. She made placemats and curtains that matched for the kitchen area, trying to give her home a country atmosphere. It might have been little, but it was comfortable. More important than that, it was hers. And Vince didn't know where she was.

Chapter Five

Vince worked for Owens Auto, a repair shop that Brian Owens, a Castle City native, owned. Brian inherited the shop from his father. Locals trusted and respected his advice and expertise. The shop was equipped with the top-of-the-line diagnostic equipment. It had four bays and a reputation for excellence. It was well-maintained and clean. Brian didn't believe in additional work that wasn't necessary. He wouldn't allow his mechanics to overcharge customers. His large customer base extended beyond Castle City.

One of Brian's customers was Christina Brown. She had been taking her cars to him for several years. The two of them had gone to school together. When Vince began working, he wasn't interacting with the customers. He was doing the required work, nothing else. After six months of employment, Brian decided Vince was ready to write repair orders.

In February, Christina and Vince discussed her transmission.

"Mrs. Brown, your transmission is slipping. If we don't do a complete overhaul, it will need to be replaced."

"Where's Brian?" Christina asked, looking around the shop for her friend.

"He's off today," Vince politely responded, backing away. "You can wait and talk to him if you'd like."

Christina gave Vince a quick review.

"No, if he left you in charge, I trust him. What if I don't do that overhaul thingy?" Christina asked, leaning against her car.

"Your transmission will stop working. It will be like driving in neutral all the time."

"Oh!" She gasped. "That doesn't sound too good. I guess you'd better do it."

"Okay, let me write it up," Vince said. "I'll be right back."

He headed for the office.

She trailed behind.

"Are you new here?"

"I've been in town for a while," Vince said over his shoulder.

"Are you married?"

"Not anymore."

"Seeing anyone?"

"No," he said with finality.

He walked into the office to write up her paperwork for the transmission overhaul.

Two days later, Christina went back and picked up her car.

Vince's quest of schools in Castle City was frustrating. His anger intensified.

Maybe Murphy was wrong. Maybe Nancy isn't in this screwed-up little town. Hell, she could be anywhere in the whole fucking world. Damn her! When I find her, she's going to pay!

Chapter Six

On the Monday after Russ' birthday party, Suzanne took her kids to school. She had arranged the following week off for spring break. That morning, Angela was clingier than usual.

"Mommy, don't leave me. I don't want to go to school," Angela sobbed hysterically. "I want to stay with you today. I don't feel good."

She was having difficulty talking through her tears.

"Baby girl, its only four-and-a-half days this week," Suzanne said, holding her daughter. "You get out early on Friday. We have next week together. The three of us. Every day," she continued, rubbing Angela's back.

"But I don't want to go today, Mommy!" she said, crying. "Russ is mean to me when we're here, and nobody plays with me."

Suzanne turned her attention to her son.

"Russ, is that true? Doesn't she have any friends?"

"How am I supposed to know?" he asked, perturbed. "I'm in second grade, and she's in the kindergarten section. I don't even see her except at lunch recess. She has a good time then," Russ answered. "Can I go now?"

"Yeah, sure. Give me a hug," Suzanne answered. "I love you. I'll see you at five o'clock."

She hugged and kissed Russ good-bye.

Turning her attention back to her sobbing daughter, she gently said, "Ange, you need to be a little angel. Dry those eyes. Go to school now, or I'm going to be late for work. Let's go find your teacher."

"Okay, Mommy," Angela said, halfheartedly.

She scuffed her shoes along the way. Suzanne and Angela went off searching for Angela's teacher as Russ ran off to find his friends.

After Suzanne found Miss Peters and explained what was happening with Angela that morning, the teacher was more than happy to help.

"Angela, I have this huge pile of papers in the back of the room," Miss Peters began, winking at Suzanne over Angela's head, "that needs a very special someone to straighten them up. Do you think you could do that for me?"

"Yes, I think so," Angela replied, smiling broadly. "Mommy, I gotta go now. Bye! I'll see you later."

She hugged and kissed her mom as she walked to the back of the room with determination, forgetting all about her worries.

Suzanne drove to work with tears running down her cheeks. Not a day went by that she didn't think about how lucky she was. But she felt guilty about everything. The three years in Castle City had been good for her. She had regained some self-confidence, but the holidays were always the hardest. She remembered all the years of family gatherings for the holidays in Greenbriar.

Her parents always had an Easter egg hunt and a family dinner in her affluent neighborhood with cousins, aunts, and uncles. There was always more food than anyone could possibly eat, and conversations would flow. Not only had Suzanne deprived her children of their own father, she had deprived them of their entire family.

There was no doubt in her mind that she would have ended up either dead or a drug addict if she had stayed married to Vince. Her children would not have a mother.

But what kind of a life am I giving them here?

They lived in a tiny little house without any family ties. They were isolated.

When she had finally decided to leave Vince, she had been advised to get counseling or go to a twelve-step program because she was a classic codependent. There was no time or means for a single parent to fit that into her schedule. Sure enough, three years had passed. And she didn't have anyone to talk to. She had to work this out on her own.

She was living a lie. She wanted to go home, just once. She wanted to stay just long enough to see her sister. This was her third Easter alone. It was time to be with family. The previous summer, her parents had died in a plane crash while going to visit Matt. She hadn't even been able to grieve with anyone. The monthly phone calls with Olivia weren't enough. She wanted to be with her family. She had gone from being lonely in a marriage, when she wasn't alone, to being lonely and alone. The only difference was that she was safe now. At least she thought she was.

Lunch was Suzanne's first chance to catch her breath. The morning had been hectic at S&S Pet Clinic. Suzanne was efficient and a valuable asset to the clinic. Dr. Bill Stevenson, a short man, was built like a chimney. At fifty-seven, he was the younger of the two vets. He remarked how smoothly the morning had run, considering the chaos.

"Suzanne, you handled that beautifully. I wonder how

we managed without you."

"Thank you, Dr. Stevenson. It was no big deal." Suzanne just sloughed off the comment.

"I agree with Bill," chimed in Dr. Sawyer, the more chipper of the two.

A couple inches taller and six years older than Dr. Stevenson, he had curly, gray hair. His twinkling blue eyes always seemed to be laughing. Suzanne had never seen Dr. Sawyer get even the slightest bit angry, no matter what the situation was.

"Well, thank you as well, Dr. Sawyer. But I think I was just doing what you two pay me to do. I'll clean up a little bit around here and see you after lunch."

After finishing the morning's paperwork, she headed out to her dilapidated ten-year-old Honda Civic. The last person she expected to see in the parking lot was Trent Brown. Seeing him always gave Suzanne's heart a little jump. He was the only person in Castle City who knew her true identity. If he was here, it could only mean bad news. The Browns and Kellers would often spend time together on weekends with their children, but it wasn't his routine to pay her a visit at work.

"Hey, Suzanne! How's it going? I heard you threw one heck of a swell party for that good-looking boy of yours!"

Trent wasn't an imposing man. In fact, he could get lost in a crowd. A mere five-foot-seven, he wasn't too heavy and not too thin. He had just enough meat on his bones to keep his clothes taut. What he had was pure muscle. He still had a thick head of curly, blond hair that was cut at collar-length. It matched his short, trimmed mustache and sideburns. His brown eyes had golden flecks interspersed throughout that would sparkle when the sun hit them at the right angle. His teeth were pearly white in a tidy row. She was always taken aback at how picture-perfect he looked.

At thirty-seven, Trent could run a man half his age into the ground and not break a sweat. All the men who served under him revered him. No one in Castle City had an unkind word to say about him. Suzanne knew Matt and Trent had been best friends growing up in Greenbriar. She knew Trent was always watching out for her best interests.

Trent had been an only child in a dysfunctional family. As soon as he graduated from high school, he entered the police academy. He wanted to remove himself from his parents as quickly as possible. His first assignment was in Castle City. His aptitude and ability quickly earned him respect and recognition. He was the youngest captain that Castle City ever had. He poured himself into his work and had paid special attention to Suzanne since she arrived.

Suzanne knew it could not be just for a friendly chat if he was there this afternoon.

"Hi, Trent! The party was fun, but it's not too hard to throw a good party for a seven-year-old. They don't require too much. As long as you keep them entertained and the cake and ice cream taste good, they're happy. What brings you way out here today?"

She was trying to hide her nervousness.

"I've been commissioned by my wife to invite you to our house for Easter. I've been given direct orders that I cannot take no for an answer," he said, smiling widely. He was leaning comfortably against her car.

"What?" Suzanne asked, bewildered at the request. "I don't get it. I just saw Christina yesterday at the party. She never mentioned anything about Easter. Besides, that's a family day, and we're not family." She had stopped about five feet away from him. She didn't really know what to do.

"Didn't you hear me? I can't take no for an answer," he said, grinning widely. "Have you ever seen Christina when she gets mad? Believe me, it isn't a pretty sight."

Trent began chuckling. He knew Suzanne was going to have to say yes. This was just fun bantering on his part. He pushed himself off Suzanne's car and headed for the police car that was parked right next to it.

"I think I've seen my side of mean. I don't think Christina ever gets that mean," Suzanne said, thinking about Vince. "If she's going to insist, then I guess there's no point in me putting up a fight."

Suzanne then headed toward her car door. She couldn't explain it to herself, but her heart was pounding wildly as Trent drove off. The idea of spending Easter with Trent and Christina was both exhilarating and scary at the same time.

Christina, a petite woman, was much shorter than Trent. She never came across as demanding. She had dirty blonde hair that often covered her hazel eyes and hid what she was thinking. Suzanne had never really warmed up to her. Actually, she didn't care for Christina at all. She tolerated her for Trent and Russ' sake. When Suzanne had first moved to Castle City, Christina's attitude had been rude and belligerent. Christina didn't believe that Trent was helping an old friend. She was certain there was more.

Suzanne wondered why, after three years in Castle City, the Browns were extending an invitation to her for Easter.

Chapter Seven

Rushing around on Easter morning, Suzanne finished baking apple pies to take to dinner. They were supposed to be there in time for the Easter egg hunt at three o'clock. That would give the children something to do to work up their appetites. Russ and Angela were glued to the television set, watching their favorite cartoons and still wearing their pajamas. As soon as Suzanne put the pies in the oven, she joined her kids in the living room. They immediately jumped onto the couch with her.

This is as close to heaven as it comes. It's so much different from Easters in the past. Vince was strung out on cocaine, and the tension was thick enough to cut with a saw. Thank you, guardian angels, for looking out for me. I am truly blessed.

After fixing a quick lunch, Suzanne put Angela down for a nap and decided to join her. Russ informed her that he was too old for naps.

"Why don't you just lie down in here and rest with us?" Suzanne suggested.

"Okay," he relented.

When Suzanne woke up at 1:45, she found her son fast

asleep on his bed right next to them. After quickly showering and dressing, she gently woke up her children, dressed them in their finest clothes, and managed to pull Angela's wild hair back in a dark blue bow to match her dress. Russ looked handsome wearing navy blue pants with a light blue shirt.

"I wish I had film in my camera!" Suzanne said. "You two are gorgeous."

"Mommy, you're gorgeous, too!" Angela said.

Castle City definitely had an affluent side of town, the northeast section. Suzanne didn't live on that side. The Browns did.

"Remember, you can never say 'thank you' and 'please' too many times," Suzanne reminded them.

"We know, Mom. You've told us a million times." Russ said, exasperated.

"We remember, Mommy. We won't forget," Angela said.

Walking tenaciously up to the front door, Suzanne was trying to hide her discomfort for her children's sake. She was actually nervous and anxious about social interactions. Although she'd been to Trent and Christina's home many times before, it had never been for a formal gathering.

"Hey, everyone, ready to find some Easter eggs? Come on in," Trent opened the door and ushered them into the foyer. "How nice! I'll take those pies," he said, reaching for the pies as Suzanne walked by him.

To her left, Suzanne saw that a formal dining room table had been set for eight, complete with china, sterling silver, crystal goblets, and linen tablecloths and napkins. Directly in front of her, she watched as her children headed to the backyard through the sliding glass door.

The aroma of homemade cooking filled the air as they entered the kitchen, which was just beyond the dining room. The kitchen was fairly large with a rectangle butcher block right in the center. The walls were decorated with a delicate rose-motif wallpaper that extended across the ceiling. A ceiling fan was spinning slowly.

"Hi, Suzanne. I'm so glad you're here," Christina said as she spun around and gave Suzanne a huge hug.

Christina was wearing an apron over her linen pants and blouse. She wasn't wearing any shoes. She was a few inches shorter than Suzanne. The hug was awkward.

"This is my sister, Crystal. Her son, Jack, and daughter, Linda, are in the backyard. Her husband, Connor, is in the den."

"Nice to meet you," Suzanne said. "The resemblance between you and your sister is uncanny."

"Same here," Crystal replied. "We get that a lot. When we were kids, people used to think we were twins."

"Suzanne's son is Brandon's best friend. Her older brother was Trent's best friend," Christina told her sister.

"Wow, what a coincidence!" Crystal said.

"Is there anything I can help you with?" Suzanne offered, trying to mask her discomfort.

"No, I think I'm good right now," Christina said. "I've set up a table outside for the kids. That way, we can eat in peace, and they can do anything they want." She looked up and continued speaking. "We're still waiting for Bill and Betty. They're old family friends. They have their three kids: Hannah, George, and Fred. And then ... Victor."

Suzanne gave Christina a puzzled looked as she paused on Victor's name.

"I hope you don't mind, Suzanne," Christina hurriedly said, trying to get it out of her mouth before she could be interrupted. "I met this man a few months ago, and he's new in town and all alone. He's having a hard time meeting people, and I thought with you being single and all ..."

Christina's voice trailed off as Suzanne's head began to spin. Her heart raced. All the color left her face as she excused herself for the bathroom. Trying to calm herself down while dabbing cold water on her face, she looked at her pale reflection in the mirror.

"Calm down. Calm down. Calm down."

She closed the toilet seat lid and sat down. Now she at least understood why they'd been invited for Easter after three years of living in Castle City.

What am I going to do? I can't get the kids and leave. What's the worst thing that could happen? I'd sit through the meal and make small talk. Big deal. I can handle that.

A few minutes later, Bill and Betty arrived with their three children. They looked like something right out of *Better Homes and Gardens*. All five of them wore matching outfits of black pants and pink shirts. The males had red ties; the females wore red scarves.

Bill and Betty actually looked like they could be brother and sister. They had the same hairstyle, including the color. Both had green eyes. They were the same height. It even looked like they wore the same size of clothes. Looking at that family reminded Suzanne of *The Stepford Wives*. She wanted to chuckle.

"Hi, Hannah, George, and Fred. Come with me. I'll introduce you to Russ and Angela," Suzanne said, grateful to get out of the kitchen.

She tried taking the three kids outside with her. Hannah was about Angela's age and very shy. She had a hard time letting go of her mother's hand. Suzanne knelt down to her and offered a hand that she reluctantly took. George and Fred were seven and eight respectively. They were ahead of her as they headed outside.

"Russ and Ange, come on over here a minute."

"What, Mom?" Russ asked.

"This is George, Fred, and Hannah."

"Hi, Hannah. Wanna come play with me?" Angela asked.

"What're you playin'?" Fred asked.

"Leap frog. Wanna play?" Brandon asked as the boys took off running.

Suzanne welcomed the moment of peace outside with the children to gather her thoughts. She couldn't believe she was being set up. She watched as the three girls sat huddled together on the grass. She longed for her sister. She didn't hear Trent come up behind her. She was startled when he put his hands on her shoulders.

"You all right?" he gently asked.

"Sure. Why do you ask?"

"You look sad," he replied.

"Just a little homesick. It'll pass. It always does," she softly answered.

"I can't even imagine how tough this must be for you," Trent responded apologetically. "I'm really sorry about this Victor thing. She'd already done it without asking me. I couldn't do anything about …"

"Don't worry. I'm a big girl. It's just dinner. I'll be fine," Suzanne said, trying to convince herself.

"Ready to find those Easter eggs?" Trent asked the kids as they whooped in response.

After thirty minutes of hunting and searching, all the eggs had been found. Christina popped her head out the door.

"Can you get the kids to wash up for dinner?" she asked Trent.

"Sure, babe." Trent answered.

"Hey, guys, come on in the house, and wash up for dinner," Trent said, turning toward the yard.

As they opened the sliding glass door into the house,

the five boys went running inside. The doorbell rang. The front door opened as Russ went in through the back door. The silhouette of Victor was framed in shadow.

"Daddy!" Russ yelled.

Suzanne's breath caught in her chest.

Chapter Eight

Russ sprinted to the front door, directly into the man who entered the house.

"Daddy!" Russ repeated, wrapping his arms around his waist.

"Whoa there, young man! I don't know who you think I am, but I am not your daddy," he said, trying to maneuver into the house. That was difficult considering Russ was wrapped around his waist.

"You're not?" Russ asked, pulling back in doubt.

"Sorry. But no."

"I'm so sorry," Suzanne managed to say to the stranger, trying to pull herself together. "My son hasn't seen his father in quite a few years. In the shadow, he must have thought you looked like him. Please accept my apology."

She turned toward her son, who had a pathetic look on his face.

She said, "Russ, come on over here."

Everyone else stared as Russ disconsolately dragged himself over to his mother.

"I hate you!" Russ spat at his mother. "I want to see my daddy, and you won't let me."

He spun around and stormed out the front door. Stilted silence filled the room. Suzanne gathered Angela and looked at Trent and Christina as tears filled her eyes.

"Thank you for including us today. I'm so sorry we ruined it for everyone. I think it's best if we left now."

As graciously as possible, she walked out the front door.

Russ was nowhere to be found. He wasn't by the car, and he wasn't down the street. She didn't have any idea where to look or what to do. Her heart felt like it had been shattered as her mind replayed the scene of Russ yelling for his daddy with such exuberance. In that exact moment of time, her world had stopped. Right now, she had to find Russ.

Suzanne didn't want to ask Trent for help. She had caused enough of a disturbance already. Putting Angela in the car and getting in herself, she rested her head on the steering wheel.

"Why don't you try the park, Mommy?" Angela suggested.

The park around the corner was a favorite place for her kids to play with Brandon. It was a good idea. She drove over there.

Suzanne turned to her daughter and smiled halfway.

"Ange, wait in the car. I'll be right back."

Even though the park was crowded with Easter celebrants, it didn't take too long to find Russ sitting under an oak tree. He had his back to her. His knees were drawn up to his chest, and his chin was resting on his knees. Tears ran down his cheeks. She quietly sat down next to him.

"Hi," she whispered, trying to soothe him without scolding him.

"Go away," he said, scooting away from her.

"I can't do that," Suzanne said, slowly pulling a blade

of grass out of the many in front of her.

"I don't want you!" Russ emphatically said, shoving his heel into the dirt by the roots of the tree.

"I know," she answered calmly. Her heart was breaking.

"Then go away!" he yelled, while digging his heels in deeper.

Hurt, she softly replied, "I can't do that." A little louder, she emphasized, "Listen, Russ, I know you're upset."

"I don't care what you know," he spat. "Go away!"

Trying to stay calm, even though his words cut to her soul and everything inside of her was telling her to cry and grab him, she said very slowly and tenderly, "I think it's time we had a talk."

"Then talk," he said, looking her straight in the face. He was daring her to say something he wanted to hear.

"Not here. At home. All three of us. Come home with Angela and me. We're not going back to Brandon's. We're going home. We'll talk when we get there."

"I still hate you," he said as he stood up and marched toward the car.

"I know," she quietly said as she followed him.

They drove home in silence.

"Mommy, I'm hungry," Angela said as soon as they got home.

"Me, too," Russ said.

"How 'bout grilled cheese sandwiches?"

"Yeah!"

"Sounds good," Russ agreed.

"Okay, you two go change into pajamas again," Suzanne instructed. "I'll make the sandwiches. We'll eat in the living room. Then we'll talk."

Suzanne contemplated her choices carefully.

I could stay here, hidden, and always be afraid. Or I could go back and face Vince.

The day had been a nightmare. Her head whirled with thoughts.

What if that had been Vince? What would I have done? If I keep hiding, there's always the possibility that he'll find us. It's time to go home. It's time to stop running. It's time to face the truth.

Finishing the grilled cheese sandwiches, her children watched her expectantly and waited.

"Mommy, what's wrong?" Angela asked. "Are you still mad at Russ?"

Suzanne sadly smiled at her daughter.

"I was never mad at Russ, Ange." She paused and took a deep breath. "I'm a little upset, but never mad. Your brother has every right to be sad. He wants his daddy. I understand that. I really do."

"Then where is he?" Russ demanded, still upset.

"I'm not really sure, but I'm going to try to find out," she answered with sincerity, never flinching from Russ's stare.

"You promise?" he challenged her.

"Yes, Russ, I promise," Suzanne replied, facing her son. She cast her eyes from her son to her daughter and back again. "First, let me tell you a few things I need to say. Come on over here with me on the couch."

She pulled them close to her and took a deep breath as her stomach lurched. She always knew this conversation was going to come. She just never knew when.

"When you were very little," she began, "your daddy and I did some things that weren't very smart."

"Like what?" Angela asked.

"We can talk about that later. Right now, that isn't important."

Russ interrupted and barked, "Maybe it's important to us."

"Okay." She sighed. "Like drugs."

"Oh," Russ said, having no comprehension what that meant.

"Anyway," Suzanne continued, drawing them closer, "things between your daddy and me weren't very good. He didn't treat me very well, and I didn't think that was a good thing for you guys to see." She looked straight at Russ and said, "I didn't want Russ to think a boy should treat a girl that way." She turned, looked at Angela, and continued, "And I didn't want Angela to think a girl should be treated that way."

Angela simply asked, "So why didn't you just ask him to stop?"

"It wasn't that easy, baby. He kept telling me that he wouldn't do it again. But he never changed. Things were getting worse and worse." Tears began forming in her eyes.

"So you just took us away?" Russ insisted.

"Not then. We were staying with Aunt Olivia and Uncle Bryce."

"Who's that?" Angela wanted to know.

"Aunt Olivia is my older sister. Uncle Bryce is her husband. They have three kids: Melissa, Nicole, and Oliver."

Suzanne wiped the tears from her eyes.

"I kinda remember them," Russ said.

"Well, we were staying there when your daddy told me that he was going to tell a judge what a bad mommy I was. He was going to take you two away from me forever. And I would never be able to see you again, ever."

Tears had started to spill down her cheeks.

"That's when you took us away?" Russ asked incredulously.

"Yes," she answered quietly.

"You did to him what he was going to do to you? You stole us first?"

"When you say it that way, I guess the answer is yes. But, Russ, there are so many things you don't know," she said, pleading with her son to try to understand.

"I don't care. Now I hate you even more!"

He got off the couch and slammed the door of his room.

This time, she didn't follow him.

At nine o'clock that evening, Suzanne affectionately placed a sleeping Angela into bed. She covered Russ, who had fallen asleep on top of his blankets. Suzanne was exhausted. This had been her roughest day since leaving Vince. More than ever, she needed to talk to her sister. Reaching for the phone, she realized this could be the biggest mistake she'd ever made.

"Hello?" Bryce answered on the third ring, wondering who would be calling that late on Easter.

"Hi, Bryce. Happy Easter. It's Nancy. How are you?"

"Nancy? Uh ... wh ... fine ... um ... Happy Easter to you, too. Is everything all right?"

"No, not really." She started to cry. "Can I talk to Oli? Please?"

"Sure, hold on. She's right here."

"Hey, baby girl, what's wrong? Why are you calling?" Olivia asked, using the nickname she'd used for her little sister from the day she was born.

Nancy immediately felt calmer hearing her older sister's voice. Olivia was three years older. She had always looked after her. She was levelheaded, wise, and Nancy's closest friend. Nancy remembered when her best friend, Sara Wells, had died. Olivia had been right beside her, solid as a rock. She'd always been there for Nancy. Right now, Nancy needed her big sister again.

"Oli, everything's falling apart. Russ hates me. I'm lonely. I just wanna come home," Nancy sobbed into the phone.

"Start at the beginning. I'm sure we can figure this out," Olivia calmly replied.

"It all started last week when I gave Russ that birthday party. He wanted to know why his daddy didn't come. He's obsessed lately with seeing his daddy." Nancy continued telling the story, including the scene with Russ dashing into his bedroom that evening.

"I haven't even told them that their names were changed. That's just another reason to hate me more!" Nancy choked out.

"What do you want to do?" Olivia asked.

"I almost fainted today when that guy was in the door and Russ yelled for his daddy. It made me realize that might happen. I can't do this anymore. I want to come home. My kids need more than just me. They need a whole family. I need to face Vince, get a divorce, and work this out. Let the chips fall where they will. If he's going to lie to a judge, let him."

"Are you sure?" Olivia asked.

"I'm not sure of anything. I have to try…for them."

"Sleep on it. We'll talk in the morning. Maybe Russ will be in a better mood tomorrow."

"Don't count on it. He's Vince's son, remember?"

Early on Monday morning, Russ snuck quietly into his mother's room. As he approached the bed, she pulled the covers aside for him to snuggle up with her. Without saying a word, he climbed into her bed and started to cry. She wrapped him tightly in her arms. Soon, they both fell back asleep.

Angela woke them up a little after seven and asked for

pancakes.

"Mmmm, that sounds good," Russ agreed.

"Let's see what we can do about that," Suzanne said, getting out of bed with her children in tow. "Who wants to help?"

"Me!"

"Me, too!"

Chapter Nine

Vince remembered the Easter tradition in the Lewiston family included a large gathering at Olivia's house for an egg hunt, traditional dinner, and family portrait. Having nothing else to do this year, he decided to take a drive to Greenbriar and see if Nancy was one of the celebrants. He figured he had nothing to lose and everything to gain. This was the third year he didn't have any family for the holidays.

She's going to pay!

Vince folded his large-framed body into a small hiding place in the bushes across the street from Olivia and Bryce's house. The moist dirt from the dew stuck to his hands as he knelt. Placing his hands between the branches, he felt the tiniest of thorns puncture his skin. He swore under his breath. This was uncomfortable, and he got madder with every minute. He scanned each person when they approached the front door. He wanted to make sure he didn't miss anyone. If Nancy came, he would know. By nine o'clock that evening, everyone had left. Nancy hadn't been there. Vince was enraged. He had wasted an entire day in an uncomfortable place for nothing!

Boldly walking to the front door, Vince poised his hand above the doorbell, ready to push it. Then he heard a phone ring inside the house. He decided not to ring the bell after all. Turning around, he ran to his truck and headed back to Castle City. That was home now.

Besides, that was the last place she'd been seen.

Owens Auto was closed, so Vince had the weekend off. He had been in this town looking for his family for more than eight months without any luck. He'd made friends with some guys from the gym, and Larry, one of the other mechanics. But that wasn't family. Holidays were the time to be with family.

Feeling despondent and lonely, he went to the liquor store. Picking up a bottle of Jack Daniels, he decided to throw himself a little party.

After all, I deserve it. I've been sober for almost two years looking for that bitch. One drink won't hurt me. In fact, I should really have a party.

Vince called Larry.

"Hey, it's Vince. I hope it's not too late to call, but I was wondering if you know where I might be able to score some coke?"

"Are you serious, Cooper? I didn't know you were a player," Larry responded, shocked to learn this information about his coworker.

Larry was in his early thirties with strawberry blond hair that hung down to his shoulders. His dirty gray eyes always looked hung-over, and he looked like he slept in his clothes. His fingernails had the constant black grease stain under them that some mechanics get, but he was a good mechanic. Brian had hired him right out of high school, so he really didn't have experience doing any other kind of work. He'd been working with Brian for more than ten years. He knew most of the customers by their first name.

"Usually, I'm not, but this is a special occasion," Vince replied.

"Give me thirty minutes, and I'll call you back," Larry assured Vince.

True to his word, Larry called Vince back. They arranged a place to meet for the drug buy. Vince bought three grams of cocaine. By Monday night, he finished the cocaine and another bottle of Jack Daniels. He spent the time plotting ways to terrorize Nancy. The only problem was that he didn't have any idea where she was.

Vince called in sick to work on Tuesday morning for the first time since he'd worked for Brian. He also lied to Brian and made up an excuse that his father had been rushed to the hospital and that was why he hadn't called in on Monday, when in fact he hadn't actually spoken with his father in over twenty years. His head hurt, and his body ached. He had the chills, and he thought he was going to die. He'd been clean and sober for more than two years and now he'd fallen off the wagon. Actually, he jumped off the wagon. Essentially, the wagon ran him over. By Tuesday afternoon, he was beginning to feel halfway normal.

"I'm going to give this til the end of the year," he said to himself. "If I can't find that cunt in this fucked-up little town by then, I'm goin' home. There's only so much a man can take, and I'm just about done takin' it."

He forced himself to get off the old couch and go to the gym. Working out would get the drugs and alcohol out of his system faster. He could get back to the business of searching for his family. He could get back to the business of revenge. His rage would again be his drug of choice.

But Vince's reign of rage had been taxing. He needed a break and craved weed.

"Do you know where to get some good grass?" he asked, pulling Larry aside at work on Wednesday.

"Uh … yeah … let me make a few calls. I'll get back to you."

The buy was set up for after work on Thursday. Larry took $100 from Vince and said he would meet him at eight o'clock. Although Vince wasn't happy with Larry being the middleman, there wasn't anything he could do about it.

"Thanks, Larry. Wanna get high?" Vince asked when they met.

"Sure, man. Love to."

"Follow me to my place. We'll stop along the way for some brews."

They drove back to Vince's apartment, stopping for a six-pack along the way.

"Nice place," Larry commented as he followed Vince into his apartment.

Vince's living room was sparsely furnished with a loveseat and recliner. A TV tray was set up in front of the couch. Dirty clothes were strewn throughout the living room. Off the living room were a tiny kitchenette, a small bedroom, and a little bathroom. They hadn't been cleaned since Vince moved in. The bedroom was cluttered with piles of clothing that were in different states of cleanliness. The entire apartment had a stale odor of sweat.

"Let me see if I can find an old can somewhere. I don't have a bong," Vince said. "Here's one."

He lifted an old Pepsi can from the garbage can. He quickly converted the can into a makeshift pipe with a little hole. They placed the marijuana over the hole and lit it as they inhaled through the original opening of the can. Within minutes, they were buzzed.

"Larry, how long you lived in this fuckin' town?" Vince asked his new buddy.

"All my life. I ain't never been anywhere else."

Amazed, Vince asked, "You shittin' me?"

"Hell no," Larry said. "What brought you here, anyway?"

Turning serious, Vince looked straight at Larry and answered, "I'm looking for someone."

"Ain't we all?" Larry said. He started to laugh at his own joke. "I'm getting a beer. Want one?" He walked into the kitchen before he noticed that Vince wasn't laughing. "Hey, man, what's wrong with you?"

"Nothin'," Vince grunted.

"Seriously, why are you here?" Larry asked.

"I told you. I'm lookin' for someone."

"You were serious?" Larry asked with a puzzled look. "Who you lookin' for?"

"My wife and two kids," Vince replied, seriously.

"Whew, that's heavy," Larry muttered. "What happened to 'em?"

"That bitch stole my kids in the middle of the night and disappeared," Vince spewed venomously. "I hired a PI. He said they were in this fucked-up town, but I can't find 'em nowhere."

"Wha?" Larry asked, taking another hit of marijuana.

"I have a wife, a seven-year-old son, and a five-year-old daughter. That bitch left me without any warning. She's a drug addict. She stole my kids from me. Ran away in the middle of the night and stole my kids. That fuckin' whore is going to pay. I haven't seen my kids in almost three years. The PI dick I hired said they're here. I'm going to find 'em. I just haven't yet."

Breathlessly, Vince completed his tirade.

"Fuck me. You're kidding, right?"

Larry's eyes were wide in disbelief.

"I'm dead serious. It's the only thing I live for."

Vince had finished the first beer. He went into the kitchen to get one more for each of them. On his way back,

55

he reached for the marijuana and took another long drag.

Larry was interested now.

"How you going to find 'em?"

"I camp out by the schools. I look for Frank and Lilly every day."

"Who are Frank and Lilly?"

"My son and daughter!" Vince turned on him. "Ain't you been listenin'?"

"Why don't you just go to the cops?"

"And do what?" Vince chortled. "Hello, I'm looking for my wife and kids. Can you find 'em for me?" His mood suddenly altered, and he looked sullen. Looking at Larry, he said, "They'd kick my ass outta there so fast."

"Yeah, I guess that wouldn't work." Larry said. He sat quietly for a few minutes, slapped his knee hard, and ecstatically said, "I got an idea. We could ask the captain's wife for help."

"Who?" Vince asked.

"The police captain."

"Who the fuck is that?" Vince demanded.

"Do you remember the tranny you overhauled last month?" Larry asked.

"Yeah. So?" Vince was irritated with Larry for this inane line of questioning.

"'Member the lady's name?"

"Hell no!"

"Christina Brown."

"So?"

Vince's irritation was obvious in his tone, but Larry wasn't picking up on it as he continued with his banter.

"Christina Brown is married to Trent Brown."

"Larry, what the fuck does that have to do with anything?"

Vince's temper was heated, and he was done.

"Trent Brown is the captain of the po-leece here in Castle City. He'll help you. If he won't, she will!"

"Why's he going to help me?"

Vince's interest was piqued now.

"Let's just say that I know his wife real well." Larry said, winking with a smirk across his face. "And I could hook you up!"

"Why would she talk to me?" Vince asked.

"She's always looking for fresh meat," Larry slyly remarked.

"Huh?"

"Trust me."

Larry winked.

"Whatever you say, Larry. Whatever you say," Vince said, shaking his head in wonder.

On Friday night, Vince didn't want to be home alone once he got there. He felt like a caged animal. He went to the gym and worked out. That killed some time. Within the past week, he'd poisoned his body with cocaine, marijuana, and alcohol. His body was craving more. At least, his mind told him he was.

"Hey, Larry, what's up? Give me a call when you get this message."

Vince left a message on Larry's phone, hoping for a call back. He made a quick run to the liquor store and picked up a bottle of Jack Daniels. Returning home, he was disappointed to find that Larry hadn't called back.

"I hate this fuckin' town," he said aloud to no one. "I don't know no one. I don't have no connections, and I'm stuck. This is hell on Earth! I swear to fuckin' God, Nancy. You will pay! I will hunt you down if it takes every day of my life. I will find you, and I will make you pay."

He poured himself a drink and smoked the marijuana, hoping Larry would call.

Waking up at ten o'clock the next morning in the recliner with the TV still on and a pounding headache, Vince realized Larry had never called. Elephants tromped through his mouth and danced on his head. That was the only explanation for how he felt. Cautiously, he walked to the bedroom and plopped on the bed.

"What the hell?" A noise in the distant fog woke him for him semi-consciousness.

Vince reached out for the ringing noise to shut it up.

"Hullo?"

"Hey, Vince, what's up?" Larry asked. He was way too chipper for Vince to handle.

"Who's this?" Vince asked. He wasn't really awake or even sure if he was on the phone.

"Larry, man. Come on. You called me. Remember? What's up?"

"What time is it?" Vince slurred.

"It's two o'clock on a Saturday afternoon. Sorry it took so long. I was … uh … occupied … if you know what I mean." Larry snickered. "What's up, man? What you need?"

"Uh … Wait a sec … I …" Vince was trying to get control of his brain and verbal skills. "Yeah, I wanted to know if …uh … I could get some stuff."

"How much?"

"Two Gs," Vince slurred.

"Two grams? Is that what you said?"

"Yeah, that's what I said!"

"Okay, I'll get back to ya. Later."

Larry hung up. Vince rolled himself out of bed and into the shower, trying to pump some life back into his body. The hot water stung his skin, but it felt good.

"I will get you, you fucking cunt. I will!" he said to the face in the mirror as he dried himself off.

His face now had bloodshot eyes and looked much more ragged than it had two weeks before. The road to revenge was back, even with the little detour.

Chapter Ten

"Can I answer it?" Russ asked when the phone rang on Monday evening.

There had been no further discussion regarding his father or the outburst from the previous day at the Brown's house or park.

"Sure, babe," Suzanne said.

Russ got up to answer the phone and quickly handed it to Suzanne.

"It's Uncle Trent," he said.

"Hey, Suzanne, I was just calling to make sure everything was okay."

"Thanks, Trent. Yes, everything's fine. I'm really sorry if we ruined your day yesterday."

"Don't be ridiculous. You didn't ruin our day," Trent insisted. "Christina shouldn't have invited that Victor guy over in the first place. He didn't belong here. I don't know where she met him or what she was thinking. He didn't say much of anything after you left. Right after the meal, he left too. Don't worry about ruining our day. You didn't."

"Thank you for saying that, but ..." Suzanne began.

"No buts about it. How's Russ doing?"

"Fine, I think," Suzanne said.

Trent responded, "Let me know if you need anything, okay?"

Suzanne could hear the sincerity in his voice.

"Okay, Trent, I will."

Russ and Angela were sleeping when Olivia called later that night to talk.

"Hey, Nance, how's it going today? Any better?" Olivia asked, concerned for her sister and her niece and nephew.

"Yeah, I think so. Russ crawled into bed with me around four o'clock this morning. I held him as he cried. We haven't really talked about it again."

"Are you still thinking about coming home?"

"Yeah, I'm tired of living a lie. I figure I should be able to find a job and an apartment and put the kids in school if I move back to Greenbriar."

"Oliver and Russ are in the same grade," Olivia offered.

"That should help a little. I hope."

"How soon are you thinking?" Olivia asked.

"I don't know." She paused. "I was thinking about the end of the school year, but I'm not sure if I should wait."

Nancy swallowed, took a deep breath to calm her nerves, and continued, "I'm going to give Russ time to settle down. Then we'll talk some more. I'm thinking I need to get a hold of Matt. I need to find a good divorce lawyer as soon as possible."

"Do you know where Vince is?" Olivia asked.

"I assume he's still in Vista Oaks. I can't imagine that he would have left."

Dropping Russ and Angela off at school the following Monday morning, Suzanne halfheartedly went to work.

Now that she'd made the decision to go home, she wanted to go. It was just a matter of time. The rest of the week had gone smoothly. Russ hadn't acted up again. He hadn't mentioned hate another time. They didn't discuss anything more about Vince or being stolen.

They haven't forgotten the conversation. Kids just need time to digest information. I'm giving them the time they need.

Expecting to see Trent waiting for her in the parking lot, Suzanne was surprised to see Christina instead. She was sitting in her car, nervously twisting her hair between her fingers.

"Suzanne, I'm really sorry," Christina said.

Her eyes were hidden behind sunglasses, but it sounded as if she'd been crying.

"You don't need to apologize, Christina," Suzanne said, trying hard to keep her immense distaste for Christina out of her voice.

"I feel like I should. This whole thing was my idea," Christina stammered.

"You shouldn't, and you don't have to," Nancy stopped her, not wanting to speak to her anymore.

"I am really sorry. Is Russ all right?"

"He will be," Nancy said emphatically.

"What's that supposed to mean?" Christina defiantly asked, changing her tactic from apologetic to offensive.

"Christina, you don't know a lot of things about us, and they need to be kept that way. It means exactly what it sounds like. He will be all right ... in time," Nancy explained. "We're going through a rough patch right now. Russ is having a tough time with it. He'll be fine ... in time."

"Well, if I caused any further strain, I'm really sorry. I really am," Christina said, sounding genuine.

"I know you are, and you didn't. Honestly, you didn't. Right now, I really need to get to work."

She turned and went inside, but she was off-kilter all

day. Her heart wasn't in her job anymore. The encounter with Christina put in her in a bad mood. By the time lunch rolled around, the doctors knew something was amiss.

"Suzanne, do you feel all right today?" Dr. Sawyer asked. "You don't seem to be yourself."

"Would you like to take the rest of the day off, dear?" Dr. Stevenson asked. "We don't seem to be too busy. I think we can handle things around here without you."

"I might just take you up on that offer. Thank you," she said.

Quickly gathering her things together and heading out the back door to her car, she became painfully aware that she would truly miss those two men.

Nancy spent the afternoon gathering her thoughts and wits; trying to figure out the best way to tell Russ and Ange what their plans were.

She put them to bed in the usual manner: "Good night. Sleep tight. Don't let the bed bugs bite. I love you all ways and always. Today, tomorrow, and forever." She said, kissing Angela once on the chin, once on the left cheek, once on the right cheek, and once on the forehead. Then she repeated the process with Russ.

As she headed out of the bedroom Russ softly whispered to her, "Mommy?"

"Hmmm?"

"Did you forget your promise?" he whispered.

"Which one?"

"The one where you said you were going to find Daddy."

"No, Russ, I didn't forget. This weekend, we're going to start on a brand-new adventure. Right now, you need to go to sleep. Okay?"

"Okay."

She started walking out of the room.

"Mommy?"
"Yes, Russ?"
"I love you."
"I love you, too."
"I love you more." Russ said.
She walked out of the room and called Olivia.
"Oli, this is what I have to do," Suzanne said.
"How soon?"
"The end of the school year. A little more than ten weeks."
"Are you serious?" Olivia asked, trying not to sound too jubilant.
"Yes, it's time to move forward and stop running. I'm tired of looking over my shoulder," Suzanne said. "Now I just have to figure out what to tell the kids or how much to tell them. I'm thinking that, if we come there for the summer, maybe we just stay in Greenbriar. I'll tell them everything, or what I think is everything, they should know."
"That might work," Olivia agreed.
"I know it's really quick, but I have this gut feeling that something's wrong here. I need to get out of Castle City quickly."
"Are you really sure this is what you want to do?" Olivia asked, sensing Suzanne's hesitation.
"Yeah. It suddenly became real and overwhelming all at the same time."
Olivia asked, "Is ten weeks enough time for you to do everything you need to do?"
"You know," Suzanne said, thinking out loud, "I could always move there and leave the house the way it is. I'll just come back and get the stuff slowly. What do you think?"
"That could work," Olivia agreed. "It's not like you

have a place here anyway.

"If I do that, then ten weeks is fine. I just need to pack up clothes and essentials until I find a place to stay permanently," Suzanne said. "Castle City is only a couple hours from Greenbriar, so I can always run back here and get what I need."

"Okay. Then I'll see you in ten weeks."

"Wow. You really will! I can't believe it."

Hanging up the phone, she had a sense of euphoria that had been missing since the night she drove away in fear.

Chapter Eleven

"Vince, get your ass up. There's someone I want you to meet! Pick up your goddamn phone."

"What the fu …"

Half-awake, Vince mumbled as he heard the voice in his semiconscious state. Then, the damn phone rang again.

"Hullo?"

"It's about fuckin' time you answered the phone. It's the fourth time I've called!" Larry yelled. "Can't you hear your answering machine?"

"Sort of," Vince drowsily answered. "Whatha fug zurproblem?" he slurred.

"What?" Larry laughed. "Was that a question?"

"What you want?" Vince growled.

"It's not what I want, Vince. It's what you want. Now the question is, 'What do *you* want?'" Larry asked, chuckling.

"What the hell are you talkin' about Larry?" Vince snapped.

"Vince, just get your ass up. Meet me at the diner down the street in a half hour. You'll want to come. Trust me."

Vince slowly put his feet on the ground and looked at

the clock. It was 11:30 in the morning. He didn't have any idea what time he'd gone to bed. By the time he'd finally gotten the two grams of cocaine from Larry the day before, it was after five o'clock. He'd been up most of the night, and it felt like he'd just gone to bed.

He struggled to get into the shower, scrounged to find clean jeans and a nearly clean shirt. Taking a quick look at himself in the mirror, he noticed stubble on his face, but he didn't care to do anything about it. He made it to the restaurant about thirty-five minutes after he was so rudely woken up.

Larry wasn't alone.

"Hey, Larry," Vince said, making his way over to the booth where he and a petite blonde woman were sitting.

She was wearing a gray sweatshirt and blue jeans. Her hair was in a ponytail. She wore no makeup. Freckles were splashed across her nose and cheeks. She could easily pass for a teenager. She was the most beautiful woman Vince had ever seen. Her hazel eyes never diverted their gaze from him.

"Hey, Vince, do you remember Mrs. Brown?" Larry asked, nodding in the direction of Christina Brown.

"Yeah ... sure ... Mrs. Brown, the lady with the transmission overhaul. How's your car running now?" Vince asked politely.

"Fine, thank you, Vince," Christina answered, chuckling. "I'm not sure we've ever been properly introduced. Please, call me Chris. I really prefer that to Mrs. Brown."

Vince slid in the booth next to Larry and sat directly opposite Chris. Reaching across the table to shake her hand, a jolt of static electricity hit him, running through his body as their fingers touched.

"Wow! Did you feel that?" he asked breathlessly.

"Magical, wasn't it?" she said, batting her eyelashes.

She didn't break her stare for one instant. The golden flecks in her eyes sparkled in the light. He thought he was looking directly into a flame.

"Yeah, somethin' like that," he muttered, completely mesmerized by her.

Larry, oblivious to the animal magnetism occurring around him, asked, "Are you hungry?"

"Starved," Vince said.

His eyes were riveted on Christina's lips.

"Ravenous," Christina answered, running her tongue across her lips for enticement.

"Well, let's order. Then we can talk business," Larry suggested.

Chris and Vince made a grand showing of looking through their menus and ordering lunch. Their feet were intertwined under the table, yet she somehow managed to slide her foot out of her shoe and maneuver it under his pants. She was massaging his calf muscle between her big toe and other four toes. He was getting an erection. She was driving him crazy. Suddenly, she took her foot away.

He looked at her mystified. She smiled.

"Vince," Larry broke into their secret game, "I've known Chris since we were kids. She knows everyone in town. Her husband is the police captain. If your wife and kids are here, I'm sure he can help you find them."

"You have a wife and kids?" Chris asked, astonished.

"Yeah, my wife left me, almost three years ago. She took my son and daughter with her. I was told they might be here in Castle City."

"That's horrible," Chris said. "Why did she leave?"

"She's a drug addict and a horrible mother," he said with conviction. "She lies and steals. She doesn't know right from wrong." He looked so convincingly pathetic that the tears almost formed in his eyes. "And I'm so afraid for my kids' safety."

Chris asked, "Have you gone to the police and filled out a missing person's report?"

Vince pounced, "No, I'm afraid that she'll lie to the police if they approach her. She's a very convincing liar." He looked her straight in the eyes with sincerity. "I have to find her myself. I'm hoping to surprise her."

"Well, I'll do anything I can to help. I'm sure Trent will, too." Chris assured him. "Trent's my husband."

"Thank you," he replied. "I appreciate any help I can get at this point. As I said, I am really afraid something has happened to my kids."

"Do you have any pictures of them?"

"At my apartment."

"Maybe I'll follow you over there after lunch and grab a few so I can show them to Trent. He'll see if he's seen her around town. Would that be all right with you, Vince?"

"Chris, that would be great."

Larry interrupted, "Aren't you glad I got your sorry ass out of bed today?"

"I am," Vince said. "I owe you big time for this one!"

Vince and Chris said good-bye to Larry as he drove out of the parking lot. She agreed to follow him to his apartment around the corner.

Vince barely had enough time to get his keys out when he felt something sliding down his crotch.

"Need some help with the keys?" she purred in his ear.

"I'm not sure it's the keys that need help," he remarked, gasping to catch his breath.

Vince was easily six inches taller than Christina. He spun around to capture her mouth with his. As he bent over she reached up and wrapped her arms around his shoulders. He lifted her off the ground. She wrapped her legs around his waist as she kissed him deeply, acknowledging the desire was clearly mutual. He carried her across the threshold into his cluttered apartment. They remained that way for several minutes, kissing right inside the door.

"Wait a minute!" Vince said, coming up for air. "Didn't you say you were married?"

"Yeah. So what?" Chris said, disengaging herself. "What my husband doesn't know won't hurt him."

She slowly scanned her surroundings, drinking in the piles of garbage, filthy clothes, empty beer cans, and dried, encrusted food bits on the coffee table.

"Vince, you live like a pig!"

"I wasn't exactly expecting company. If I'd known you were coming, I would've cleaned things up a bit," he tried explaining as he quickly cleared a spot on the couch by throwing the clothes onto the floor. "Here, I've cleared you a spot. Can I get you a beer?"

"No, thanks. Is the bedroom this messy, too?" she asked as she headed in the general direction of the bedroom.

Vince could not believe what he just heard. Was she really going into his bedroom?

He followed like a flea on a dog.

"No, it's a little cleaner, but not much." He giggled. "I'm sure I can find a clean space though."

Chris immediately took control of the situation and maneuvered Vince between her and the bed. She gently, but firmly, shoved him down. Once she was on top of him, they began kissing again. They spent the next two hours in arduous lovemaking with Christina in control. Vince had never been dominated in the bedroom before. He wasn't sure whether he liked it or not.

"What about your husband?" he asked.

"What *about* my husband?" she countered.

"Where is he today?"

"Sunday is his day with Brandon," Chris answered between kisses.

"Who?"

"Our son."

Vince stopped her.

"You didn't tell me you had a kid."

The situation suddenly made him uncomfortable.

She purred into his ear, "You didn't ask." She was eager to continue their playing.

"How old is he?" Vince demanded, still disinterested in continuing.

"Almost seven," she answered. "He's a good kid, a little too whiny for me. But he's a good kid," she said, nibbling his earlobe.

"What would happen if your husband ever found out about … uh … this?"

"He won't," Chris chuckled.

"How can you be so sure?" he asked, pulling away.

"You think you're the first?" she asked mockingly. "Or the last?"

"You're already tired of me?" he asked playfully.

"Did I say that?" she said, feigning a yawn.

"How long do these normally last?" he asked.

"Depends on my mood," she said, twirling his chest hairs between her fingers.

"What kind of mood are you in now?"

"Well, right this minute, I'm not really in the mood to talk."

She caught his mouth for a passionate kiss, their last passionate kiss of the day.

Chris went home to her husband and son around five o'clock. Vince went back to his plan of annihilating his wife. Suzanne continued with her plan of returning to her life as Nancy Cooper.

Chapter Twelve

Suzanne cherished Saturday mornings. Russ was an early riser and would stealthily creep into her bedroom, where she would silently lift the covers aside. He would then climb into bed with his mom. They would cuddle, usually falling back asleep until Angela came in to wake them up. The three of them would then venture into the living room. The kids settled in front of the television with the Saturday morning cartoons. Suzanne would make herself coffee and whip up a batch of pancakes for everyone.

After breakfast, the usual routine included discussing what had to be done that weekend and determining necessities and desires. Necessities always came first; desires were prioritized. This particular weekend, Russ and Angela had clean slates. There were no birthday parties or T-ball games to attend. They had neither necessities nor desires.

"As long as you two don't have anything you need to do, you can help me," Suzanne said, getting up and shutting off the cartoons. "I need you to go through all of your toys and make two piles."

"Two piles?" Angela asked. "Why?"

"One pile is for toys you want to keep. The other pile is for toys you don't want to keep."

"What if we want to keep them all?" Russ asked.

"Then I'll come in and separate them," Suzanne answered, smiling. "I mean it." She continued, "If there's something in your room, at the bottom of the toy box, or back of the closet that you don't play with anymore, put it in the pile of toys not to keep."

"What are we going to do with 'em?" Angela asked.

Suzanne lovingly looked at her daughter.

"I'm going to donate them to charity. A lot of children don't have any toys, and they would love to have anything they can get."

Angela thought hard for a minute and looked up at Suzanne.

"What about my animals?" she asked.

"Them, too," her mother answered.

"Not Zeke?" Russ asked, horrified.

"No, not Zeke," Suzanne assured her son, referring to the black mountain gorilla that he slept with every night. "We're not getting rid of Zeke."

"Or Little Bear?" he asked, frightened he might not get to keep both of his animals.

"Not Little Bear either. Only the things you don't want anymore," she reassured him.

Russ asked, "Why are we doing this?"

"Because …" she began, inhaling deeply, "we're moving out of this house. We need to take only the things that we absolutely want to take with us."

"Where we going?" Angela asked.

"When are we leaving?" Russ asked.

"Hold on. One at a time. We're going to Aunt Olivia's house to start. Then we're going to find a place of our own," she said. "We're going to finish the school year here. When you guys get out of school, we'll leave. If something changes, I'll let you know."

Russ looked up at her and sheepishly asked, "Is that what you meant by keeping my promise?"

"Uh-huh," she said, nodding, but dreading the inevitable meeting with Vince.

"I love you, Mommy," he whispered in her ear as he threw his arms around her neck and hugged her.

"I love you more, Russ," she whispered back.

Sorting toys took most of the weekend. Whenever a toy came out, it got played with. Suzanne began doubting that ten weeks was enough time. She slowly rummaged through closets, organizing things to donate and things to move. She began accumulating bags to donate to the women's shelter.

"Mommy?" Angela broke into Suzanne's thoughts.

"Hmm?"

"Should I tell Miss Peters that I'm going to find my daddy?"

"What?" Suzanne came to full attention. "What, honey?"

Angela repeated herself, "Should I tell Miss Peters tomorrow that I'm going to find my daddy?"

Suzanne thought about her answer and replied carefully, "No, sweetheart, I'll take care of telling your teachers that we're leaving. You don't need to tell anybody anything. Okay? Actually, I think it'd probably be a good idea if you didn't say anything."

"Okay," Angela said and went back to sorting her toys.

"Promise me," Suzanne requested.

"I promise," Angela said over her shoulder.

"Russ?"

"Okay. What's the big deal?" he responded, annoyed at

being disturbed.

Suzanne carefully chose her words.

"It's not really a big deal, but I think it'd be best if I tell the school what's going on instead of it getting confusing."

"Can I at least tell Brandon that I'm leaving?" Russ insisted. "He's my best friend."

"Yeah, I don't see how that could hurt," she agreed.

Chapter Thirteen

The following Sunday morning at eleven o'clock, Vince awoke to hear a thudding noise.

"What the fu …"

Fwack, fwack, fwack!

"What the hell?"

Bang, bang, bang!

"What the hell is that noise?" Vince said out loud as he unsuccessfully attempted to ignore the racket coming from his living room.

Thud, thud, thud!

Fwack, fwack, fwack!

He rolled out of bed, shuffling into the living room. The noise only got louder.

Thud, thud, thud!

It was coming from his door. Something was hitting it.

"What the fuck is the matter with you?" he said, opening the door quickly.

"If you would just give me a key, I could come climb into bed with you. I wouldn't have to stand out here like an idiot banging on the goddamn door," Chris sarcastically answered.

"Did I call you?" he asked. "Did you call me? Did we have plans today? Am I missin' somethin'?"

"Just this," she said as she ran her hand back and forth along his crotch.

"Wait. Hold on a minute here, Chris. I gotta pee."

The room was spinning out of control. He'd just gotten to bed. Now she was waking him up. The dry taste inside his mouth insisted on water. Leaning under the spigot, he sloshed cold water into it. It didn't really help. The two-ton gorilla pounding on his head told him to get back into bed. He felt like crap.

"Why are you here?" he asked, slowly making his way back towards the living room, where Chris was waiting for him.

"Aren't you glad to see me?" she purred.

She'd already stripped down to a black, lacy G-string and nothing else.

"It's my day to play. You're my favorite playmate right now, so I came over. But I can go somewhere else if that's what you want."

She began reaching for her clothes. Vince grabbed her. He wasn't tired anymore. His attention had been aroused ... all of it.

"Why would I want that?" he asked, tenderly shoving her down on the bed.

"I see someone has woken up," she murmured in his ear as she looked down at his crotch.

She fondled and caressed him while kissing him. She tickled him with her tongue. She was driving him crazy. Vince had never been with a woman like this in his entire life. He'd always been in control.

"Come over here, Chris," he pleaded.

"Oh, not so soon, mister! You'll have to wait until I'm done with you!" she growled back.

She continued with her teasing and tormenting. Every time he'd try to dominate the situation, she'd back off.

"I said wait, and I mean wait. Or I'll just leave right now."

She worked him up into a frenzy several times before finally straddling him and allowing him a release. A few minutes later, she was ready for more. Vince was exhausted.

"Hey, now it's my turn," she said. "This is no one-way street, pal."

Vince could not believe his ears.

What the heck does she want?

"You gotta give me a minute to catch my breath. I'm not a machine," Vince said.

"You were a machine last week," Chris said. "What happened?"

"Last week, I didn't have a hangover," he muttered. "Last week, I wasn't yanked outta bed."

"You weren't complaining two minutes ago!" she sniped.

"I ain't complaining now. I jes said to gimme a damn minute to catch my breath!" he said irately. "Is this what you call foreplay? Get your man fuckin' mad first?"

"Is it working?"

She batted her eyelashes.

"Kinda. It's not exactly my favorite way of getting turned on, but it's working," he gasped.

They managed to work up an appetite over the next ninety minutes, when Vince barely gasped out, "Let's go get something to eat."

Chris answered as she started to put her clothes back on, "I don't think that's a good idea."

"Why not?"

"Vince, I'm married to the captain of the police

department. Everyone in this town knows who I am. I can't be seen in public with you."

Vince was hurt.

With baleful eyes, he said, "You were seen in public with me last week."

"That was different. We were with Larry."

Now he was confused.

"How was that different?"

"Larry and I have known each other since grade school. No one would start any rumors about us," Chris replied. "But, if I were to be spotted with a new guy, the rumors would fly."

"Oh," he said sarcastically, "so you can only see me inside these four walls?"

"Yup." She nodded, as if it were the clearest thing on earth.

"That sucks."

"Take it, or leave it," she said matter-of-factly, leaving him no options.

"I'll get us something to eat," he said.

Then he stormed out of the apartment.

Chapter Fourteen

April quickly slipped into May. Suzanne's little house was filled with boxes marked and ready for moving. She had gathered several bags that were set aside for donations. Russ and Angela had completed their task of going through their toys. All that was left in their drawers and closets was what they needed until school was over. By the last weekend in May, everything was ready for their new adventure.

"Oli, I can't believe I'll see you in two weeks," Suzanne excitedly rambled over the phone. "This is going to be our last Memorial Day apart. I told the landlord that the house would be vacant by July 1. That should give me two weeks to find an apartment after we get there."

Olivia shared in her excitement.

"You can stay here while the kids have a chance to reacquaint themselves with their cousins. Bryce will help you find the perfect place to live," Olivia said.

"I can hardly wait. I miss you so!"

"Me, too!"

Suzanne decided to tell Drs. Sawyer and Stevenson on Friday afternoon that she would be leaving at the end of the following week. She anxiously waited for the right opportunity. It finally arrived in the late afternoon. She quietly approached them.

"I need to talk to both of you," she said.

"This sounds serious," Dr. Sawyer said.

"I'm afraid it is," she said. She lowered her head as she wrung her hands together, fighting back her tears. "I'm really sorry to have to do this to you. I wish there was some other way, but my last day here is going to have to be next Friday."

"Oh, my dear," Dr. Stevenson said, concerned. "Is everything all right?"

Suzanne replied without meeting his gaze, "Not really. I have a family emergency to take care of. I'm leaving Castle City. I hope you won't think ill of me for leaving you without enough notice."

"Don't worry about us," Dr. Sawyer reassured her. "We'll be fine. We're worried about you. Is there anything we can do for you?"

"I don't think so," she said, unable to hold back the tears any longer.

She started to cry. Her nervousness of the day had caught up to her. Their kind reaction came as a welcome surprise. She simply came unglued.

"I just wish there was some other way. I'm so grateful to both of you for giving me this job, and I've enjoyed my time working with you. The two of you have been so kind to me that I'm going to miss you so much."

Suzanne was having a difficult time talking through her sobs.

"Now, dear," Dr. Stevenson said, hugging her.

He held her for quite a while before saying, "Things have a way of working themselves out for the better. What we think is black today will be gray tomorrow and white the next day. If your situation changes and you find your way back to Castle City, we'll still be here. The door will always be open for you. You are welcome here. Anytime! Any day!"

"If you need to leave sooner than next week, we would understand. Don't worry about us. We can pay you through next week and make today your last day," Dr. Sawyer offered. "Would that make things easier for you?"

"I could never ..."

"We won't take no for an answer," he interrupted. "Consider that our going-away gift to you. We've enjoyed working with you, too."

Suzanne gathered her personal belongings from the office. She hugged the two doctors good-bye several times. She promised she would keep in touch with them. As she drove out of the parking lot for the last time, she wondered if she was making a mistake.

I've made a good life for the kids and me here. What are we going back to?

Without finishing her reverie, the loud blast of a car horn surprised her. She'd just cut off a pickup. Quickly glancing in her rearview mirror, she noticed something familiar about that truck. It was the same style and color as Vince's. In fact, it looked just like Vince's old truck.

Swiftly moving to the right lane, she allowed the truck to pass her. Snatching a glimpse at the driver, she was positive it was Vince. She turned at the first corner and pulled over to catch her breath. If he was following her, he would be coming around the corner any second. She waited thirty minutes. No truck came. Still shaking, she went to pick up her children.

"Hi, Mommy! I thought you forgot us!" Angela said, running up to Suzanne.

"Why would you think that?"

Suzanne feigned happiness while still shaking inside.

"It's late, and almost everyone is gone," Angela replied, stating the obvious.

"Oh ... well ... I'm just a little late, but I'd never, ever, *ever* forget you. You're my little angel. Remember?" Suzanne said, swooping down and giving her daughter a huge hug.

"I remember."

"Where's Russ?"

"In the other room."

"Let's go get him."

"Okay," Angela said, grabbing her mother's hand and leading the way into the room where Russ was waiting.

Suzanne was jittery. She kept scanning every direction and looking over her shoulder. She wanted to make sure there was no pickup on the street outside of the school as she escorted her children to the car.

"Mom, whatcha lookin' for?" Russ asked. "You keep lookin' back and forth. Like you lost something?'"

"I ... uh ... um ... there ... I dropped something. I think it was out here, so I was looking for it."

"Want us to help you look for it?" Angela asked.

"No, that's okay. It's not that important," Suzanne answered, trying to cover up her fear...and her lie. "It's late, let's just go home."

The three of them got into the car.

Suzanne hadn't been able to eat any dinner. She was distracted during the evening with the kids. After putting them to bed, she sat atop her bed, debating what to do. Nervously twisting the ends of her hair with one hand and biting the nails of her other, she finally reached for the phone to call Olivia.

"Oli, I swear it was him. I would know that truck anywhere. It was his. He's here," Suzanne ranted after explaining the events of the day.

"Nance, calm down. It could've been anybody. You're just wound up. You know how you get when you're tired," Olivia calmly said.

It was after ten o'clock on Friday night. They'd been going over this for more than thirty minutes.

"Think logically for a minute. If it was Vince and he knew it was you, don't you think he would have followed you?"

"I suppose so."

"Did he?"

"Uh ... no."

"Well?" Olivia left the question hanging.

"Maybe he's waiting for a sneak attack."

"Nancy, you know you're being ridiculous!" Olivia said, gently scoffing. "You cut off a guy. Okay. That shook you up. You saw a truck that looked like Vince's and a guy that looked like Vince. That does not mean it was Vince!"

"Maybe you're right," she started to agree. "What if you're not? Oli, what if it was him? What if Vince is here and he's watching me?"

"Nancy, you know I'm right," Olivia said.

She'd always been levelheaded and able to break a problem down to its simplest form.

"You're right. You're right," Nancy relented. "Of course, you're right. If it had been Vince, he'd have followed me all the way home. I'm so stupid."

"No, Nancy, you're not stupid," Olivia reassured. "You're just tired. Tired and lonely. You need to come home."

"Yeah, maybe."

"Not maybe. Definitely. Now what's the plan?"

"Now that I don't have to go back to work next week, I can leave the kids at school for their last week. I can start bringing things to Greenbriar and look for an apartment."

"Why don't you let the kids finish school?" Olivia interrupted. "Finish up the house. Donate the bags to charity. Take the things you need with you, and put the rest in boxes. When we are ready to move you, they'll be readily accessible."

"That sounds like a good idea."

"Next Saturday morning, the three of you come here with enough clothes for two weeks," Olivia spoke excitedly. "Then you can look for an apartment. After that, we'll figure out a way to get your furniture and boxes from Castle City to Greenbriar."

"Okay," Nancy said. "Oli?"

"Yeah?"

"How come you can always calm me down?"

"I don't know. I guess that's what big sisters are here for. I love you, Nance. I'll see ya next week!"

"Okay, I'll let you know if anything changes during the week. I love you." Nancy said, hanging up.

Chapter Fifteen

"Larry, that bitch is a nymph."
"No shit. I could of told you that."
Larry laughed at Vince as he bit into his ham sandwich. Vince looked at him.
Astonished, he asked, "Why didn't you?"
Larry simply replied, "You didn't ask."
Vince and Larry had started taking breaks and lunch together since they had become party buddies. At first, Vince didn't think it was such a good idea to let on that he and Chris were sleeping together, but he had to talk to someone about her.
"You mean she's always been like this?" Vince questioned in disbelief.
"Depends what you mean when you say 'like this'," Larry chuckled. "If you mean, 'Has she always been crazy in the sack?' Yeah. She was like that in high school."
"You're shittin' me, right?"
Larry shook his head.
"No way, man. She was the class slut. She'd do anybody. Anytime. Anywhere."
Vince furled his brow and asked, "How'd she marry the

police captain?"

"He moved here from out of town. She latched on to him almost as soon as his feet hit the pavement. He never really stood a chance. He didn't find out about her reputation before he married her. No one told him about it after they were married." Larry stopped to take a sip of his drink. "Now he's like that ol' ostrich. Keeps his head buried so far that he doesn't know what's goin' on. She gets herself a new boy toy whenever she feels like it. Looks like you're the new flavor of the month," Larry continued. "Enjoy the ride, cowboy. You never know how long it'll last."

"It's more like the merry-go-round from hell," Vince said.

"Well, I suggest you ride it as long as you can until the devil shows up!" Larry cackled.

Vince moaned. "All I wanted was help findin' my family. I wasn't lookin' for a wild ride."

Larry winked. "Yeah, but when was the last time you were laid like that?"

"Uh ... never," Vince admitted. "Honestly, Larry, I'm not sure that I've ever been laid like that before. Chris is wild and insatiable. She can take everything I've got, and she still wants more. She wears me out. I don't know what I'd do if it was more than once a week."

"Don't worry. She usually burns out on her boy toys after about a month. You'll be lucky if you last through July."

On Sunday morning, Vince was ready for Chris. He'd cleaned up the apartment ... a little. He'd moved the piles of clothes into the closet and taken the trash outside. He'd even gone to the grocery store on Saturday so there was food in the house. Even though he'd complained to Larry, he was actually looking forward to her coming over.

He opened the door before she had a chance to knock.

"Oh, you're awake this week. How nice," she gibed, sarcasm dripping from every word. "Were you waiting for me? Anticipating what I have for you?"

She sashayed right past him, carefully avoiding any physical contact.

"I see you've cleaned up a little, too. Trying to impress me?" she snidely asked. "How nice! I might have to reward you for being such a good boy!"

"I ... um ... wanted to talk to you," Vince sputtered, trying hard not to let his lust get the better of him.

"Talk? You want to talk?" she asked dubiously. "You would rather talk than ..."

She sidled up against him like a banana peel against the fruit. He backed away.

"I didn't say I wanted to talk instead," he snapped. "I just said I wanted to talk to you. Can't we talk first?"

"Oh, all right!" she said, flopping down on the couch. She was obviously annoyed. "What do you want to talk about?"

"Do you remember the morning we met?" he asked, sitting down next to her ... but not too close.

"Yeah, Larry introduced us. I remember. So what?" she said, yawning and examining her fingernails to show her disdain for this discussion.

"Do you even vaguely remember what I needed help with?"

"Not really. My mind was somewhere else," she said, sliding closer.

"Chris, I'm tryin' to be serious here for a minute."

"Okay, okay," she said, scooting back. "What did you need help with?"

"Finding my family," he said, trying not to sound desperate.

"Yeah, I kinda remember that. Your drug addict of a

wife stole the kids during the night. They might be here. Was that it?" she asked.

"Yeah," he said, wondering if this was going to get him anywhere.

"Let me think about it and figure out what I can do to help. Can I get back to you on it?" She asked, slyly grinning as she shimmied out of her tight jeans.

"Yeah, I suppose so."

"Don't look so sad. I'm sure I can make it up to you in a different way," Chris said, wriggling her way onto his lap.

The rest of the day became a blur, just like the Sundays before.

Vince left work early on Friday, hoping to catch a glimpse of Frank or Lilly at the new school he was staking out. He'd painstakingly scanned each child as they exited the school. His spirits lifted each time there was a brother-and-sister duo. One came close to his children's age and height range.

Hesitantly, he got out of his truck and crossed the street toward them. He was fifty yards from them. His heart was racing.

"Jamie, Naomi, over here!" he heard a voice coming from behind him.

"Mommy!" both children screamed at once as they raced around him toward their mother.

Vince swiftly turned around to garner a look at the mother. This could be the moment he'd been waiting for. The woman was almost as tall as Vince and probably as wide as she was tall. Her dirty brown hair hung like clumps of yarn beneath her shoulders. Her clothes bunched up around her bulging rolls of fat. Each child was engulfed within a monstrous arm of flab. She escorted them toward her van.

Dejected, he headed home. Meandering aimlessly through the streets of Castle City, he got lost. He was finally on a main street he recognized when a beat-up Honda Civic pulled out of a driveway and cut him off. He slammed on the brakes and laid into his horn.

"Goddamn driver, watch where you're going!" he yelled at the back of the car.

The Civic moved over to the right lane and let him pass. He glanced over and flipped off the driver.

Damn woman driver.

He continued his drive home.

Chapter Sixteen

"Hello?" Suzanne wondered who could be calling her at home on a Wednesday afternoon at two o'clock. No one knew she was even there. She was supposed to be at work.

"Mrs. Keller? This is Mr. Jeffries from Open the Door Elementary School. I'm sorry to have to call you this way, but there's been a little problem with your son."

"Russ? Is he all right? He's not hurt, is he?"

"Oh, he's just fine. The other boy wasn't so lucky."

"Other boy?" she said, her heart pounding. "I don't understand."

"Russ apparently started a fight when one of the other boys said something he didn't like. By the time the teachers could break it up, Brandon was pretty banged up. We don't think it's anything serious, but we can't take any chances."

Mr. Jeffries spoke, but she wasn't focused anymore. As soon as she heard it was Brandon, her mind began to wander.

"Brandon? I don't understand. Russ and Brandon are best friends."

"I need you to come get your son."

"Oh. Of course, I'll be right there." Suzanne hung up, confused and concerned.

What could have caused Russ to turn on Brandon?

That morning, she loaded the car and drove to the thrift store whose proceeds went to the women's shelter. She was surprised to find Christina working behind the counter.

"Christina, I didn't know you worked here," Suzanne said, surprised.

"I have to do something to occupy my time," Christina sardonically remarked. "What brings you in here?"

"I'm just bringing in some toys, clothing, dishes, and other things as donations."

"That's very kind of you, Suzanne," Christina said. Then sarcastically, she added, "Aren't you a little late for your spring cleaning?"

"Actually," Suzanne replied, "we're moving. I'm trying to lighten the load a bit."

"Moving?" Christina was interested now. "Where are you going?"

Suzanne was prepared for this question, and she was using the same response for everyone.

"I'm moving back home. There's been a family emergency."

"Oh, Brandon is really going to miss Russ," Christina said sincerely. "Will you be coming back?"

"I'm going to try. We really like it here," she lied.

Suzanne wasn't about to tell the truth to this woman about anything, especially when she knew deep inside that Christina never had a nice word to say, ever.

"Well, let's take a look at what you've got there," Christina said, changing the subject.

They moved the boxes in and exchanged small talk. Suzanne left. Christina was one woman that Suzanne was definitely not going to miss.

Driving over to the school, Suzanne could not stop wondering what caused Russ to fight with his best friend.

"Thank you for coming so fast, Mrs. Keller," Mr. Jeffries said as he escorted her into his office.

Russ was sitting in a wooden chair outside of the office with his hands folded in his lap. He was in a narrow hallway with one empty chair on either side of him. His head was down so his blonde hair was shielding his eyes. She could see he had been crying. She only wanted to run over to him, gather him in her arms, and tell him everything would be all right. But she had to talk to the principal first. She winked at him instead. One side of his mouth turned up in a half-smile.

"As I said on the phone," Mr. Jeffries began after Suzanne entered his inner office, "all we know is Russ started the fight over something Brandon said. Russ will not talk to anyone. He won't tell anyone what Brandon said, and Brandon isn't talking either."

Mr. Jeffries was a slender, average-sized man. His horn-rimmed glasses and dark brown mustache looked like the Halloween masks people wore. It was difficult for Suzanne to look at him without smirking.

"Is Brandon all right?" Suzanne asked.

"He appears to be. He has a few nicks and cuts. Might bruise up a bit, but nothing a few days won't cure. His mom just took him a few minutes ago."

"The school policy on fighting is quite clear about punishment," he began. "I'm not sure if you recall reading that when you signed all the paperwork at the beginning of the year or not?"

"Uh … no … not really," Suzanne said, unable to hold his gaze for fear of laughing.

"Most parents skim over that part, thinking that'll never

happen to their kids," he chuckled. "The punishment for fighting is immediate expulsion."

"Expulsion? For his first fight? Don't you think that's a bit extreme, Mr. Jeffries?"

"Well, actually Mrs. Keller, as you recall, Russ has been in a few scuffles this year. His teacher has sent home notes about his behavior."

Suzanne did recall that Russ's behavior was changing and that she'd been worried. "I appreciate all that you've said, Mr. Jeffries. Thank you. I might as well tell you now, both Russ and Angela are being removed from this school, we are leaving Castle City and moving back home to Greenbriar." She gathered as much of her dignity as she could and walked out of his office, walked by Russ and reached for his hand and continued to walk.

As soon as they reached the car, Suzanne hugged Russ for a few minutes.

She asked, "What did Brandon say to you that was so bad that you had to hit him?"

Russ looked down at his hands and mumbled, "He told me I didn't really have a daddy and I was making it all up."

"What?" she exclaimed, not sure she had heard him correctly.

"That's what he said," Russ said, "I didn't really have a daddy."

"Okay, I heard that. Now start from the beginning," she prodded him.

"It was lunch recess. I wanted to tell him that we were leaving. He didn't believe me," Russ softly told her. "So I said, 'I am too leaving. I'm going to find my daddy.'"

"Oh no. You didn't," she said.

"I did. I know you told me not to tell anyone that, but I kinda forgot that part 'til it was too late."

Russ started to cry.

"Okay, go on," she said, pulling him closer to her.

She wanted to let him know that she wasn't upset with him for sharing their secret.

"He said, 'You don't have a daddy.' I said, 'I do have a daddy. Everyone has a daddy. I just have to find mine, and that's why we're leaving,'" he said, barely stopping to catch his breath as he retold the story.

"He started to laugh at me. Not like a joke laugh, but a mean laugh. I'd never heard anything like that before, Mommy." He stopped to catch his breath as the tears streamed down his face. "I wanted to cry. I told him to stop laughing, but he wouldn't. Then he said, 'You don't really have a daddy. You're making it up!'"

Russ stopped talking and started crying harder. Suzanne enveloped him in her arms and held him until his sobbing subsided.

"I got so mad that I just started hitting him. I don't remember anything else until the teachers pulled us apart." Russ stopped to catch his breath. "Mommy, I'm not sorry that I hit him. He was really mean to me today."

"I know, sweetheart."

Suzanne comforted her son and just held him close to her for a few minutes.

"Mommy?" Russ asked after a few minutes of silence.

"Yes?"

"I do really have a daddy, don't I?" he whispered.

"Yes, sweetheart, you do."

You have a daddy, but you might not like him once you find him.

"Russ?" she asked after a few more minutes of silence.

"What, Mommy?"

"I don't want you to think that it's okay to hit when you get mad. Hitting is never okay. We need to come up with a better way to handle anger than hitting."

"Okay, Mommy."

"I think, after we find a new place to live, we maybe need to find someone who can help us figure that out, too. Okay?"

"Okay."

Together, they went to find Angela.

By Friday morning, Suzanne's little house was completely packed. The Honda was loaded with all their clothes, stuffed animals, and as many toys as they could fit. The rest of their belongings were neatly marked in boxes and stacked in the living room. Suzanne's goal was to rent a U-Haul and make one trip from Greenbriar. She wanted to get everything quickly as soon as she was ready. She had one stop to make on her way out of town.

Pulling in front of the Castle City police station brought back memories. Three years ago, she had pulled up in front of this very station. That night, she was coming from Greenbriar. This morning, she was going back.

Am I making a mistake?

"Hi, Trent," she said as she was escorted into his office with Angela and Russ beside her.

"Good morning, Kellers. To what do I owe this honor?" Trent asked, bowing courteously and smiling.

"We've come to say good-bye and thank you," Suzanne said, her heart beating wildly.

"Oh, so the rumors are true." Trent grinned.

"There are rumors?"

She gasped.

"Just kidding! Christina said she saw you the other day."

"Yeah, I forgot about that," Suzanne asked. Then she remembered and asked, "How's Brandon?"

"Fine. Why?"

"She didn't tell you anything?"

"No, what's up?" Trent asked, puzzled.

"Russ, can you take Angela to the machines and get her a candy bar?" Suzanne asked.

"Sure, Mom!" he said.

He took the dollar she gave him and rushed out to the vending machines.

"Trent, Christina didn't tell you that Russ and Brandon got into a fight on Wednesday?"

"No," Trent answered.

"Why wouldn't she tell you?" she asked.

"I dunno. Why'd they fight?"

"Apparently, Brandon laughed at Russ when he told him we were leaving to find his dad," Suzanne said, sitting down in the chair across from his desk.

"Is that why you're leaving?" Trent asked, astounded by the news.

"That's not what I'm telling people, but yes," she said, facing him.

"You've got to be kidding me!" Trent exclaimed, perplexed.

He leaned against the front edge of his desk. .

"Trent, I can't run and hide anymore. I'm tired of living a lie. Russ needs his father," Suzanne tried to explain. "That became very clear to me on Easter."

"Do you think this is wise?" Trent gently asked.

"I'm not sure if it is or isn't, but I don't think I have any other choice," she said.

She couldn't look him straight in the eyes when she was talking to him. Her heart was pounding wildly, so she diverted her attention to her twitching hands.

"I'm going home. I'm filing for divorce. I'm going to find Vince and do what I have to do. That way, at least the kids will have more family around them. They'll get to know their father."

"Standing in your backyard on Easter, I realized it was one thing to be lonely in a marriage when there was someone there, but I'm lonely, and no one is around. I need my family. I need my sister. I have to face my fears."

"You are one brave lady, Nancy." Trent said, admiringly. "I'll give you that. I'm not saying it's smart, but, if that's what you think you have to do, then ..."

"I do," she said, not giving him a chance to finish. "Trent, I can't run all my life. I'm tired of looking over my shoulder. What would've happened if that had been Vince at your house? What would I've done?"

"I don't know what to say."

"Me neither, and I don't want to find out." She stood up and brushed off her jeans to keep her hands occupied. "Thanks for everything, and I mean everything. I couldn't have done any of this without you."

"I'm here if you need anything. Just call, and I'll come. Day or night. Remember that." As he gave her a hug, she started to cry. "What's that all about?"

"I'm not really sure," she said. As she wiped away the tears, she said, "You know, you're the only friend I've had for the past three years. I'm going to miss you."

"Same here. I mean it, Nancy. Anytime. Day or night. If you're in Greenbriar, I'm only a couple hours away."

"Okay, I'll remember. I promise. Now where did my two children go?"

Chapter Seventeen

Vince hid his surprise Thursday morning when Chris drove her van into Owens Auto and complained her transmission was slipping. She insisted on speaking to the "damn mechanic" who fixed it the first time.

"Cooper!" Brian bellowed. "Did you work on Mrs. Brown's transmission?"

"I don't remember, Brian," Vince answered, trying to look calmer than he felt. "I work on so many people's cars. I can't remember which ones I've worked on, and if I have, what I've done to 'em. You can't really expect me to remember all the cars I've worked on and exactly what I did to every car. If the paperwork says I did, then I must've done it. What seems to be her problem?"

"Mrs. Brown says that it's slipping."

Vince raised his eyebrow and looked at Chris. Luckily, Brian didn't catch it.

"Let me take her for a test drive and check it out, boss."

"Okay," Brian agreed. "She's been a customer for a very long time. I want her car fixed and fixed right!" He turned his attention toward Christina, "Christina, you know we'll do whatever it takes to fix it. Vince is a top-notch mechanic. In fact, he's the best mechanic I have. He'll take it around the block and see what the problem is."

"Why don't I ride along and show him what I'm feeling?" she suggested.

"If that would make you feel better, sure," Brian agreed.

Vince and Chris pulled out of Owens Auto in her car. It became immediately apparent to Vince that there wasn't anything wrong with it.

"What the hell are you doing, Chris?" Vince seethed with anger. "Are you trying to get me fired?"

"No, I'm trying to help you," she answered innocently, smiling sweetly and batting her eyelashes. "I didn't have your number, and I wanted to invite you over for a barbeque on Sunday. I figured that would be the best way for you to get Trent to help you find your family. I couldn't come up with a better idea."

"Barbeque? At your house?" He pulled over to the curb and stared at her in disbelief. "With your husband? You are kidding, right?"

"No, I'm dead serious," she responded with a straight face. "I bring home strays all the time. You should've been there on Easter. I invited this guy, Victor, over. Some kid thought he was his dad. It was a riot!"

"Wait a minute. You are serious," he said, shaking his head as he headed back to the repair shop.

"Yeah, I am. You said you wanted my help. Here it is. Be there by two o'clock. Don't be late," she said just as they pulled back into the parking lot.

"Well?" Brian inquired as they both exited the car.

Chris immediately became apologetic.

"I must've been wrong, Brian. What I thought was slipping was really shifting. Vince explained the difference to me."

"So, there's nothing wrong with the transmission?" Brian asked dubiously.

"Not as far as I can tell," Vince assured his boss.

"Okay. Thanks, Vince."

"Don't hesitate to bring it back if you have any other questions or problems," Brian said to Chris.

"Don't worry. I won't," she said.

She drove off.

Chapter Eighteen

Nancy drove from Castle City to Greenbriar, wondering if she was doing the right thing.

It's time to face my fears and stop running.

She stopped at the park she'd played in every day as a child. She was home. It was time to tell her children the rest of their story. Her emotions were wreaking havoc with her stomach. She'd hardly eaten anything in days. Constantly looking over her shoulders, she was certain she was being watched. Being back in Greenbriar reminded her of the last time she was there and Vince's awful threats.

"Why are we stopping at the park, Mommy?" Angela asked.

"Because we need to talk before we get to Aunt Olivia's."

"More talking?" Russ asked, exasperated. "Aren't we ever done talking?"

"Almost. I promise," she assured him. "I just need to tell you one more thing. Then all the talking about the past is done."

"Okay. What now?" he asked as they gathered on a park bench.

"The last thing I have to tell you might be a little harder to understand, but I need you to try real hard. Okay?"

"Okay, Mom, what is it?" Russ impatiently asked.

Taking a deep breath, she decided to jump in feet first.

"Our last name is not Keller. My first name is not Suzanne. You're not Angela, and you're not Russ."

"What?" he asked.

"Huh?" Angela said.

"I thought that would be a little confusing. Okay, here it goes a different way. When we moved to Castle City, I had to hide, so I changed our names. Your daddy's name is Vincent Cooper."

"Even if Daddy was looking for us, he couldn't find us?" Russ asked, jumping off the bench in outrage.

"Right," she answered softly.

"Mommy, were you that scared?" Angela asked.

"Yes, Ange, I was."

Nancy was constantly amazed at her daughter's astuteness. She was much wiser than a typical five-year-old.

"Are you still scared?" Russ asked, coming closer again.

"Yes, Russ, I am." She admitted, looking him square in the eyes.

"Then why are we coming back?" he asked.

"Because I made you a promise, and I don't break my promises to you. It's time for us to find your daddy. You guys need to know him, and it doesn't matter how scared I am. Sometimes, you need to face your fears and work through them. As long as you two remember that I love you, I have always loved you, and I will always love you, that's all that matters. I have to face this fear. And you guys need to know your daddy."

"So, what is my real name?" Russ asked, sitting down

next to her on the bench again.

"Yeah. Mine, too?"

"You are Frank Cooper. You are Lilly Cooper."

"Who are you?" Russ asked.

"Nancy Cooper."

"How did you pick our new names?" Angela asked.

"I picked Angela because you are an angel sent from above to save me. I picked Russ," she said, turning towards him, "because it is like the wind rustling through the leaves. It is everywhere, and I carry you with me everywhere."

"How do we just go back to our real names?" Russ asked.

"I guess you can choose which one you want. Then we figure out what to do next," Nancy answered. "I'm going back to Nancy Cooper. If I want to find your dad, I have to. That's me. If you want to continue to be Russ, that's okay. If you want to go back to being Frank, that's okay, too. Same with you, Ange. Whatever you want. I know this is a lot for a child to understand. That's why I kept it for last. I promise there is nothing else. You guys know everything now."

"What is Aunt Olivia going to call us?" Angela wanted to know.

"Whatever we tell her," Nancy said.

"Frank, Russ, Frank, Russ, Frank, Russ," Russ said out loud.

Angela mimicked her older brother, "Lilly, Angela, Lilly, Angela, Lilly, Angela."

Nancy chuckled to herself. This had gone much differently than she had expected. She figured Russ would be maddest about this, and he was actually taking it in stride.

"Mom, call me Frank. I want to see how it sounds."

"Okay, Frank. How did that sound?" she said.

"Weird."

"What's my whole name?"

"Franklin Vincent Cooper."

"Am I named after him?" he asked gleefully.

"Yup," Nancy answered.

"Then that's the name I want," he decided.

"Okay. Then I'll start calling you Frank, Frank." Both started laughing. "This might take us a few days to get used to."

"Call me Lilly. I want to see what that sounds like," her daughter said.

"Okay, Lilly."

"I like that. What's my whole name?"

"Lillian Rose Cooper. I used to call you my lily flower."

"I want to go back to that one, too. Okay?"

"Okay, little lily flower, whatever you want. Remember, this might take us all a few days to get used to. Don't get mad if we slip up and call you Russ or you Angela or whatever."

"What if we call you Dad?" Lilly asked.

"Huh?"

All of them laughed.

They left the Keller family behind in Castle City. It was time to put their lives back together as the Coopers in Greenbriar. They played at the park for a little while before heading over to Olivia's house.

Olivia opened her front door before Nancy could ring the doorbell. It had been a very long three years for the two sisters. Tears were flowing.

"Mommy, what's wrong?" Lilly insisted. "I thought you wanted to come here."

"Come here, Lilly. I want to see you," Olivia said. "You've grown up so much since you went away."

She hugged her niece, who had suddenly grown shy.

Frank was cowering behind his mother, not wanting to get anywhere near his aunt. Olivia was shorter than Nancy and bubbled over with enthusiasm. Her goal in life was to make sure those around her were happy. After one look into her emerald green eyes, worries melted. Everything was perfect. She was neat and tidy, and her home was comfortable. She escorted her sister and children into her home and asked how the trip was.

"Fine. It was too early for traffic," Nancy said, feeling immediately at ease as the bonds of family began to envelope her.

"We stopped at the park and played," Lilly offered.

"You did?" Olivia asked. "What's your favorite thing to play on?"

"I like the swings," Lilly said.

"What about you, Frank?" Olivia asked.

"I like the monkey bars," he answered softly.

"So does Oliver," Olivia said, pretending that Frank wasn't hiding.

"Who's that?" Frank asked.

"Your cousin," Olivia answered. "That's my son."

"Where is he?" he asked as he ventured out of his hiding place behind his mom.

"At school. He'll be home this afternoon. You can meet him then. He's just finishing the second grade ... just like you."

"Really?" Frank asked. His face lit up.

"Uh-huh."

"Am I going to go to school with him?"

"Would you like that?" Nancy asked, interjecting herself into the conversation.

"Yeah. Then I'd know someone, and I wouldn't be so afraid."

"Well, let's see what we can do about that then," Olivia said, winking at Nancy without Frank seeing.

"What about me?" Lilly asked. "Did you forget 'bout me?"

"Never," Nancy said. "I would never forget my lily flower. There are two girls here, too. But they're older. Melissa and Nicole. Melissa's nine, and Nicole's eight."

"Does that mean they won't play with me?" Lilly said, beginning to pout.

"I don't think it means that at all," Olivia said. "They've been looking forward to you coming all week."

"They have?" she asked, wide-eyed. "Really?"

"Really. They keep arguing about whose bed you're sleeping in. They both want you."

"Nu-uh, you're makin' it up, Aunt Olivia," Lilly said.

"I am not! Wait, you'll see when they get here. Now who's hungry for lunch?"

"I am!" Frank said, forgetting he was supposed to be shy.

"Me, too!"

Chapter Nineteen

"Matt had arranged everything when Nancy fled. Now that she was coming out of hiding and needed help, she turned to him again. He and his wife, Julie, also a lawyer, lived in Connecticut with their two small children. They hadn't been back to California since the year that Nancy left. When he was told of her return, he made arrangements to join the family in California.

"I'm really going to see you that soon, Matty?" Nancy asked in disbelief.

"Really," he said.

"You're not disappointed in me after everything you did to help me get away?" she asked, sobbing as they spoke over the phone.

"Nance, I've never ever been disappointed in you," Matt said. "If this is what you feel you have to do, then I'll help you any way I can. You should know that by now."

"I do, but ..." Nancy began.

Matt interrupted, "No buts about it. I want you to be happy. If you think this is what you need to do, and this is the best thing for Frank and Lilly, or Russ and Angela, whatever we're calling them," he chuckled. "Then that's what we'll do. I'm going to make a few calls before we get there and line up a lawyer we can talk to. How's that sound?"

"Great!" Nancy said, relieved he was on her side.

"Why don't you find a place to live? That way, when I get there, Bryce and I can move all your stuff for you."

"Seriously?" she asked in stunned disbelief.

Matt countered, "Yes, Nancy, seriously. What are brothers and brothers-in-law for, you big dope?"

"I dunno. Thanks, Matt."

"For what?"

"Being you," she simply replied.

"Let me talk to Oli."

"Okay."

Nancy handed the phone to her sister.

"Hey, Matt," Olivia said.

"How's she doing?" he asked, sounding concerned.

"Seems okay," Olivia said, walking out of the room. "But I think she's still a little shell-shocked. Right now, her main concern is the kids. Frank wants to find his daddy, and that's what's driving this whole thing. I'm not sure how she's going to handle any of this when we find Vince or if Vince finds her."

"Did you find out if he still lives in Vista Oaks?" Matt asked.

Olivia answered, "Yeah, I found out he's long gone. No one knows where he went."

"Then he could be anywhere."

"Yeah," she agreed.

"Okay, is Bryce near you?"

"Yeah, right here," she answered, looking toward her husband. "Wanna talk to him?"

"Yeah," Matt answered. "Hey, Oli?"

"Yeah?"

"Love you. Thanks for helpin' her."

"Love you too, Matty. You don't have to thank me any more than I have to thank you," she stated simply.

She handed the phone to Bryce.

"Hey, Matt, what's going on?" Bryce asked.

Bryce had married Olivia eleven years earlier. He was a successful graphic designer with his own firm in Greenbriar. Bryce was an average-sized man, firmly built with square shoulders, a chiseled chin, deep blue eyes, and dimples in his cheeks when he smiled. He was fiercely loyal to Olivia and her entire family. As far as Matt was concerned, they were brothers, not brothers-in-law.

"Hey, Bryce, Oli told you Vince wasn't in Vista Oaks anymore, right?" Matt asked.

"Yeah."

"So he could be virtually anywhere," Matt said, "including Greenbriar. For all we know, he could be watching your house. Be careful, okay?"

"You know I will be," Bryce assured him. "I'm going to take the next couple days off and help Nancy find an apartment. I'm thinking, if I work it right, I can get her into a place with security. What do think?" Bryce asked.

"I think that's a smart idea." Matt agreed.

"Now, I just have to figure out how to trick her."

Matt disagreed, "I think you're better off telling her the truth. Tell her that we talked and we think she would be safer in a complex with security than trying to trick her. She's had enough deception in her life. We don't want to be any party to that."

"Yeah, you're probably right. I didn't think of it that way," Bryce acquiesced.

"Okay, I also told her that, when I get there, we'd go to Castle City and get her stuff. You okay with that?" Matt asked.

"Sure. No problem."

"Okay. See you in a few. Give my love to the girls."

"Bye."

When Bryce got off the phone, he, Nancy, and Olivia started making plans.

"I can't believe I'm actually here!"

Nancy started crying again.

"Well, believe it, baby girl. You are," Olivia said. She hugged her sister. "We're here for you anytime."

"I've been so lonely by myself," Nancy spoke into the nape of Olivia's neck. "I'd sit there with Frank and Lilly and dream about being with everyone else."

"You don't have to dream anymore," Bryce said.

"Where are those kids anyway? It's awfully quiet," Nancy wondered out loud.

"Yeah, too quiet," Olivia agreed.

They found Melissa, Nicole, and Lilly playing with dolls in the girls' room. Oliver and Frank were quietly watching a movie.

"And you were afraid they wouldn't get along?" Olivia asked Nancy.

"Mommy, you look funny!"

"Thanks a lot, Ange ... er ... I mean ... Lilly!" Nancy said, scooping up her daughter.

Olivia had just finished bleaching Nancy's hair back to its natural blonde color. Lilly didn't remember ever seeing her mother as a blonde.

"This is actually the color my hair's supposed to be. Don't you like it?"

"I guess so," Lilly said, unconvinced. "It just looks funny. I'll get used to it. Let's go show Russ ... er ... I mean ... Frank!"

Lilly ran off to find her brother.

"At least I won't have to worry about dyeing my roots anymore," Nancy said.

"Wow, Mom! That looks great!" Frank said, following Lilly back into the room.

"You really think so?" Nancy asked.

"Yeah. Can I go play now?"

"Sure," she said, watching Frank run off to find his cousin.

"He seems so happy." She sighed. "Oli, it's weird looking in the mirror and seeing me again. There's been a stranger looking back at me for so long, I kind of forgot who I was. Even though I'm really scared and I don't want to see Vince, I'm so tired of hiding. I know this is the right thing for to do. It's not just for the kids, it's for me, too. I need to come out of the shadows and find myself again."

"I can't even imagine what it's like to look in a mirror and see someone else," Olivia said. "Nance, we really are here for you. Whatever you need."

"I know you are, but I think this is something I might have to do by myself."

Bryce and Nancy found a three-bedroom apartment close to the Howard's house in a secured complex. The parking garage required a key for entry. The only way into the building was either through the garage or the guarded front entrance. A security guard was on guard twenty-four hours a day. Nancy's apartment was on the third floor in the back. It was available on June 28.

Matt, Julie, and their two children, two-year-old Stephanie and six-month-old Peter, arrived in Greenbriar early on the morning of June 22. Nancy met them at the front door. Matt and Nancy clung to each.

"I thought I'd never see you again," Nancy said through her tears.

"You really thought you were going to get rid of me that easily?" her brother teased.

"You know what I mean."

"Yeah, I do."

"Hi, Julie. I'm sorry. I didn't mean to be so rude," Nancy said, backing away from Matt to say hello to her sister-in-law.

"Don't worry, Nance. You're not being rude. I understand completely," Julie said, holding a sleeping Peter. Stephanie was peering out from behind her leg. "Hey, Steph, this is your Aunt Nancy. Do you want to say hello?"

"Nuh-uh," Stephanie said, shaking her head from side to side.

"That's okay," Nancy said. "I understand. I didn't want to say hello to strangers when I was two, either."

She was still wiping the tears out of her eyes.

"Why you kying?" Stephanie asked.

"I'm crying because I'm happy to see my brother," Nancy answered.

"Who dat?" Stephanie asked, confused.

"That's your daddy, and your daddy is my brother."

"Huh?" Wonder filled her little face as her nose curled up and tiny blue eyes squinted.

Nancy squatted down to get to Stephanie's level.

"Just like Peter's your brother, your daddy is my brother. Here, come with me. I'll show you something."

Stephanie shyly looked at Nancy's outstretched hand, glancing toward her mother for reassurance.

"It's okay. You can go with her," Julie assured.

Stephanie took Nancy's finger and wrapped her hand around it. Slowly, Nancy led her into Olivia's house. They quietly went into the family room, where the walls were lined with pictures. One of the pictures was Matt, Olivia, and Nancy as children. Nancy lightly lifted Stephanie up to show her.

"See that little girl?" Nancy asked Stephanie.

Stephanie slowly nodded.

"That's me," Nancy said.

"Ree-ddy?" Stephanie asked, wide-eyed.

"Yes, really," Nancy smiled. "See that boy there?"

"Uh-huh," Stephanie said, nodding.

"That's your daddy when he was a boy."

"Ree-ddy?" she said, even more wide-eyed. This time, it was a look of mistrust.

"Really," Nancy said. "He's my big brother. That other girl is your Aunt Olivia. I think I hear her coming around the corner right now."

"Whatcha got there, Nance?" Olivia asked as she came into the room.

"I found me a new niece. Stephanie, meet your Aunt Olivia. Aunt Olivia, may I introduce you to Stephanie?"

"Very pleased to meet you, Stephanie," Olivia said, bowing deeply.

Stephanie giggled as her parents came into the room. She squirmed out of Nancy's arms and ran up to her dad.

"Daddy! Daddy!"

"What, punkin?" Matt answered.

"I thaw you!"

"You did? Where?"

"Ober dere!"

She dragged Matt over to the picture Nancy had just shown her of the three of them.

"Nice pics, Oli. Where did you find these?"

"I got them off Mom and Dad's walls when I had to empty their house out last year."

Their parents had been very clear on funeral and memorial arrangements. Everything had changed when

Nancy went into hiding. Neither one had wanted a memorial service or an elaborate funeral. Both had been cremated, and their ashes were in urns in Olivia's living room. The plan had been to spread the ashes at sea when the three children were together, whenever that would be. Their parents had taught them to rejoice in life, not dwell on death.

"I think we should go out to the bay and celebrate their lives," Matt said as he picked up his daughter. "They would be glad to know we are together again, and they would want us to put them to rest."

"Sounds good," Olivia said. "I think that's a great way to start Nancy's new life."

"I'm okay with that," Nancy sadly agreed.

It was time to put the past behind her and face the future with whatever it might bring.

Chapter Twenty

Matt had made contact with Jackie Kelly before he left Connecticut. She was a prominent divorce attorney in Greenbriar. He and Nancy had an appointment early in the week after his arrival.

As they were ushered into a plush office decorated in subtle tones of navy blue and silver, Matt whispered to Nancy, "She's very highly recommended." Jackie Kelly walked in, and her very presence commanded attention. A petite woman with long, jet-black hair tied loosely in a bow, she had sparkling navy blue eyes. She wore very little makeup and carried herself gracefully. Her firm handshake immediately put Nancy at ease.

"Nancy, I'm not going to lie to you and tell you that this is going to be easy," Jackie said after listening to Nancy's story. "You did technically kidnap your own children. We do, however, have time on our side."

"I don't understand," Nancy said.

"Well, Mr. Cooper should have filed a police report immediately upon your disappearance. He didn't. He could have filed any number of charges against you, including kidnapping. You abandoned your husband, and you fled the county with your children. He could have required that you and your children return to Vista Oaks immediately, but, as I said, he didn't do any of those things. Now he has waited too long for any of that to be effective."

"Is that a good thing?" Nancy asked.

"I would say so. We do have a few obstacles in our way," she continued. "California is a community property state, so I recommend we do this one step at a time."

"What does that mean?" Matt asked.

"As long as Nancy and Vince are still legally married, he's entitled to one-half of everything she has."

"Everything?" Nancy asked in disbelief.

"Yes, Nancy. Everything. That's how a community property state works."

"He could get half of my share of our parents' estate?" she asked. Tears welled in her eyes.

"He can try," Jackie said. "But, as I started to say, let's take this one step at a time. First, we file a stipulation to bifurcate marital status from dissolution of proceeding an order. That is, we ask the judge to grant us dissolution of the marital status only. And we reserve judgment pertaining to property, child custody and support, community property, attorney's fees and costs, and any other arrangements."

"Good idea," Matt agreed.

Nancy interrupted, "Someone want to explain what that means to me?"

"We get you divorced from Vince. Then we deal with alimony, child support, and property issues later," Matt clarified.

"Okay, I don't want any of his money anyway. As far as property goes, there isn't any. There's just money. I don't want his, and I don't want him to have mine. So let's get this thing started because I sure don't want to be married to him anymore. What do we have to do to accomplish that?"

"We will serve him with papers for the dissolution. At the same time, we will petition the court requesting a bifurcation. It has been my experience that this court rarely denies this type of request," Jackie explained. "Do you have an address for Vince?"

"Only our old house in Vista Oaks," Nancy answered.

"Does he still live there?"

"I really don't know. What if he doesn't?"

"We'll send the papers there. If he's left a forwarding address, they'll be forwarded. If not, they'll come back here. Then we'll put an ad in the paper looking for him. He has six months to petition the court. If he doesn't make an appearance, you'll be granted an uncontested divorce."

"Six months? Then I'll be free?" Nancy asked in astonishment.

"Nance, I don't think you'll be free as long as you have his kids," Matt said.

"Yeah, you're probably right," Nancy gloomily agreed. "Let's just deal with this right now. I want to get this divorce as quickly as possible, please."

"Okay, I'll draw up the papers. We'll file as quickly as possible. If all runs smoothly, you could be divorced as early as the New Year," Jackie said, standing up to indicate their meeting had ended. "Nancy, remember, I'm here if you have any questions. Anytime."

"Thank you."

Nancy was quiet as she and Matt left Jackie's office and walked back to the car. "So what did you think?" Matt asked her as they were driving back to Olivia's house.

"She seemed like she knew what she was doing, but then she hasn't met Vince yet. What about you?"

"I agree with you. Then I also know that she's very highly recommended. Let's just take this one step at a time. Let her file the paperwork to get this ball rolling. The first thing we have to do is get you into the family court system and have the divorce proceedings started. I don't think the sparks are going to start flying until Vince finds out and starts fighting over the kids," he said.

"I'm just scared about what's going to happen when he finds out. Period."

"He is going to find out. Sooner or later, he will," Matt said emphatically. "Bryce said you guys found an apartment with a security guard, right?"

"Yeah," she responded. Her mood was now altered.

"Just be careful every time you go in or out. Never let anyone in without checking."

"Yes, Matt, I know," Nancy pretended to be annoyed, but he knew she wasn't.

"When you get the kids into a school, let the teachers and the principal know exactly what's going on. You can't keep him from getting in, but you can make everyone around them aware."

"I know. I've thought of all of that and a hundred million other things a billion more times. It doesn't mean I'm not scared all of the time. I am. But I'm tired of being scared all the time. Do you know what it's like to be scared every minute of every day of your life?" She was crying so hard that she was having a difficult time talking. "You don't. I wake up scared. I go to sleep scared. I have dreams that I'll never see my children again."

"Nance, I'm just trying to help," Matt softly said.

"I know you are, and I don't mean to unload on you. But I have to do this by myself."

"No, you don't. We're here for you. All of us. Me, Julie, Olivia, and Bryce. Let us help," her brother pleaded.

"I'm trying. I really am."

On Sunday morning, Nancy woke up with Frank and Lilly in her bed. She couldn't have been happier. This was her first weekend in a very long time with the entire family. They had never been all together like this before. When she was married, Vince had kept her away from her family. She hoped she was the first one awake. She wanted to make pancakes for everyone. She quietly crept into the kitchen with her children. Julie and Peter were already there.

"I was going to surprise everyone and make pancakes," Nancy whispered, hoping not to wake anyone else up.

"I think that's a great idea," Julie replied. "Need help?"

"Can you make the coffee?"

"Already ahead of you. It's brewing as we speak!" Julie said.

Julie was soft-spoken and kind. She'd managed to win the heart of Matt when many women had failed before her. Her open, down-to-earth nature and sheer goodness shone through in everything she did. Compared to her husband, she was tiny, but she managed to keep up with him. They'd dated for more than ten years before they actually married. They didn't think a piece of paper was necessary to cement their relationship. Nancy and Olivia accepted Julie as a sister almost the first moment they met her, which was before Olivia was even married. Julie had been around through all of Nancy's troubles and had stood by Matt as he helped Nancy. She was there for Nancy and any of the Lewistons, whatever the price.

"Frank and Lilly, why don't you go see if you can find Melissa, Nicole, and Oliver," Nancy whispered. "But please don't wake up Aunt Olivia, Uncle Bryce, or Uncle Matt."

"Okay, Mommy, we'll be very, very quiet," Lilly said as they tiptoed down the hall.

"Where's Stephanie?" Nancy asked.

"Snuggled up with her daddy. It's her favorite place to sleep."

"Yeah, I kind of remember he used to be my favorite teddy bear, too," Nancy said, smiling.

"It's nice to see you smiling again, Nancy," Julie said.

"You mean I haven't been smiling?"

"Not for a long time! Now we have to fatten you up a little. You might actually be your old self again." Julie said, with a wink.

"Huh, I'm not even sure if that old self exists anymore," Nancy replied. A faraway look shadowed her face.

Five kids came trudging down the hallway into the kitchen just as the first batch of pancakes came off the grill. Nancy and Julie made a good team keeping the pancakes and syrup going until all the kids had their fill. They hadn't even noticed they were being watched.

"Where are my pancakes?" Olivia asked slyly as she snuck into a chair at the table.

"Oli! Happy Sunday!" Nancy said, putting a pile of pancakes in front of her big sister.

"Coffee?" Julie asked.

"But, of course," Olivia responded.

The three women laughed. An outsider observing would instantly know these women were sisters.

"What's all this commotion?" Bryce said as he came into the kitchen. Matt, carrying Stephanie, followed.

"Pancake breakfast. Come join me," Olivia said to her husband as she patted the chair next to her.

"Mmm. I think I will."

"Daddy, me, too," Stephanie said, squirming out of Matt's arms. "Hi, Mommy!"

"Hi, Stephers!"

Nancy served everyone pancakes until they could eat no

more. The children were anxious to go outside and play."

"What's goin' on, Nance?" Olivia asked, noticing that tears had begun to stream down her sister's face.

"I'm happy. I'm scared. I'm sorry. A little bit of everything," she said, embarrassed at being caught crying.

"That's not so unusual," Matt said. "But what are you sorry about?"

"I'm sorry I'm putting you all through this again."

"Would you cut that out?"

"I'm going to pop you one."

"If you don't stop that ..." they all seemed to speak at the same time.

"Okay, I'm not sorry."

She laughed.

"That's better," Bryce said. "Now, your apartment is ready next week, so Matt and I will go to Castle City while you get it ready. We should be back here by noon. Does that give you enough time to do whatever you need to do?"

"I think so," Nancy said. "Oli, are you going to help me? Is Julie going to help me? Who is going to watch the kids? How are we handling that?"

"I thought it would be best if I watch the kids. Peter's still nursing. Olivia can help you with the apartment," Julie suggested.

"Okay," Nancy agreed.

"Seriously, guys, I'd be lost without all of you!" Nancy said.

Matt scooted over on the couch and put his arm around his sister.

"Yeah, we know. That's why we'll be sending you the bill in July. Julie and I are really expensive."

Nancy punched her brother in the stomach. Soon, the room broke out in bedlam.

Chapter Twenty One

At two o'clock on that same Sunday afternoon, Vince nervously stood outside Trent and Christina Brown's front door, contemplating whether or not he should ring the doorbell.

What the hell am I doing here?

His moment of quandary was interrupted. Chris opened the door and briskly escorted him into her house.

"Vince, this is my husband, Trent," Chris said, introducing him. "Trent, this is Vince."

"Pleased to meet you," Vince politely said, shaking Trent's hand firmly.

"Same to you," Trent replied, returning the shake amicably. "I hear you're one heck of a mechanic."

"Thank you, sir," Vince said modestly. "I don't know if I'm any better than anyone else."

"Well, come on in. Make yourself at home," Chris said, breaking up the boys. "Would you like a drink?" She led him into the living room. "This is my sister, Crystal. Her husband, Connor, is in the den."

"Hi, Crystal," Vince said. "I can certainly see the family resemblance." Crystal was a taller version of

Christina, but her hair was shorter and darker.

"I'm not sure if that's good or bad," Crystal coyly answered.

"I'd say that's good," Vince responded.

Chris and Crystal Thomason had grown up in Castle City. Crystal was two years older than Chris, but they were often confused as twins. Their father had left the family home when Chris was ten. Their mother basically checked out after he left. Her attention soon turned toward anything that would keep her warm at night. She forgot she still had two girls at home who needed a mother.

Crystal took over the role as the mother figure. She made sure she and Chris went to school every day, there was food on the table, and they had clean clothes to wear. She'd taken a job at the diner when she was fourteen. She brought in enough money to buy food. Their mother's activities brought in enough to pay the rent and utilities, but she was rarely sober enough to be a positive role model.

As a junior in high school, Crystal met Connor. They fell in love and were married the day after graduation. They took Chris in to live with them, but she was rarely home. Chris sought love and acceptance elsewhere, following her mother's example. She'd lost her virginity by the age of fourteen, learning that boys would give lavish gifts in return for the promise of sex. Her plans were to graduate high school and leave Castle City. Then Trent Brown arrived, and everything changed.

Trent appeared four months before she was to graduate. He immediately became her next target. When she got pregnant, he did the only thing he could do. He proposed. There went her plans to leave. They were married the summer after graduation. Brandon was born the following winter. It didn't take long for Trent to realize what he'd married. He made a conscious decision to turn his back on his wife's activities. As long as she provided a decent home for him and their son, he would not object. That was before the night he met Nancy. As soon as Nancy arrived in Castle City, Trent realized his marriage was a sham and there was the possibility of a better life. He was biding his time awaiting the right opportunity to make his move.

"Come on, Vince. You don't need to be gabbing with the girls," Trent said. "Let's go grab a beer and watch the game."

"Sounds good to me," Vince said, following Trent into the den. The Brown's den was a room designed for watching TV. One wall of the room held nothing but a wide-screen television set that was directly opposite two recliners and a sofa. The dark paneling, bookcases, and shelves along the walls gave the room a definite masculine air.

"Nice setup!" Vince commented, genuinely impressed.

"A man has to have a place to call his own. I work too damn hard not to have my own space," Trent said. "This is my brother-in-law, Connor. You just met his wife, Crystal, in the kitchen. Their kids, Jack and Linda, are hanging around somewhere, along with my kid, Brandon."

"Hey, Connor, nice to meetcha," Vince mumbled.

"Right back at ya," Connor said, not lifting his eyes from the game.

"Where are you from, Vince?" Trent asked.

Vince answered as he kept scanning the room, "Originally, I'm from Wilton, Ohio. It's a little town outside Columbus."

"What brought you to California?"

"I moved here when I got out of the service. What's not to like about Southern California?"

"That's true," Trent agreed. "Do you have any family here?"

"Trent, can you start the coals?" Chris poked her head in the door. "We're starving."

"Babe, you've outdone yourself," Trent said, stretching. "That meal was wonderful." The only thing that remained on the table were empty plates that once held barbequed chicken and ribs, coleslaw, a fresh fruit salad, homemade biscuits, corn on the cob and peach cobbler.

"I agree. That was delicious," Vince agreed. "Thank you again for inviting me. I don't remember the last time I had a home-cooked meal."

"Here, let me help you clear, Chris," Crystal said, getting up.

Connor excused himself to finish watching the game as the kids scattered.

"So, Vince, Christina mentioned you needed my help finding someone," Trent said after they were alone at the table.

"Yeah," Vince solicitously said, "I told her I thought my wife and kids were here. She thought you might be able to help me."

"What makes you think they're here?" Trent furled his brow in consternation as he asked.

"A PI told me they were," Vince simply answered.

Bewildered, Trent asked, "Why would you hire a PI?"

Vince placed his hands on the table, folded them together as if in prayer, looked Trent solidly in the eye, and spoke evenly, "My wife stole my kids in the middle of the night three years ago. She's a drug addict and pathological liar. I'm afraid something terrible has happened to my kids. I hired a PI to locate them."

"So this PI found them in Castle City?" Trent asked. His police instincts were kicking in.

"Uh-huh." Vince nodded.

"But he didn't give you an address?" Trent's brow furled again.

Vince snapped back defensively, "I fired him before we got that far."

"Why?"

"He pissed me off."

"Okay," Trent said, suspiciously.

Trent had been a cop too long not to know that something didn't add up. There was a something about the story Vince wasn't telling him. His gut sense told him there was more to it. He wasn't quite sure what it was, but he was going to have to find out.

Stalling for time, he asked, "Do you have any pictures of your wife or your kids?"

"When she left me, my son was four, and my daughter was two. I have no idea what they look like today," Vince explained. "But I do have a picture of my wife." Vince reached into his wallet and pulled out his wedding picture. "Here's the bitch on a happier day. Nancy Cooper."

Trent had to stop himself from leaping across the table to clutch Vince's throat. He slowly picked up a glass of water and took a long drink. Attempting to calm himself down, he slowly and deliberately took a deep breath.

"Let me think how I could assist you," he began. His mind was racing with thoughts on how to get this maniac out of his house. "First, have you filed a missing person's report?"

"No, as I said, she's a fucking liar. If I filed that report and she were to be found, she'd blame me."

"Blame you for what?" Trent asked. Again, his brow was furled.

Vince answered angrily, "Hell if I know. She's the liar. She'd make some fucking thing up!"

"Judging by that picture ..." Trent said, looking at the

picture of Nancy again. Her long, blonde hair captivated him. He had to force himself to look away. "No one around town looks like her."

She's absolutely radiant.

"I can take the picture and show it to my men if you'd like," he said in a voice much calmer than he felt.

Gratefully, Vince said, "That would sure be a start. Thanks."

Trent's reaction startled even him.

"Why don't you go ahead and give me the picture. I'll get back to you if I find anything out."

"Great," Vince said. "I appreciate any help I can get."

Trent took the picture from Vince and put it in his pocket.

"Will you excuse me just a minute?" Trent asked.

"Sure, Trent," Vince said.

Trent went into the other room, returning a few minutes later.

"Vince, how have you been looking for … uh Nancy? Was that it?"

"Yeah, that's the bitch's name," Vince spat venomously. "I've been camping out at the schools looking for my kids. I started out on the other side of town last September. I had planned to switch to this side of town in a few months. I've been through eleven different elementary schools. I'm giving it until the end of the school year. If I haven't found 'em by then, I'm going home."

Trent asked pleasantly, "Where exactly is that?"

"Vista Oaks."

The phone rang. Chris yelled for Trent to pick it up. He went into the den.

Trent walked back into the dining room and apologized, "I'm really sorry, but I have to go. Duty calls."

"Trent, it's Sunday," Chris whined.

"I know, babe, but I'm the captain," Trent explained. "It can't be helped."

"I guess I should be leaving, too." Vince said.

"No, Vince," Trent insisted. "Don't leave on my account. It's still early. You can stay and visit with Chris awhile. What else have you got to do?" he asked, giving him a piercing look.

Vince never really had a chance to take the bait.

Crystal said, "We really need to head out, too. Come on, kids. Get your stuff together. We're going to go. Come say good-bye to Uncle Trent. He has to go to work."

"Bye, Uncle Trent."

"Bye, munchkins," Trent said, hugging them.

"I'll try not to be too late," he told Chris hurriedly, giving her a kiss on the cheek.

"Where's Brandon?"

"In his room. Watching a movie," Chris answered. "Brandon, come out here and say good night to your dad."

"Leave him alone," Trent said.

Trent left for work. Connor, Crystal, Jack, and Linda left right after him.

"I really should get going, too," Vince said, heading for the front door.

"What's your rush?" Chris asked, slithering next to him and rubbing her body close to his.

"You've got to be kidding!" Vince asked in astonishment.

"Who?" She batted her eyelashes. "Me?"

"I'm outta here," Vince said.

He walked out the front door.

That crazy bitch is going to get me killed.

Trent drove straight to his office. He had to make some phone calls. He didn't want to be overheard or interrupted.

There was no emergency that needed his attention. He'd called his dispatcher and asked him to call his house back five minutes later. Trent had arranged the emergency so he could get out of his own house. Nancy was in serious trouble, and he had to figure out how to help her. But he didn't know exactly where she was. She just said she was going home, but home where?

Trent opened his locked drawer and pulled out the file he'd created three years earlier. It had all of the phone numbers he needed to reach Matt or Olivia in case there was an emergency regarding Nancy. This was definitely an emergency.

It hadn't been his place to ask Nancy where she was going when she left. He really didn't have any idea where she went. He assumed Matt or Olivia would know. Dialing Matt's home number first, he restlessly strummed his fingers atop his desk.

"You've reached Matt and Julie. We're not here. Leave a message after the tone," the answering machine said after the fourth ring.

Debating whether or not to leave a message, Trent hung up. He decided to call Olivia. If he received an answering machine there as well, he would call Matt back and leave a message. Dialing again, he was taken by surprise when Bryce answered the phone.

"Hello, this is Trent Brown in Castle City. I'm so sorry to bother you."

"Hey, Trent, this is Bryce. You're not bothering us."

"I was wondering if you knew where Nancy might be."

"Sure, she's right here. Did you want to talk to her?"

"Yes, if I could. Thanks, Bryce."

"Hold on a sec. Let me get her for you."

At least I know she's in Greenbriar. I wonder how long she'll be there.

His thoughts were quickly interrupted.

"Hi, Trent! How sweet of you to call!" Nancy said. "Are you checking up on me?"

"Yup, just want to make sure you made it all right. You sound great, so I assume you did. How is everything?"

"Everything's going good. I found an apartment with a twenty-four-hour security guard around the corner from here. I move in next week. Matt and Bryce are driving to Castle City to get the rest of my stuff. Then I'm going to find a job." She was rambling, but he didn't care. It was so good to hear her voice. "The kids start school with Oli's kids in September. I'm filing for divorce. I'm moving forward. Still scared. But I've got to do it."

"Remember what I said when you left. I'm only a couple hours away. Call me if you need me," Trent reiterated.

"I remember. I won't forget. I won't forget everything you've done for me, Trent. I could never do that," she said. Her heart was pounding wildly.

"Hey, did you say my buddy Matt was there?"

"Yeah," she replied. "Do you want to talk to him?"

"I'd love to!" Trent answered, trying not to sound too anxious.

"Hang on. I'll get him for you."

Nancy went to find her brother. She couldn't explain to herself why the phone call from Trent made her feel like a teenager. She was giddy.

Chapter Twenty Two

"Hey, Trent. How are you, man?" Matt said with delight, picking up the phone to talk to his old friend.

"Not too bad, buddy."

"Thanks for everything you did for Nancy. I don't think words can ever express our appreciation."

"It was easy. She's become special to me," Trent said. He lowered his voice and continued tentatively, "I need to tell you something, and it's important."

"Okay. Let me go somewhere that's not so noisy. Hang on a minute so I can switch phones." Turning to Julie, he said, "Can you hang this up for me when I get it in the bedroom?"

"Sure," Julie said. "Is everything all right?"

"He needs to tell me something important," Matt explained. "I'm going to the bedroom where I can hear better."

"What's going on?" Olivia asked.

"I don't know. I'll let you know when I find out," Matt replied, getting up to go into the spare bedroom where there was a telephone.

"What's up?" Matt asked, getting settled in the bedroom.

"You'll never believe who was in my house for a barbeque today."

"Who?"

"Vince."

"What! Why?" Matt exploded in disbelief.

"That's another story for another day," Trent answered. "Let's just say that my marriage is a sham and my wife brings home her boy toys to dangle in front of me. This month, it must be Vince."

"I'm so sorry, Trent."

"Anyway," Trent continued, "the premise she used to bring him over was that he's looking for his family."

"Okay," Matt asked, "how did he end up in Castle City?"

"Apparently, he hired a PI who traced them here. But he got pissed off at the PI before he found out her address, and he fired the guy."

Matt chuckled, "Sounds like something Vince would do."

"The way he's telling the story is that Nancy's a drug addict and pathological liar. She kidnapped the kids."

Matt exploded, "He said that?"

"Hold on; it gets better!" Trent continued. "He can't fill out a missing person's report because, if they were to be found, she'd just lie and tell them some made-up story about him."

Matt was dazed.

"How long is he staying in town?"

"No way to know that one. Best I can tell, he plans on staying here until the end of the school year, whatever that means. If he can't find 'em by then, he's moving back to Vista Oaks."

"So she did see him last week," Matt said in a speculative voice.

"What?" Trent asked, bewildered.

"You mean she didn't tell you?"

"Tell me what?" Trent asked, puzzled.

"On her last day of work, she was upset about something, and her mind was wandering. As she pulled out of the parking lot from work, she cut off a pickup. She was sure it was him. She called Olivia, and she was shaken up pretty badly. She was positive it was his truck and it was him. Oli managed to calm her down. The funny thing is that Nancy's always had this intuition about things. She must've known inside that he was getting closer. I'm surprised she didn't tell you about it."

"She didn't even tell me she was moving away until she came by my office to say good-bye on Friday morning," Trent said. "I can't blame her though. On Easter, my *wonderful* wife had a different boy toy over."

"Yeah, that one I heard about," Matt said. "Actually, I think that's what started this whole thing."

"Maybe that's a good thing. Imagine what would have happened if they were still here today."

"God, I hadn't thought about that," Matt said. "I'm supposed to be picking up her stuff in a few days. What if he sees me?"

"Nancy mentioned that to me. She said you and Bryce were coming, right?"

"Yeah, that's the plan."

"Let me see if I can work something out here to load the truck. I'll drive it to you. Hell, I haven't seen you in a while. It would be great to get together anyway."

"That sounds great!" Matt exclaimed. "In the meantime, I have to let Nancy know what's going on. I can't keep her in the dark. We went to a divorce lawyer a couple days ago. The papers are being filed soon. Now we have to figure out if we send them to his old address in Vista Oaks and pretend we don't know where he is. Or do we tell the attorney we have a new address for him?"

"Hell, I don't know where the bastard lives! I only had him over for dinner. For all I know, he lives in a cardboard box!" Trent laughed.

"Yeah, I see your point," Matt agreed.

The old friends remained on the phone for a few minutes longer catching up on other things before they hung up, having made tentative plans for Trent to bring Nancy's belongings to Greenbriar the following week.

Rejoining the family in the den, Matt informed Nancy about Vince's whereabouts. Nancy's euphoric state turned sour.

"Why was he at Trent's house?" Olivia asked.

"Apparently, Christina invited him for a barbeque. She was unaware of his family ties," Matt answered.

"You mean she never knew that Suzanne Keller was really Nancy Cooper?" Bryce asked.

"I made Trent promise not to tell anyone in Castle City who I really was ... even Christina," Nancy explained. "I never trusted her anyway. There's something off about that woman. I can't really put my finger on it. From the very beginning, she never trusted that Trent was only helping me. She always thought there was something more."

Nancy said worriedly, "If Vince was really in Castle City, I really did cut him off in the pickup. I wasn't imagining things."

"I think so, too," Matt agreed.

"Now what?" Nancy pleaded.

"Nothing changes. The only deviation we have to make is that Bryce and I can't go to Castle City now. We run the risk of Vince seeing us. Trent has volunteered to bring your things here," Matt explained. "He'll get the truck loaded. We'll meet him at your apartment and unload it."

"So Trent's coming here?" Nancy asked.

Excitement over Trent replaced all feelings of dread regarding Vince.

"He's going to let me know if he can work it out. If he can't, we'll have to figure something else out."

"What about the divorce papers?" Nancy asked. "Now we know he isn't in Vista Oaks, shouldn't we send them to Castle City?"

"I think we should let Jackie file the papers as planned," Matt began.

Julie interjected, "Let her office mail them to his last-known address in Vista Oaks. When it comes back with no forwarding address, then you can forward it to his employer in Castle City. That at least gives you a head start."

"What good does that do?" Nancy asked.

"If Vince's taken by surprise, he might not contest the divorce," Matt answered. "I'm sure he'll still put up one hell of a fight over the kids and support payments, but you'll at least be divorced."

Around noon on moving day, Trent arrived at an apartment in Greenbriar that was spotless and ready for furniture. Between Matt, Bryce, and Trent, the van was unloaded in less than an hour. Nancy was overwhelmed. As she unpacked her meager belongings into her new home, tears rolled down her cheeks.

"What's wrong, baby girl?" Olivia asked, wrapping her sister in her arms as they finished putting dishes in the cupboard.

"I'm not too sure. This is really scary. It's suddenly very real."

"What is?" Olivia asked.

"Living alone again. Being here. Waiting."

"You're not really alone," Olivia whispered, lovingly rubbing Nancy's back. "I'm right around the corner. You can't get rid of me that easily."

"I know, but I don't know. It's hard to put into words," Nancy sniffled as they disengaged from their hug. "I'm just so tired of being scared all the time."

"What's going on in here?" Matt barged in and asked.

"Nothing," Nancy said, quickly drying her tears. "Are you guys about ready for lunch?"

"We're starving!" Bryce said. "I think we could eat everything you have in your fridge. Oh yeah, there's no food in there."

"Funny, Bryce. Very funny!" Nancy said, punching him in the arm.

"Okay, guys, I've got to head back," Trent interrupted.

"What? You're not going to stay for lunch?" Matt asked. "Come on, that's the least we can do for you."

"I really need to head back …" Trent began.

"Please, Trent, just stay for lunch," Nancy pleaded. "You've been such a big help. Besides, the kids would love to see you."

"Well, if you put it that way, how could I possibly refuse?"

"Uncle Trent! Uncle Trent!" Lilly ran up to him as soon as he walked in the door. "Did you see our new house? I get my very own bedroom this time! Did you see it?"

"I did see it!" Trent answered. "It's very nice, Ange."

"My name's not Angela anymore, silly. It's Lilly!" she scolded Trent.

"I forgot. Sorry," he apologized.

"And Russ isn't Russ anymore. He's Frank."

"I knew that, too. Where is he?" Trent asked.

"In the backyard playing. Come on. I'll show you."

She dragged Trent by the hand into the backyard.

"Wow, she adores him," Julie said as she greeted everyone when they came in.

"He's been really good to my kids for the past couple of years," Nancy said, watching him walk away.

"Looks like someone else adores him, too," Matt commented.

Chapter Twenty Three

As people prepared for their summer vacations, Owens Auto became overwhelmed with business. Vince rarely had time for a break. That didn't stop him from partaking in his nighttime festivities though. After leaving the Brown's house, he decided he needed something. Meeting Larry at the diner, Vince replayed the events of the day.

"I couldn't believe that bitch made a play for me in her own house," Vince told his friend.

"That's nothing," Larry commented. "She probably would've taken you into her own bedroom if you'd shown any interest!"

"With the kid in the house?" Vince asked dubiously.

"Hell, if she could get away with it, she'd do it in front of the kid."

"And you think Trent doesn't know a thing?" Vince asked doubtfully. "I don't think he's that dumb."

"I don't know," Larry said. "What's your plan now? Is she still coming over every Sunday?"

"I don't fucking know anymore, and I'm not really sure if I care. She's going to get me killed. I swear she is."

Christina showed up the following Sunday at Vince's apartment at the usual time. He could tell something had changed.

"This is over," she said, storming through the front door. "God, you live like a pig."

"I don't remember you complaining before," he remarked defensively. "And what'd you just say?"

"You heard me. It's over," she reiterated.

He asked defiantly, "Fine. But why the sudden change?"

Pacing around the room like a caged animal, she replied, "Trent knows all about us."

"He said that?" Vince asked, raising one eyebrow in disbelief.

"No," she answered him. "I can just tell."

Her eyes didn't meet his gaze.

"You what?" he mocked her.

"It's just the way he's acting," Chris exploded. "I've been married to that man for almost ten years, and I can tell he knows. He's acting differently. He doesn't care. That means he knows."

"Oh, you can tell. I see. Okay. Fine with me," Vince said, trying not to let his hurt feelings show.

"I thought it was best if I told you in person. See ya around," she said, walking out the door.

Great! Fucking great!

He called Larry to get himself good and wasted.

On Nancy's first night in her new apartment, Frank and Lilly wanted their cousins to sleep over. Lilly's room had the Disney curtains and comforter from the old house, but Frank's room wasn't decorated.

"Nance, he's a boy. He really doesn't care about that stuff," Olivia said. "Stop beating yourself up about it. You don't have to be supermom. It's just a bedroom."

"I just want them to be happy."

"Decorations in a room are not going to make or break happiness," Olivia admonished her.

"Yeah, I guess you're right," Nancy conceded.

Near the end of July, Jackie Kelly's office received the stipulation for dissolution that had been addressed to Vincent Cooper in Vista Oaks. Addressee unknown was written across the face of the envelope.

Brian noticed the quality of Vince's work had diminished. Vince had fallen into his old habits. He would either go to work with a hangover or call in sick. When Brian approached Vince about it, Vince became extremely defensive.

"What the fuck do you mean? I made a mistake? It wasn't my mistake. The lady told me it was her front brake, not the rear. I didn't make the mistake."

By the beginning of August, Brian was fed up and had had enough. He'd seen an apt mechanic become an inept employee, and there was no explanation. Brian just knew that Vince was hurting his business.

"Vince, I'm really sorry," Brian said, "but I have to let you go."

"What?" Vince asked, dazed. He didn't what he'd just heard.

"You're fired," Brian repeated. "Here's a check with everything I owe you, including today's pay."

He handed Vince an envelope and tried to guide him toward his car.

"Why? I'm the best damn mechanic you got here, and you know it," Vince spat.

"Not anymore you're not," Brian said, shaking his head. "At one time, that was true. But it isn't now. I'm not sure what got into you, but, whatever it is, man, get rid of it. For your own sake."

"Ah, fuck you, Brian. Fuck you and this fucked-up town," Vince said.

He stormed off in a huff.

Vince decided his firing was a sign to go home. He loaded everything he possessed into his pickup, called the landlord, and told him he was leaving.

"I'm outta here, and I ain't payin' August's rent."

He started driving out of town, but he changed his mind. He turned around at the edge of town and headed straight for the police station.

"Can I see Trent Brown?"

"Captain Brown?" the receptionist asked.

"Yeah, Captain Brown," Vince answered, mocking her.

Vince was wearing stained jeans and a dirty T-shirt. His hair was messy, and a foul odor was coming from his direction. The receptionist was having a difficult time taking this person seriously as she calmly looked over her wire-rimmed glasses at him.

"Let me check. May I say whose asking for him?"

"Vince Cooper."

He almost reached over the glass paneling that was separating them and grabbed the cocky receptionist by the throat.

Who the hell does she think she is, anyway? She's no better than I am!

"Just a minute."

She picked up the phone and spoke quietly into the receiver.

She hung up, turned toward Vince, and said, "You can go down that corridor. Captain Brown will meet you at the end of the hall."

Vince headed down the long, narrow corridor that was

lined with walls of half-wall and half-glass. He could see the tops of people's heads as they sat at desks.

Too many desks in too little space. This looks like one hell of a fun place to work.

He noticed that everybody seemed to either be on the phone or typing away at a computer. At the end of the hall, Trent was waiting for him.

"Vince, what can I do for you?" Trent asked, extending his hand.

"I came by to see if you had any luck with my family," Vince said, taking the extended hand and shaking it firmly.

"Come on in my office. I'll tell you what I found out," Trent said amicably, as he ushered Vince to the end of the hall into his enclosed workspace.

He quickly noticed Vince's deteriorated state.

"So you did find something?" Vince asked in anticipation.

"Not exactly," Trent hesitantly replied. "I actually came up with nothing. There was or is no Nancy Cooper living in Castle City. I'm not sure what the PI you hired found. If you want, I could call him and see if he'll talk to me."

"Nah," Vince scoffed. "I think it was a crock. I'm leavin' today. I quit my job. I don't think she's here, and I'm not sure if she ever was here. I'm goin' home. Maybe she'll show up there."

"Okay," Trent said. "Let me know if there's anything else I can do for you, Vince."

Vince hesitated a moment and then said, "There is something I think you should know."

"What's that?"

"Your wife ... how should I say this ... is making a fool out of you," Vince said.

"Excuse me?" Trent asked, completely taken aback at the turn of this conversation.

"Your wife ... Christina."

"Yeah, I know who my wife is," Trent countered defensively.

"She's not who you think she is."

"Do you know who you are talking to?"

"Yeah, I do," Vince said, holding his ground. "And that's why I think you need to know. I like you. You seem like a really honest, nice, decent guy. She's making a fool out of you."

"Vince, I really appreciate what you're trying to do and say here, but she's not making a fool out of anyone but herself."

"You know?" Vince asked, taken aback.

Trent inquired, "Know what?"

"What she is."

"What is she?" Trent asked.

"A slut."

"Yes."

Trent opened the door to his office, escorted Vince to his pickup, and watched him drive down the street and out of his town.

Jackie Kelly's office forwarded the dissolution stipulation to Vincent Cooper c/o Owens Auto in Castle City, California, via certified mail in the second week of August. He never received it. It was returned unopened to Jackie's office.

Chapter Twenty Four

Christina knew something had changed in her marriage. She just didn't know what. Trent hadn't been the same after Vince came over for the barbeque. She assumed he finally figured out what she'd been doing for all these years.

Did that idiot Vince tell him? I'll just bide my time. I'm the best thing that's happened to Trent. He'll come around. I can outlast him.

Trent rarely came home for dinner. When he did, he didn't speak to Christina. He went straight to his den.

"Is everything all right?" she asked near the end of July. She'd had enough of this game.

"Yeah," he responded nonchalantly.

"Are you sure?" Christina pressed. "It seems like something is bothering you lately."

"Nope, just busy. That's all."

His attention was focused on the television, not the conversation.

"You'd tell me if something was wrong, right?"

"Sure."

"Okay."

But she had a nagging feeling inside that he wasn't telling the truth. He never wanted to make love to her anymore, not that she minded. He was boring and dispassionate anyway. It was like riding a bicycle. But he didn't even bother trying to come near her. She wondered whether there was someone else.

Trent's life changed dramatically on the afternoon he saw Nancy's picture slide across his table and heard the lies coming out of her husband's mouth. He knew at that moment how much he cared for Nancy. After spending the day with her entire family in Greenbriar, he became painfully aware that his marriage was a shell and that he'd been going through the motions of life without enjoying himself. He was too young for that. He watched Matt and Julie with envy. He could visibly see the love, admiration, and respect that Bryce and Olivia shared for each other. He wanted the same out of life.

He drove back to Castle City, determined to make some changes. First, he had to leave his wife. Then he had to leave his job. Or should he do it the other way around? He had to put out feelers for open positions in surrounding areas. Maybe his marriage was salvageable. Maybe it wasn't.

Vince left Castle City and drove straight to Vista Oaks, bunking with some buddies for a few nights before finding a dump he could rent. He lined up a job and quickly resumed his old way of life. He worked to feed his habit. Time whirled by in a blur. He quickly looked like the Vince that Nancy had left. He was large, unkempt, and slovenly. Months passed. He hadn't even noticed.

On Thanksgiving, Vince was just wasted enough to try the phone number he had for Olivia's house. He would see if he could find his wife. Dialing the number, he wasn't overly optimistic.

Olivia and Nancy were in the kitchen, preparing for the family gathering. The five kids were outside. When the phone rang, Nancy said, "I'll get it."

As soon as she heard his voice at the other end of the phone, her face drained of all color. Her hands began to tremble. She dropped the phone as she fell to her knees. Olivia came running when she heard the phone hit the floor.

She took one look at her sister and became alarmed.

"Nance, what's wrong?"

"It's him," Nancy whispered as she shakily pointed to the phone.

The kitchen whirled around her as she remained on the floor. Beads of cold perspiration formed on her lip and brow. Shaking uncontrollably, she brought her knees to her chin, wrapping her arms around herself to cocoon them.

"Hello?" Olivia asked the receiver as she picked up the phone. She looked at her sister, wrapped up tightly on the floor.

"Hello, Olivia," Vince smugly slurred. "I didn't mean to frighten my wife. I only asked her how she'd been."

"Hello, Vince." Olivia dryly responded to her brother-in-law. "I think shock is more like the right word, not fright. We're right in the middle of getting dinner together. Can we call you back in a little while?"

"Yeah, you guys aren't really trustworthy ... if you get my drift," Vince sarcastically scoffed. He was suddenly sober. "How 'bout if I call you back in two hours? Does that give her enough time to get over her shock and still give her time to stay put?"

"Give us three hours, Vince, " Olivia acidly replied. "And she'll still be here."

Nancy's day had been ruined, but she tried her best to

remain upbeat for her children's sake. They sensed something was wrong. Her appetite was minimal. The day she'd been dreading had arrived.

Three hours later, Vince, true to his word was on the phone. "Nancy, I just want to put our family back together. I'll do whatever it takes," Vince pleaded. "I'll move to Greenbriar. I'll get a job as a janitor if I have to. I'll do anything to prove to you that I've changed. You name it. I'll do it."

"Vince, it's not that easy," she said. Her heart was beating wildly. Her mouth felt like it was full of cotton. "I've filed for divorce."

"You've what?" he quietly asked.

"I filed for divorce," she repeated. "I've been trying to have the papers sent to you, but I didn't know where you were. They were sent to Vista Oaks, and they came back. Someone said you were working in Castle City, but they came back from there, too. I need an address to give to the attorney so you get your copy."

She spoke so fast that she wasn't even aware of the room around her. This was her worst nightmare coming true. She pictured him at the other end of the phone, and her stomach churned with nervous tension.

"You ... filed ... for ... divorce," he slowly repeated each word in disbelief. "I gotta go."

He hung up.

"What did he say?" Olivia asked as Nancy entered the kitchen in a dazed stupor.

"He wants to put the family back together. He'll do whatever it takes to prove he's changed," she said with a glazed look on her face. "When I told him I filed for divorce, he got real quiet. Then he said he had to go. The next thing I knew, he hung up."

"He never even asked about the kids?"

"Not once," Nancy replied, beginning to cry. "Not 'How are they? Can I see them?' Nothing." Tears were pouring from her eyes. "He only cares about himself and what he can have. He doesn't care about them." She took a deep breath and looked forlornly at Olivia. "What am I supposed to tell Frank? I found your dad, but he didn't even ask about you." Nancy sobbed uncontrollably. "We have this conversation every night before they go to bed. I'm looking for him. As soon as I find him, I'll let them know. Now that I found him, how do I tell my children that their dad isn't interested in them?"

"First, baby girl, you have to calm down," Olivia comforted her. Holding Nancy in her arms, she softly said, "You and I both know he's going to call back. He's stewing right now. He's hurt and angry. He's figuring out the best way to come back at you. Did you give him your home phone number?"

"No, we weren't on the phone long enough for me to even tell him I wasn't living here," she said, swatting away at the tears.

"So he thinks you live here?" Olivia asked, amazed.

"I don't know what he thinks," Nancy said. "That's the problem. I don't think I ever knew what he was thinking."

Vince did eventually call back, ninety minutes later. Nancy took the call in Olivia's bedroom, closing the door to speak privately to her husband.

"Hello, Vince," Nancy said, trying to remain calm. "How have you been?"

"I've been all right, Nancy, as if you really care," Vince added sarcastically. "Are you living with your sister now?"

"No, I have an apartment here in Greenbriar," Nancy answered, ignoring his sarcasm, "It's close to Olivia's house."

"That must be nice for you."

"It is," she conceded. "It's good for the kids. They get to be close to their cousins."

"I want to see them, Nancy," Vince demanded.

It wasn't a request or question. It was a demand. Nancy had been expecting nothing less from him.

"Of course," she answered. "Anytime. You name it. You can see them."

"Tomorrow."

Nancy was stunned that it was that soon.

"Vince, they have plans tomorrow with their friends. You can come on Saturday or Sunday, if you want."

"No, I have to work. Bring them to me on Monday," he commanded.

"Vince, I can't do that. I have to work, and they have school."

"Screw you, Nancy. You stole everything from me. I want to see my kids."

"Come here and take them to dinner, Vince. They have to go to school," she said, standing her ground for their sake.

Her insides were doing flip-flops the entire time.

"Fine, I'll come there. I'll check into a hotel, and they're going to stay with me for a couple days," Vince said. "I'll take 'em to school and pick 'em up. They're going to get to know their dad again."

"Uh, okay. What time are you coming?" Nancy asked.

"I don't fucking know what time I'm coming!" he yelled. "What difference does that make?"

Nancy tried to remain calm, even though her heart was pounding so loud in her chest that it was all she could do to get the words out of her mouth.

"Vince, I need to know what time to have them ready."

Same old Vince: nice one minute, nasty the next.

Vince spat out, "I'll be there Monday night at five o'clock."

"Okay, you can pick them up at Olivia's house. I'll leave clear instructions on where they go to school."

"What? You're not going to be there?" he yelled.

Nancy disbelievingly responded, "Yes, Vince, I'm going to be here."

"So you don't trust me?" he asked in disbelief.

"No, Vince, not really," she admitted.

"Nancy, I'm not the one who stole the family and disappeared. You are. I don't think you have a lot of room to talk about trust here, do you?" he asked.

She could hear the venom in his voice. "No," she answered in a half-whisper. Waves of guilt enveloped her.

Calmly, Vince again spoke in a subdued tone, "Nancy, I'm serious. I'll do anything to prove to you that I want to put our family back together."

"First, just spend a day with your children. Get them to school on Tuesday morning. I'll pick them up from school on Tuesday afternoon."

"Okay, see ya on Monday," he said, jovially, as if he hadn't just finished yelling.

He then hung up. Nancy conveyed the conversation to Olivia.

"Are you sure that's what you want to do?" Olivia asked doubtfully.

With her heart in her throat, she said, "I'm not sure of anything anymore, but I promised Frank I'd find his dad. Now that he's surfaced, I don't want to keep him away. I think it's time they were reintroduced to him."

"You're probably right," Olivia agreed.

"I doubt if I'll be doing much sleeping for the next couple nights," Nancy said.

Nancy left work early on Monday to pick up Frank and

Lilly from school. They had started a new school in September with Melissa, Nicole, and Oliver. Nancy took all five kids to school in the morning and Olivia picked them up after school. Nancy would swing by Olivia's house after work and pick up Frank and Lilly. Frank and Oliver were both in the same classroom in the third grade. Lilly was in first grade. So far, the first ten weeks of the year had been an easy adjustment for them.

She hadn't told them yet about Vince.

"Mommy, why did you pick us up instead of Aunt Olivia?" Lilly asked.

"Because I have a surprise for you."

"What kind of surprise?" Lilly bounced up and down with excitement. "A present?"

"Not exactly, Lilly. This one's an answer to a promise."

"My promise?" Frank asked.

"Uh-huh." Nancy nodded.

Frank beamed in anticipation.

"You found him?"

"Yep."

Excitement spread across Frank's face as if he'd just heard he'd won first prize in a contest.

"Do I get to see him?"

"Tonight," she offered.

"Really?"

"Yes, Frank, really."

"Mommy, you're the best!" Frank said.

Nancy calmly tried to put into plain words what was going to happen to her children without conveying her trepidation.

"Here's the deal. Your dad is going to pick you both up at Aunt Olivia's house around five. He's staying at a hotel, and you're going to spend the night with him there. He's going to take you to school tomorrow, and I will pick you up after school tomorrow. How does that sound?"

"Great!" Frank said.

"Okay," Lilly said, not too excitedly.

"Just okay?" Nancy asked her daughter.

"Mommy, I'll miss you. I've never spent the night anywhere away from you before. What if I can't sleep?" Lilly asked. Her lower lip began to quiver.

"Sweetie, I'll miss you, too," Nancy comforted her daughter. "But I always have you with me, and you always have me with you."

"You do? I do?" Lilly was confused.

"Uh-huh. I carry you everywhere I go. You're right here," she said, pointing to her heart. "I carry you in my heart. If I ever start to get lonely or miss you, I can feel you by feeling the thumping of my heart. I know yours is doing the exact same thing."

"I can do that, too!" Lilly excitedly exclaimed, as she put her hand over her own heart. "That means you're always with me!"

They pulled into the parking garage of their apartment and raced into the elevator.

"What should we take with us?" Lilly asked.

"Pajamas, your toothbrush, clothes for school tomorrow, and …"

"Can I take Zeke?" Frank asked.

"Of course, you take Zeke. Lilly, you take Bailey."

"Is he going to take us out to dinner?" Lilly asked.

"I think so," Nancy answered.

Chapter Twenty Five

"Mommy, where is he?" Frank asked for what must have been the fiftieth time.

It was 5:30, and Vince hadn't arrived yet. It was difficult for a child to understand that his father didn't have any concept of time. Vince hadn't called to say he was running late, and Nancy didn't have any idea when he would be getting there. Frank's face was pressed against the windowpane, searching for his father's car.

"He's here! He's here!"

Frank began jumping with glee. Nancy could not catch him before he darted out the front door. As Vince opened the door to his truck, Frank ran up to him.

"Daddy! Daddy!"

"Hey, little buddy! I've missed you so much!" Vince said, whisking Frank up off the ground. "Wow, you've grown up! Where's your sister?"

"She's inside. Come on, I'll show you," Frank said, grabbing Vince's hand and dragging him toward the front door of Olivia's house.

"No, I think it'd be better if you just brought her out here," Vince said, disentangling his hand from Frank's.

"Okay, I'll go get her."

Frank raced inside to get Lilly as Nancy came to the front door.

"Hello, Vince."

"Hello, Nancy. Wow, you cut your hair," he said, leering.

The way he looked at her made her skin crawl.

"Oh." She touched the back of her hair and felt the length. "Yeah, I did. Where are you staying?"

"Motel 6 on Brandies Street."

"Okay. Here are my numbers in case of an emergency and directions to the kids' school. They start at 8:30. Don't be late," she instructed.

The whole time she was talking, he wasn't really listening to her. He was staring instead.

"Their bedtime is nine o'clock."

"Um, is there any way we could talk for a little bit?" he asked.

"Now?" Nancy responded, trying not to sound shocked.

"Yeah, now," he said in a tone ringing with superiority.

Why can he make me feel stupid again within five minutes of seeing him?

"Vince, the kids have been waiting for you for almost an hour. You do realize you're late, don't you?" she asked, trying not to let him see what she was really thinking.

"Yeah, so?"

"I think it would be best if you just took them and spent some time with them."

"Hi, Daddy," Lilly shyly said, creeping out from behind Nancy's leg.

"Well, hi there, li'l darlin'," Vince said, kneeling down to Lilly. "Do you even remember me?"

"Nu-uh." Lilly shook her head.

"I'm your daddy, and I remember you. Are you ready to

come and have a good time tonight?" he said, speaking softly and slowly as he held out his hand to his daughter.

Lilly nodded. Then she looked at Nancy for reassurance. Nancy winked at her daughter. She was trying very hard to be brave for her children's sake, even though her insides were doing somersaults.

Nancy hugged Frank good-bye and whispered in his ear, "Remember that no matter what happens, I love you. You have to listen to your heart above all else."

"Lily flower, you remember what I told you about always being with me, okay?" Nancy said, tapping her daughter's heart and hugging her good-bye.

"Okay, Mommy," Lilly whispered back.

"If you get lonely, it works the other way, too. You put your hand on your heart and know that mine is beating for you. I love you always and all ways, no matter what."

Nancy held back her tears as she hugged her children good-bye. She watched them climb into Vince's truck and drive away. As soon as they were out of sight, she sobbed. Driving home to her empty apartment, Nancy's stomach felt hollow.

What if he takes the kids away from me? I'd be lost. But that's exactly what I did to him.

It suddenly hit her. She could not remember what Frank or Lilly was wearing. She didn't have any recent pictures of them. She didn't have any idea where Vince would take them, his past behavior and history of lying and manipulation left her with a feeling of uneasiness. She had no reason to trust Vince.

The emptiness of a three-bedroom apartment overwhelmed her. She walked from room to room, sitting on each of the children's beds and holding one of their stuffed animals. She put her head on their pillows to capture their scents. Wandering into the kitchen and

163

opening the refrigerator, she realized she wasn't even hungry. She curled up into a ball in the corner of the couch and cried. The phone ringing at 7:30 startled her.

"Hello?"

"Hi, Mommy! I wanted to say good night."

"Hi, Lilly. I'm so glad you called. Are you having a good time?"

"Yeah! Daddy let me have ice cream, and I didn't have to finish my dinner," Lilly excitedly said. "He said we could watch television until we fall asleep tonight."

"That was nice of him," Nancy said.

"Uh-huh. He says you lied to us, too."

The comment caught Nancy completely off guard.

"Huh?"

Lilly continued with her conversation, not realizing what she was repeating.

"He said you stole us and he was never going to hurt us. It was your fault."

"Okay, Lilly. We can talk about this when you guys come home, okay?"

"Okay. I love you, Mommy. Good night. I hope you sleep good. Don't let the bug beds bite!" Lilly said.

"You either, lily flower!" Nancy said, laughing as her daughter mixed up "bedbugs." "Can I talk to Frank?"

"Uh-huh, here he is."

Nancy could hear the shuffling as the phone was transferred from her daughter to her son.

"Hi, Mommy!" Frank said softly.

"Hi, Frank. How is everything?"

"Good." Frank answered in a flat voice.

"Good. Are you having a good time?" she asked.

"Yeah."

Nancy could sense that Frank wasn't going to say more than that over the phone.

"Okay, sleep good. I'll see you tomorrow."
"Okay, bye."
"Frank?"
Nancy tried to catch him before he hung up the phone.
"Yeah?"
"I love you."
"I love you, too, Mom. Daddy wants to talk to you."

She heard the rustling of the phone being exchanged between her son and husband right before the explosion of language was catapulted upon her. "You fucking cunt, I can't believe you told them you couldn't find me. That's why they haven't seen me in over three years. I stayed in Vista Oaks at the same fucking job for almost two years, waiting for you to come back. You have the balls to tell my kids that I left?"

"Where are the kids right now?" Nancy asked, alarmed he would be speaking to her that way in front of Frank and Lilly.

"Here. Why?" he responded.

"They hear you talking like this?"

"So fucking what? You will pay for this, you fucking piece of shit. You'll be lucky if you ever see your children again."

The phone disconnected.

Nancy stared at the receiver in a daze, listening to the dial tone, trying to obtain some sort of a clue as to what just happened. The room was a blur around her. It was as if everything was in slow motion.

What have I done? I should have waited until the divorce was final and a custody arrangement was in place before letting the kids see Vince. Now I have no legal standing if he takes them. He could do the exact same thing to me that I did to him. All because I wanted to keep a promise to Frank.

The phone rang. She quickly snatched it.

"Hello?"

"Listen, cunt. I don't know what game you're playing or what you think you're doing, but these kids are miserable. And it's all your fault."

She begged, "Let me talk to them."

"Fuck you. If you had just stayed and tried to work it out, none of this would have happened. But you ruined our family, and these kids are the ones who have to pay for it. You will suffer. I promise you that."

"Let me talk to them."

"Fuck you, cunt!"

He hung up.

She might have thought she was ready to come out of hiding and face her fears, but facing her fears and facing Vince were two different things.

Nancy tossed and turned all night, unable to fall asleep until after two o'clock. She arose unrested and went to work. Calling the school after nine, she was relieved to find that Frank and Lilly had indeed been dropped off. She spent her lunch in Jackie Kelly's office, relaying the events of the past twenty-four hours.

Once again, the stipulation for dissolution of marriage was sent via certified mail to Vince in Vista Oaks. This time, it was received.

Chapter Twenty Six

Vince's reign of revenge had returned. His vow of vengeance was vehement as he vied for his children's affection. He had a new goal, and Frank and Lilly were the prize. Nancy treasured them more than anything. Turning them against her would be sweet revenge.

He wanted to find the one lawyer who wouldn't back down, no matter what. He wanted the one lawyer who would go all the way and get him his kids. Asking around the courthouse, the only name that kept coming up was Carol Toranado. He hired her, but she wasn't cheap. Vince had to come up with a $5,000 retainer before she would even talk to him. He knew exactly how to come up with that much money and more.

Vince rededicated himself to destroying Nancy. He had to say good-bye to his lifestyle of working and partying. His income was enough to survive, but there was plenty more income to be made. Vince was an excellent mechanic, and he could make a decent living when he worked. His downfall had always been the money he spent on drugs. He knew that if he'd quit once, he could quit again. He lined work up with two different shops under the table, and he began dealing drugs again. Within two months, he had saved enough to have the retainer for Carol Toranado.

Her law offices were located across the street from the courthouse in a four-story building. Her outer office was sterilely decorated with three armchairs and a matching, mint green sofa, forest green pile carpeting, and an assortment of magazines and newspapers. The walls were lined with modern art that looked like color swatches and two, oversized mirrors.

After sitting in the lobby for forty-five minutes, Vince was seething with impatience. He had begun to pace and asked the receptionist several times how soon he would be seen.

When he was finally ushered into the inner sanctum of Carol's private office, he was surprised to meet the petite lawyer. She couldn't have weighed more than one hundred pounds. Her perfectly tailored suit of tan complimented her blonde hair.

"Mr. Cooper, I am so sorry to have kept you waiting," she apologized, speaking in a long, slow sentence.

She shook his hand as she led him in. Her demeanor made him feel completely at ease.

"No problem," he responded. His impatience ebbed instantly.

"I've been looking over your paperwork. Your wife apparently filed for divorce last June, and it went through uncontested. Unfortunately, you have brought me a stipulation for dissolution that is too late to act upon. Your divorce was final six weeks ago. You are no longer married."

Vince jumped in, "So there's nothing I can do about it?"

"I didn't say that," she interrupted. "Let me finish,

please. I also see that she set aside all other matters for ruling later."

"What does all that mean?" Vince asked.

"Although you are divorced, the matters of custody and support have not been determined yet. They are still open for a court to decide," she answered. "I see that you have two children."

Vince answered, "Yeah, what's that got to do with my marriage?"

"We're going to ask her for child support and get you as much custody as we can," Carol said, looking directly into Vince's eyes.

His eyes opened wide in surprise.

"I'm going to get support from her?"

"You did say she makes more money than you, didn't you?"

"Hell yeah!" he said, slapping his knee. "She always has. She went to college. I didn't. Now I found out her parents are dead. I'm sure she got a nice chunk of change from them as well. Can I get some of that?"

"We'll have to see what her income looks like," Carol answered. "The way support is calculated in California is all computer-generated. It is based on numbers. It is the percentage of time that each parent has the children and how much income each parent makes. Simple math. If she makes more money than you, that is one-half of the equation. The second half will be the percentage of custody we can arrange for you. If we can get a large percentage of custody time for you and her income is substantially greater than yours, I think we have a good shot of you getting child support from her."

"Shit, you are good!" Vince declared with admiration.

"First," Carol continued, "I'll need your tax returns from the last three years."

"Uh, that might be a problem," Vince stammered.

"Oh?" she questioned, lifting an eyebrow.

"I haven't filed any tax returns since my last return with Nancy."

"Then go file today," she commanded.

He looked at her hesitantly.

"File anything?"

"I didn't say that." Carol answered, again looking directly into his eyes. "I said, 'Go file.' We need to fill out an income and expense statement for the court to determine child support. We need tax returns to back up our numbers. We will request that Nancy do the same thing. She will also have to provide tax returns."

"Okay," Vince nodded, thinking about how much money he would have to claim on his return and how much money he could get from Nancy.

"As far as the custody arrangements go," Carol explained, "the state of California requires mediation for all child custody cases. There is a mandatory Child in the Middle course that the courts run before mediation starts. You need to go as soon as possible."

"Okay." Only partially listening, he agreed.

"Let me know when you've attended that, so I can schedule the mediation. Until then, I'll see what I can do about a temporary custody arrangement."

"Anything else?" Vince asked.

"My office will be in touch if anything else comes up," she said, standing to indicate their meeting had ended.

"Thank you," Vince said.

He stood up and shook her hand. He left with a jubilant feeling.

I'm going to get money from her.

In the middle of March, Nancy attended the Child in the Middle course. Vince kept putting it off. He was granted temporary visitation every Wednesday night, for dinner only, until the court could rule on permanent custody arrangements. By the third Wednesday night, Nancy finally gave Vince her address to drop the kids off at the apartment complex.

When he tried to enter the front gate, the guard would not let him in.

"What the fuck do you mean I can't come in? I need to take my kids home," Vince insisted.

"No, sir. Their mother is on her way down."

Enraged, Vince shouted at the guard, "Bullshit! I'll take 'em up."

"I'm sorry, sir," the guard calmly said. "I can't let you in."

"Why the hell not?" Vince was irate.

The security guard was an older man who worked in the evenings to supplement his retirement income. The management had given him specific instructions to never allow Vince into the building. Matt gave these directions when Nancy first moved in.

At the first sign of trouble, the guard set off a silent alarm that went directly to the Greenbriar police. Two patrol cars were on their way with their lights and sirens off.

"Daddy, why are you so mad?" Frank asked.

"Frank, shut the hell up!"

Turning toward the guard, he challenged him by saying, "I asked you a question. Why the fuck am I not allowed in this building?"

"I don't know, sir. Those were the instructions I was given."

"Who gave those instructions?"

Nancy opened the door as the police cars pulled up in front of the building.

"Mommy!" Lilly exclaimed. "Daddy's mad! The guard won't let him in, and he's mad!"

"What seems to be the problem here?" the police officer asked as he walked up to the cluster of people.

"No problem, officer," Vince said, turning to the policeman. "I'm bringing my kids back from dinner, and this asshole phony fuzz wouldn't let me in the fucking building."

"Sir, watch your language in front of the children. Why don't you step over here with me?" the officer said, leading Vince away from Frank and Lilly.

"Are they going to hurt him?" Lilly asked.

"I don't think so, sweetie. What happened?" she asked, looking toward Frank.

"He wanted to take us up, and the guard wouldn't let him in. He got really mad," Frank said. "Does he always get that mad?"

"Uh-huh." Nancy nodded. "Come on. I think it would be best if we went inside now."

"Can't we wait and say good-bye?" Frank asked.

"No, I think it's better if we just go inside."

"Okay," Frank sadly said.

Nancy had put Frank and Lilly to bed and was just getting ready for bed when her phone rang. It was after ten. "I will get you for this, you cunt. First, you steal my kids. Then you won't even let me say good night to them. You'll pay for this. You will fuckin' pay for this, you piece of shit."

Vince's telephone rant went on for several minutes. By the time he'd actually been allowed to leave Greenbriar and gotten home to Vista Oaks, it was too late to say good night to Frank and Lilly, who had already gone to bed.

"What do you want me to say?" Nancy asked.

Vince jumped at his chance.

"I want you to say that you'll go out with me."

"What?" she asked in disbelief.

"You heard me. I told you I'd do anything you wanted to prove to you that I have changed. I want you back. I want to put this family back together."

Nancy grimaced.

"Yeah, your actions tonight show me how much you've changed."

"Fuck you, bitch."

He hung up. Nancy looked at the dead receiver in her hand as the tears slowly began to stream down her cheeks. She didn't bother to wipe them away.

He's right. This is all my fault. If I'd just stayed there, none of this would be happening now. We'd still be in our house in Vista Oaks. The kids would've adjusted. I'm such an idiot! I've made such a mess of things.

She fell asleep to her own thoughts of unworthiness.

Vince had moved to Vista Oaks from Castle City because he really didn't know where else to go, but he was lonely. Even though he hated Nancy for destroying his life, he wanted her back. He wanted his family back. He hated being alone.

Vince was the only son born into a dysfunctional family. His older sisters had raised him as his mother drank her way through life. He'd been a lonely boy who turned into a lonely man. Drugs became his escape from reality. The only time he'd ever been happy, or at least thought he was happy, was when he had his own family. He needed to get them back, and he would stop at nothing to do just that.

Vince attended the Child in the Middle course during the second week in May. Mediation for child custody was set for July 12.

Chapter Twenty Seven

The family court building housed the California mediation centers. The court-appointed mediator had access to the case file. Both parties had to sign in upon entering the center. Both had to fill out a questionnaire with personal information and what he or she hoped to accomplish through the mediation session. The appointment time allowed thirty minutes for paperwork.

Nancy arrived ten minutes early for the appointment and proceeded to complete her questionnaire. When asked what she hoped to accomplish through the mediation process, she filled in that she wanted to have every Mother's Day and her birthday. She would alternate the kid's birthdays, Christmas, Thanksgiving, and Easter. She also wanted to be primary custodial parent, giving Vince visitation every other weekend. He could pick Frank and Lilly up from her house on Friday nights and return them on Sunday afternoons. Also, she was asking assistance from the court to make him stop swearing in front of the kids and calling her names.

Vince arrived fifteen minutes late for the appointment and began filling out his questionnaire. He wasn't done when the mediator called them in.

"My name is Stan. I'm a licensed mediator with the state of California. This is one of the many states that have adopted the policy of mediation for all custody hearings. The judge takes into consideration any recommendations that we make prior to ruling on child custody. First, let me explain to both of you how this process works and answer any questions you might have," he paused. "We will take about forty-five minutes to talk about the two of you and your children. Together, we will assess what the best interests of your children are, and we will come up with a recommendation. Do you have any questions?"

He was a balding man in his early fifties with horn-rimmed glasses. His bushy mustache hid his lip and twitched when he spoke. Stan's eyes darted between Nancy and Vince as he detailed the purpose of their visit, trying to take them in with his diatribe.

"No," Nancy answered.

"I don't think so," Vince responded.

"Good, then let's get started. Who wants to go first?"

"I will," Vince said. "She fuckin' stole my kids. Now she wants to arrange something with the court where I can only see 'em some of the time."

"Vince, is it?" Stan asked.

"Yeah, Vince."

"I'd really prefer it if you could watch your language in here. That's also one of the things your wife requested as well."

"Ex-wife, you mean," Vince sarcastically said. "Okay. Getting on with what I want," Vince continued, "I want to see my kids more often. She took 'em away from me for almost three years. I'm just beginning to get to know 'em again. I want to see 'em all the time. I want 'em every weekend, every Christmas, every birthday, and every holiday. All the time. I don't even think she should be allowed to have 'em at all. It's my turn to get 'em."

Vince continued telling Stan how he'd been wronged. His heartfelt plea was genuine and sincere. He told stories of what a devoted father he'd been and how he woke up one morning to discover that his wife and children were gone. He was horrified. Then he discovered that she'd disappeared from her sister's house on top of that.

"Maybe she should only get 'em on the weekends. Then she can know what it feels like to not have a family around. Why should I be the one who has to suffer more? I'm not the one who took 'em away! I want to put this family back together. She's the one who filed for divorce. Not me. I want my family back!"

Stan turned his attention toward Nancy and simply asked, "Nancy?"

She was stunned. She'd been listening to Vince convincingly tell a perfect stranger what an absolutely wonderful human being he was. She knew that none of it was true.

She told Stan exactly what Matt and she had discussed, "I want whatever's best for our children. I don't think living with Vince would be the best thing for them. He doesn't have a steady job. He never has. I live around the corner from my sister. The kids have their cousins to play with."

She was having a hard time holding back her tears. She couldn't believe that Vince could once again get away with lying. She proceeded to tell Stan her side of the story. Vince had lost his job right after they were married. She also told him about Vince's continued battle with drugs and alcohol. She didn't mention the sexual abuse she endured during their marriage. She was too ashamed to bring that up.

"I don't want to keep Vince away from his children, but I think they should be here every other weekend because he lives a hundred miles away. What if they have a birthday party or something else they want to do on the weekend? They can't do that if they're in Vista Oaks."

"How old are your children?"

"Lilly is six and a half. Frank is eight and a half," Nancy answered.

Stan paused for a moment. Then he said, "I usually recommend children retain a bond with both parents. When parents live a distance apart, especially a hundred miles, it becomes exceedingly difficult to have frequent visits. Let me explain. The traditional visitation of every other weekend and every Wednesday for dinner, as an example, would not work in this case. It is just not practical to drive two hundred miles for dinner."

"So are you saying I'm not going to get to see my kids because I live so far away?" Vince shot off.

"Please, hold on just a minute, Vince. Let me finish," Stan said. "This case is extremely different than most cases I handle. In this situation, the father is really trying to reestablish a relationship with his children. It is a 'rebonding,' for lack of a better phrase."

Nancy had a sinking feeling in her stomach. Stan obviously bought Vince's sob story of being wronged. He was siding with him.

"In cases of children needing to bond with a parent, I recommend more visitation, not less. In this particular case, I'm going to suggest just that." Stan remarked, looking straight at Nancy. "I am going to recommend that Vince be allowed to have Frank and Lilly every weekend."

Nancy's stomach dropped. She had played out almost every possibility in her mind over the past few weeks. This scenario never entered her mind. Never in her wildest imagination did she ever think that Vince would get every weekend.

"In light of the fact that it is a lengthy drive, I also think that the burden of the drive should be split between both parents. Vince, are you able to pick up the children on Fridays?"

"Yes, sir," Vince responded immediately.

"Nancy, can you drive to Vista Oaks on Sundays?"

"Yes."

Stan looked from Vince, to Nancy, and back at Vince again.

"Then that's what I'm going to recommend. I'll send a copy of these recommendations to each of your lawyers and a copy to the residing judge for your custody hearing. I assume the date has been set with the court?"

Vince gave him a blank look.

"I'm not sure," Nancy said, still dazed by what was happening around her.

"Okay, if there is nothing else to discuss, I guess we've covered everything we can today. Good luck to both of you."

Nancy staggered out of the courthouse in a stunned fog. She sat on the concrete bench outside of the building for a few minutes trying to regain her composure, unsure that the preceding had actually occurred. As she watched people pass her, unaware of her condition, she envied them. Their worlds had not just been completely uprooted…hers had. She sat in this dazed stupor for thirty minutes before walking to her car, picking up her kids and telling her sister her bad news. Vince was elated.

"Nance," Matt said later that night on the phone, "your court date's next month. There's always the possibility that the judge won't rule in favor of the mediator's recommendation."

He'd been trying to calm her down for almost two hours because she'd been crying uncontrollably. It took almost ninety minutes for him to get the whole story out of her.

"Yeah. How often does that happen?" she sniffled.

"I'm not sure."

"I don't think very often. You should have seen Vince's smug face when that Stan guy made his recommendation. It was like he'd just won the biggest award ever," Nancy sobbed. "I just can't believe that everyone sees me as the bad guy here. The worst part is that Frank and Lilly are the ones who really end up losing. I really screwed everything up."

"Cut it out. You know you did the right thing by leaving him. Now you just have to do what's best going forward. Frank and Lilly will be just fine. Go give them a great, big hug and a kiss for me, will ya?"

"Okay. Bye, Matt."

Nancy hung up the phone feeling guilty and ashamed. She wished she'd never gotten herself into this mess. Maybe she should just go back to Vince. Everything could be put back together, and the family would be together. That way, the kids wouldn't be stuck going back and forth.

Vince drove back to Vista Oaks in a jubilant mood.

Round 1 ... Vince.

This deserved a celebration. He had a large purchase of cocaine and marijuana arranged for that evening. He hadn't planned on dipping into the stash. But, in light of today's accomplishments, his plans changed.

"Hey, Louie, how's it going?" Vince said, meeting the dealer at the designated location.

"Not bad, Vince. How's with you?"

"Absolutely fantastico!" Vince responded ecstatically.

"Really?"

"Yup! I just came from the courthouse. I am whooping the shit out of my ex-wife!"

"Well, good for you, man! Good for you!" Louie said, even though he couldn't care less.

"Okay, dude, I'll settle with you in a few."

"Okay, see ya then," Louie said.

Vince stopped for a bottle of Jack Daniels before heading home. He let his old buddies know he was back in business. As people filtered in and out, Vince dipped into his stash.

"The party's on me tonight!" he insisted as four of his friends showed up.

By four o'clock in the morning, they'd managed to go through five grams of cocaine, two twenty-four packs of beer, and the bottle of Jack Daniels. Vince had managed to front a party that would cost him as much as a full month's rent.

The party ended two days later. Vince had blown through all the cocaine, and he had very little money to show for it. He was supposed to pay Louie back the next day. He called the dealer and arranged another buy.

"Vince, you still owe for the last one."

"Louie, have I ever stiffed you before? I'm good for it. I'll give you everything I owe by the end of next week. You have my word on it."

Vince's sincerity was genuine.

Chapter Twenty Eight

Nancy's promise to her children to never be too busy for them included not allowing her own depression or guilt to impact any time she spent with them. So, when she picked them up after school on the day of the mediation, she refused to allow her depression to hinder the time she spent with Frank and Lilly.

"I have some really big news to tell you guys," she said on Monday night as they sat down for dinner.

"What?" both asked.

"Today, we were told that it would be the best thing for you guys to spend the weekends with your dad." She tried sounding upbeat and happy. "Doesn't that sound like fun?"

"I think it sounds like fun," Lilly said.

"Can we call him as soon as we're done with dinner?" Frank asked.

"Of course," Nancy said.

"Mommy, why doesn't he answer his phone? I've left him a bazillion messages, and he never called me back. What if he got in an accident?" Frank asked. His lower lip was quivering. It was time for him to go to bed. He still hadn't been able to reach Vince, and he'd been trying since dinner, almost two hours before.

"Sweety, I'm sure he's fine. Maybe he's just busy. He'll call you back. I'm sure of it," Nancy assured her son.

How am I supposed to tell him that his dad is probably stoned, high, or drunk?

Along with her promise to never be too busy, she had also promised herself never to say anything bad about Vince. She figured that Frank and Lilly would find out soon enough.

When Frank finally reached his dad on Wednesday night, after calling him Tuesday after school and receiving only his answering machine again, he asked, "Daddy! How come you didn't call me back?"

"Did you call me, buddy? I didn't get any messages," Vince answered convincingly.

"I left you a bunch of messages on your answering machine. You didn't get any of 'em?"

"My machine must be busted. Did you hear the good news? You get to come stay with me every weekend!"

"I know. You're gonna pick us up from school this Friday, right?" He asked, excited, having forgotten all about his disappointment at not having been able to reach his father for two days.

"I'll be there!"

Nancy's trepidation didn't stop her from helping prepare her children's belongings for their weekend with their father. She made sure they had enough clothing for the weekend and their toothbrushes, pajamas, and favorite stuffed animals. She dropped off their bags with them at school on Friday morning.

Hugging Lilly, she whispered in her ear, "I love you so much, no matter what. I'm always in your heart, and you're always in mine. I'll see you on Sunday."

Turning to her son, she whispered the same thing and added, "Please take care of your sister."

"I will, Mommy. I will."

Nancy's feeling of loneliness overwhelmed her as she opened the door to an empty apartment. Never had the sound of silence been so loud before. She knew Vince had picked Frank and Lilly up. She'd called to make sure. Wandering down the hallway, she peeked into the empty bedrooms, but that only intensified the loneliness and depression. She curled up on her bed and began to cry. The whirlwind of the past few months had finally caught up to her.

This is your new life, Nance. Weekends are free. No kids. Better get used to it.

The ringing of the phone brought her out of her trance.

"Nance, are you okay?" Olivia asked.

"No, not really." She sniffled. "But I guess I have to get used to it."

"Want to come over and let us cheer you up?" Olivia suggested.

"Not really," Nancy responded.

"Want me to come over there?"

Nancy said, "No, not really."

Olivia asked, "You gonna be okay?"

"I guess so." Nancy tried not to cry. "Oli, I just wish I hadn't made such a mess out of my life."

"Nance, I don't think anyone expected the mediator to give Vince every weekend," Olivia spoke calmly and kindly. "Let's wait and see what Jackie comes up with. Maybe she can get the judge to change the order."

"I hope so," Nancy glumly said.

"This is his first whole weekend with them. He might not be able to handle them anyway," Olivia added, trying to cheer Nancy up. "Give it time. Call me if you need anything."

"I will."

Nancy tried to call Frank and Lilly at Vince's house to say good night, but there was no answer. She left a message asking for a return call. At 9:30, she tried again with similar results. She didn't leave another message.

An empty house has a different sound than a quiet house. Nancy had never noticed the difference until that night. She could not fall asleep. She could not get comfortable in her bed. She couldn't remember what Frank looked like. She had a hard time remembering how long Lilly's hair was or what color pajamas she'd packed for her. Her mind began to play tricks on her.

What if Vince takes them away and I never see them again? Can I describe them to the police? Do I have recent photographs of them? Do I know what clothes they have with them? Why haven't they called me back?

The more she thought, the more distraught she became. Finally, at two o'clock in the morning, she dozed off.

The ringing of the phone at 8:30 woke her up. She fumbled to reach it, hoping ...

"You fucking cunt! How the fuck am I supposed to feed your daughter when she refuses to eat anything but 'Mommy's pancakes'? I will get you for this!"

Then the phone went dead.

Nancy stared at the receiver in shock. Numbly, she dialed Vince's number.

"Can I talk to Frank, please?"

"No, you can't!"

Vince hung up the phone.

Nancy's stomach began to churn. Her feeling of helplessness intensified as she sat staring at the phone, wondering what to do. She remembered Jackie telling her to document everything that occurred between her and

Vince and the children. She made notes of her inability to reach the children the previous evening and Vince's refusal this morning to allow her to even speak to Frank.

The day dragged slowly as Nancy tried to keep herself busy with household chores. Olivia checked on her several times during the day, only to be rebuked at suggestions of getting together. The telephone's chime at three o'clock was a welcome break.

"Hey, Nancy, how are you?"

"Trent! I'm doing all right. How are you?" Nancy responded, utterly pleased to hear from her friend.

"I'm all right as well. I thought I'd check up on you. I hadn't heard from you, so I figured you must be doing okay there. Staying out of trouble at least."

"I guess you could say that. How's everything in Castle City? How are Brandon and Christina?"

"Actually, I'm in Greenbriar. Christina and I are getting divorced."

"Oh!" Nancy said, surprised.

"I was wondering if …" Trent stammered, "maybe I could come by and see you."

"Sure! That would be great!" she said without hesitation.

"Are you still in that apartment we moved you into?" he asked.

"Yup."

"Okay, I'll see you in a few minutes."

"Okay, I'll see you then."

Nancy hung up the phone with delight.

Within five minutes, she hugged Trent when she let him into her apartment.

"Can I get you anything to drink?"

"No, I'm good. You look great! Your hair is getting longer. You look much better as a blonde."

Nancy's hair had been shoulder-length the previous year. Now it was five inches down her back. Her natural blonde sheen had taken over. The wavy curls gave her a youthful look.

"Thanks," she said, self-consciously running her fingers through her hair. "What brings you to Greenbriar?"

"Besides you?" he asked, sitting on the front of his chair and looking her straight in the eye.

The sparkle in Trent's eyes mesmerized Nancy. She found it difficult to look away. His golden locks and trimmed mustache were as she remembered. It took an effort on her part to speak.

"You're being serious, aren't you?" she asked self-consciously.

"Yes, I am."

"Trent, I'm a mess. You're married. You live over a hundred miles away. My ex-husband is a … I don't know what you'd call him. I'm in the middle of a child custody disaster. I don't know if I'm coming or going." She stopped to catch her breath, and tears started flowing down her cheeks. "I am not something you want to be interested in."

"First," Trent said, reaching for her hand and searching into her eyes, "you are not a thing. Second, you are someone I am very interested in. I didn't realize how interested I was until you were gone. I don't live over a hundred miles away anymore. I am not married. I don't care about your ex-husband, and I don't care about the disasters. I want to help. I want to be here for you. I want you to be here for me. Now that we've said all of those things, don't you think we should maybe start this conversation at the beginning? Assuming you still want to have this conversation?"

"Oh, I want to have this conversation," Nancy said. "You have no idea how long I've wanted to have this conversation. It's just that you really caught me at a bad time."

"Do you want me to go away and come back another day?" Trent suggested.

"Yes ... er ... no ... I don't know," Nancy said, shaking her head, as if she was trying to clear out cobwebs.

"Well, as long as that's clear," he said, grinning widely. "Why don't you tell me what's going on right now? We'll shelve the other talk."

Chapter Twenty Nine

Nancy encapsulated the mediator's decision, her inability to reach Frank and Lilly the previous evening, Vince's morning phone call, and her overwhelming sense of emptiness and guilt. In expressing her feelings, she began crying again.

"Trent, I am so sorry to unload on you."

"You don't need to apologize for anything, Nancy," he tenderly said. "What are you most afraid of?"

Without hesitating, she responded, "I think he's going to hurt them."

Trent cocked his head to one side and thought for a moment before softly asking, "Do you really believe that, or is your mind running wild?"

"I'm not even sure anymore," she replied, wiping her tears away. "I don't know if I think he will or won't."

"Has he ever threatened to hurt them?"

Nancy thought about that question for a moment or two and then confessed, "No, he's only threatened to take them away from me."

"All right. Then let's try to think like Vince for a minute," Trent said, stopping to take a deep breath and look straight at Nancy. "Even though it would be impossible for you and I to ever think like that man, let's give it a shot anyway." He smiled at Nancy. She actually smiled back. "Who on this earth does he really want to hurt?"

She looked down at her hands, laced her fingers together, and then unthreaded them several times before looking back up at Trent.

She responded meekly, "Me?"

"Right," he said, nodding in agreement, "that would be my best guess, too. His whole pattern has been to get even with you." Trent's eyes remained focused on Nancy. "What's the easiest way to hurt you right now?"

"I don't know," she answered without any thought.

"Yes, you do. Who do you value more than yourself?"

Without even thinking about it, she responded, "Frank and Lilly."

Suddenly, the light went on. Nancy was aware of what Trent was trying to make her see.

"That's right. And Vince knows that. He's going to do everything he can to keep them away from you. If you want to talk to them, he won't let you. He's going to try to brainwash them into believing you're a horrible mother and you stole them from him. He's going to bribe them with toys and fun and games. He's going to become the Disney dad. Every time they're with him, it'll be fun. Every time they're with you, it's going to be reality. School, chores, homework. The real world."

"But that's not fair," Nancy angrily retorted.

"Who said anything about fair?"

"How do I stop him?" Nancy asked. The spark returned to her voice.

"You can't. The only thing you can do is talk to the kids and tell them how much you love them. Be consistent in everything you do. Try to call them when they're with

Vince. If he refuses to let you speak with them, document it for your lawyer."

"How do you know all this?"

"Christina did the exact same thing to me."

"She turned Brandon against you?"

"She's trying."

"I am so sorry, Trent."

"Why? You didn't have anything to do with it. If anything, you helped me to see that I had a horrible marriage. I was living a lie. If you had the strength to face up to the truth, I realized I could do the same thing."

"Right now, I don't feel very strong," Nancy mumbled, slumping into her couch.

"I know," Trent acknowledged. "I don't feel very strong a lot of times either. Why don't you try to call the kids again and see if he'll let you talk to them?"

There was no answer at Vince's house. Again, Nancy left a message. She didn't expect a return call.

"I decided to leave Christina quite a while ago," Trent told Nancy over dinner. "It just took me a long time to finally do something about it. She had been playing me for a fool almost since the day we got married."

"What do you mean?"

"I didn't realize it at the time, but my darling wife had quite a reputation around town. She'd slept with every man within a fifteen-mile radius of Castle City. She didn't really care if they were married or not. Our marriage didn't stop her activities."

"That must have been awful for you."

"I fooled myself into believing that motherhood would change her, but it didn't. After a few years, I pretended it didn't bother me. I did my thing and let her do hers. As long as she didn't flaunt it in my face, I figured it wasn't doing any harm. That was until you arrived in town or, should I say, until you left town," Trent admitted. He kept his eyes fixed on Nancy while he talked.

"I don't understand," Nancy said, confused.

"The day I brought your things here to help you move in, I watched Bryce and Olivia and Matt and Julie. I realized it was possible to have a happy marriage with a partner you enjoyed being around. That's what I want, and I couldn't stop thinking about you, Nancy."

"Trent, I don't know what to say."

"You don't really have to say anything. I need you to know how I feel. I don't want to pressure you into anything. I've left Christina. My divorce is final next month, and the Northville Sheriff's Department just hired me. I'm only fifteen minutes away from Greenbriar now. I'd like to see you and the kids."

"Wow! I'm not even sure how to respond to this. I've always thought of you as a friend, a truly good friend."

"That's a pretty good place to start, don't you think?"

Nancy picked her kids up Sunday in Vista Oaks. They chattered all the way home from Vista Oaks.

"Mommy, we got to watch movies all night long. Daddy let us sleep on the couch!" Lilly said.

Frank asked, "How come you never let us sleep on the couch?"

It's as if I'd done something wrong.

"You have beds to sleep in. Does your dad have beds for you to sleep in at his house?"

"No, but it's so much more fun to sleep on the couch anyway," Frank retorted. "He said that it's all your fault he has to live in a one-room apartment. You stole all his money when you stole us. He can't pay any bills, so he can't afford to pay for beds. But we don't care as long as we're together as a family."

"Yeah, we don't care as long as we're together," Lilly chimed in.

"I'm glad you had a good time," Nancy said. "What else did you do besides sleep on the couch?"

"We went miniature golfing and bowling. We went out to dinner on both days," Frank said.

"He tried making pancakes, but nobody makes pancakes like you do, Mommy." Lilly interjected. "He got really mad at me when I said that. I said I was sorry, but he didn't care. He just started calling you bad names."

"That's okay, sweetheart. Remember what I told you. Sticks and stones can break your bones, but words can never hurt you." The words rang empty because she didn't believe them herself. She continued for her daughter's sake, "It might be better if you don't talk about me when you're with your daddy. He's still pretty mad at me."

"Okay, I'll try," Lilly agreed.

"I'm glad you guys had a good time. Did you know that I tried to call and say good night to you both nights?"

"No," both answered.

"Well, I did. For some reason, you never got the message. If that happens again next week, just know that, even if I don't talk to you, I'm still thinking about you. Okay?"

"Okay," Lilly said. Then she stopped and got really serious. "Mommy?"

"What, sweetheart?"

"I missed you."

"I missed you, too," Nancy responded.

"I had a really hard time falling asleep because I missed you so much. I started crying, and Daddy got mad at me. That only made me cry more. The more I cried, the madder he got."

"I'm so sorry, Lilly. We'll figure something out that will help you sleep better."

"Okay, Mommy."

Chapter Thirty

Monday, August 23, was the day that Nancy had feared for months. It had been five years since she had left the little house in Vista Oaks.

Her stomach was churning, her heart was pounding, and her head was throbbing.

Pull yourself together, Nance. You knew you had to face the music. You knew this day was coming.

She meticulously chose a navy blue dress with a tiny pink floral print. The dress was tailored with an empire waist and three-quarter-length sleeves. Her blonde hair was held back with a pink floral barrette. She wore very little makeup. She looked sophisticated yet simple at the same time. She didn't want to come across as snooty or arrogant to the judge. This was the day that Vince and Nancy Cooper faced each other in court to settle custody issues for Frank and Lilly.

Dropping her children off at day care, Nancy pretended the day was similar to all other days. But the truth was diametrically opposite. She hid her nerves with laughter and joviality. They talked about the Labor Day party they were going to have at Aunt Olivia's and how exciting it was going to be to see Uncle Matt and his whole family again. She also told them she had a big surprise for them at that party.

Frank and Lilly didn't know that Trent and Nancy had been seeing each other. Trent had arranged for Brandon to be with him for the long weekend, and they would be joining her family for the Labor Day party. That was the big surprise Nancy promised her children that morning as she dropped them off on her way to face Vince in court.

Thinking back over the past eighteen months, Nancy realized she had changed a great deal since she had thrown the dinosaur birthday party for Frank in Castle City.

It's strange how so much can change in such a short time. Frank, more than Lilly, has grown more distant. Perhaps that's to be expected. He's rebuilding a relationship with his father.

Nancy and Olivia waited for Jackie to join them at the courthouse. Standing outside the century-old stone building with the words "justice for all" etched into the stone, Olivia spoke calmly, trying to reassure her sister that things would work out all right.

"Nance, you're their mother. The judge is not going to take them away from you," she said, soothingly rubbing Nancy's back the entire time. "You know that Vince says anything he can to rile you up. He's full of hot air."

"What if he's convinced his lawyer that I'm unfit?" Nancy whined.

Olivia rebutted, "How is he going to prove that?"

"I kidnapped them!" Nancy whispered.

"I don't think he's going to do anything like that today. Just calm down. We'll wait and see what happens. Here's Jackie now."

Jackie strode up the walkway, exuding confidence. She walked with her eyes facing forward. She had a straightforward air about her. She was dressed smartly in a pale gray suit, white blouse, and low black pumps. Her long, flowing hair was held back with a white bow. She held a black satchel in one hand and a steaming cup of coffee in the other. Her smile and sparkling eyes instantly calmed Nancy down.

"Good morning. Sorry I'm running a little behind schedule. Has your ex showed up yet?" Jackie asked as she kept in stride.

"I haven't seen him," Nancy answered, scanning the surrounding area again for Vince.

"Maybe we'll get lucky and he won't show up!" Olivia joked, stepping into stride with Jackie.

"I wouldn't count on it," Jackie said. "Not after what I received in the mail yesterday."

"Oh?" Nancy asked, turning her head toward Jackie. "What did you get?"

Together, the three women entered the building and headed for the courtroom where their hearing was to be held.

"He's going for full legal and physical custody of the children. He wants you to pay child support and all his legal fees."

"He what?" Olivia faltered, taken aback by the news.

Nancy stopped in her tracks as all the colors and shapes melded together around her. Her toes went numb. Her insides began to shake, and she immediately lost all color in her face. Pins and needles ran up and down her spine.

She whispered, "He can do that?"

"I'm afraid so," Jackie said, nudging her along through the security gate and into the elevator up to the family court.

She located their courtroom and turned toward Nancy and Olivia.

"I guess I get to be the bearer of more bad news. We pulled Judge Decker. He tends to favor fathers."

"What does that mean?" Olivia demanded.

"I guess time will tell," Jackie answered matter-of-factly. "Let me go file these papers with the bailiff. You two will sit here. I'll be right back."

Olivia comforted Nancy the best she could, but the two women really didn't have any idea what to expect.

Vince and Carol walked into the courtroom five minutes before the judge. Vince had painstakingly chosen his attire for this appearance as well. He'd borrowed a sport coat from a friend and wore a light blue shirt and navy blue tie. He was clean, sober, fit, and trim, the ideal picture of a man. His attorney was also sharply dressed in her navy pin-stripe suit with matching navy heels. Her blonde hair was elegantly pulled back off her no-nonsense face. As Vince passed Nancy, he grinned and winked.

Judge Richard Decker entered the courtroom through the back door of the judge's chambers. His long, black robes rustled. The only visible parts of his body were his chubby hands and round, bald head with three short wisps of hair that stuck straight up. His face was round, reminiscent of the old man in the moon, with a bulbous nose right smack in the middle.

Judge Decker was a very large man. When he plunked his 380-pound body behind his bench, his very demeanor commanded silence. The entire room heard the creaking of his chair as it held his overbearing weight.

Judge Decker hadn't started out his tenure on the bench as a vile, vindictive, vicious man. Many years of hard drinking, lonely nights, and a cheating wife had soured his views on life. His disposition toward women was especially disagreeable. Although he wasn't supposed to be biased, he actually hated women. Judge Decker didn't usually sit behind the bench in family court. Under normal circumstances, this was Judge Allen Arnold's courtroom. Today, Judge Arnold was sick. Judge Decker had been called in to substitute for him. With a quick rap of the gavel, the court was called to order.

Vince kept glaring at Nancy. She had an overwhelming feeling of trepidation. Olivia squeezed her hand in reassurance. When their case was called, Nancy was sure the entire courtroom could hear her heart pounding. She gingerly made her way through the swinging doors toward the front of the courtroom, concentrating on staying upright. Meanwhile, Vince pranced forward, as if he were going to the county fair and was expecting to win the blue ribbon. They followed their respective attorneys and sat at their designated tables.

Judge Decker noisily began flipping through the pages of a file. He cleared his throat in a phlegm-filled chortle.

"Mr. Cooper?"

"Yes, sir!" Vince responded loudly, as if replying to a roll call.

"I see here that you are seeking full legal and physical custody of your children. Is that correct?"

"Yes, sir!" he said emphatically.

"Do you believe you are better equipped to care for your two children than Mrs. Cooper?" The judge peered at Vince over his glasses as he questioned him. "And you can do this by yourself, even though I see here that you are seeking monetary compensation from Mrs. Cooper as well?"

"Yes, sir. I do. I believe I am a much better parent than Mrs. Cooper, and I need her money to support them." Vince answered the judge in a voice that was loud enough for the back row of the courtroom to hear.

He didn't seem to notice the chuckles coming from

behind him.

"I also see that you don't have a permanent job. You live in a one-bedroom apartment, and you make very little money." Judge Decker had removed his glasses and looked straight at Vince. "Is all of this true, Mr. Cooper?"

"Yes, sir." Vince replied, a bit more quietly this time.

The judge looked right at Vince, glanced over at Nancy, peered at Carol sitting next to Vince, and continued, "Yet you still feel that you are the one who is better equipped to be a parent?"

"Yes, sir. I do," Vince said with conviction.

Nancy sat very quietly while the judge was asking Vince these questions. Her stomach felt like hundreds of worms were squirming inside. With the judge's last question, she was almost certain that Vince wasn't going to get his wish and Judge Decker saw right through Vince's attempt to take Frank and Lilly away from her. Based on everything he was asking, it seemed like the judge didn't believe that Vince could care for their children as well as she could.

Judge Decker unremittingly glanced at Nancy. Then he turned his attention back to Vince.

"I also see here that you both went to mediation and the mediator recommended you have your children every weekend. You signed that agreement, did you not?"

Vince hesitated.

"I did, Your Honor." He regained his confidence. "If I might just speak for a minute?"

"Go ahead," Judge Decker said, waving a chubby hand toward Vince.

"I've been spending every weekend with my kids. I realize it just isn't enough. I want more. I deserve more." Vince turned toward Nancy. Hatred was now in his voice. "She took my children away from me for almost three years, and it's my turn to have them. By the time we start to get to know each other on the weekend, it's time for them to leave again."

"How do you plan on caring for them?" Judge Decker asked.

"I've got a job. When I'm at work, they'll be at school. Then I'll pick them up every day after work. We'll be together every night. I'm their father," Vince started to tear up. "Don't I deserve a chance to be with my own children?"

"I see that you've accused your wife of kidnapping your children, but I don't see that any charges were ever filed against her. Can you explain that to me?"

Nancy's heart sank. This was the one thing she had feared the most, and it was coming true. He'd actually brought it up.

Why isn't Jackie objecting or something?

Vince answered, "One day, I woke up, and she was gone. She took our children and simply vanished. I kept waiting for her to come home, but she never did. That was almost five years ago. Then I called her sister's house last November, and she answered the phone like nothing had happened. She told me she had filed for divorce and asked if I wanted to come see our kids."

Judge Decker looked at Nancy expectantly.

"Mrs. Cooper?"

"Yes, sir?" Nancy responded, choking back tears.

I can't believe Vince is doing this. He's lying to a judge.

"Can you please explain all that to me?" he asked harshly.

"Yes, Your Honor," Nancy answered softly, trying not to cry.

"A little louder, please. I can't hear you," the judge

reprimanded.

His tone made Nancy even more nervous. Her voice quivered as she spoke.

"I left my husband five years ago because I was afraid. I was afraid for myself and the safety of our children. Vince had threatened to kill me on several occasions. He had also threatened to take the children away from me." Tears were slowly streaming down her face. "I had endured years of emotional, physical, and sexual abuse from him, and I didn't feel that it was safe any longer. I went away."

"Did you ever call the police and file charges against him?" Judge Decker looked over his glasses at Nancy. "Ever get a restraining order? Ever go to counseling?"

"No, Your Honor, I didn't."

The judge pushed his glasses to the top of his domed head.

"Do you have any proof of these allegations, Mrs. Cooper?"

"My brother and sister both heard his threats when I was at my sister's house five years ago."

"Let me see if I have this straight," he said, mocking her. "You were in fear for your life, and you disappeared. But you came back? Is that about the size of it?"

"Yes, sir," Nancy said. "Our son was asking about his father, and I was tired of hiding. I felt it was time for our children to get to know their father."

"I see."

"Did Mr. Cooper ever hit the children?"

"No, sir."

"Did he ever hit you?"

"No, sir."

Nancy twisted her hands together on top of the table as her eyes refilled with tears. Vince was sitting at the table with his attorney. He was gloating. He was sure this was going to be his day to wreak the revenge he had worked so hard to attain. Nancy was going to lose. He could just feel it all the way to his bones.

"All right, I just want to make sure I'm clear. You were married for seven years. One day, you decided you'd had enough. You never called the police. You never went to counseling. You never even told your husband that you were having problems. You just left. Is that about right?" His beady eyes glowered straight at her as if they were penetrating through her.

Nancy had never felt more violated in her life.

"Your Honor?" Jackie interjected.

"Counselor, I'm not speaking to you!" the judge spat at Jackie.

"Mrs. Cooper? I asked you a question," the judge said through clenched teeth.

"Er ... I guess you're right if you put it that way ... but ..." Nancy stammered.

"Thank you, Mrs. Cooper. Mr. Cooper, your motion for full custody is granted. If you choose to let Mrs. Cooper see your children, that is completely up to your discretion. You are not legally bound to do so. Mrs. Cooper, you are ordered to pay $750 per child per month for child support. Each of you is responsible for your own legal fees."

He rapped his gavel on the bench and dismissed the Coopers.

Chapter Thirty One

Round 2 ... Vince.

He was elated. His revenge had begun. The cards were finally turned in his favor. Judge Decker just gave him the open door to Nancy's world. He got the very thing she cherished the most, their children. Nothing was keeping him down anymore.

He hugged Carol and said, "I don't know how to even begin to thank you. You've given me everything I've ever wanted."

He spun around and walked down the center aisle of the court, right past a dazed Nancy.

He winked at her and slyly whispered, loud enough for everyone to hear, "You win some, and you lose some. Babe, you just lost!"

Outside the courtroom, he asked Carol how soon he would get to pick up his kids and move them to Vista Oaks with him. He wanted to do it that very afternoon.

"Vince, you have to wait for my office to prepare the stipulation ... after, of course, you pay me. Then you will need to come in and sign it. We will then send it to Jackie Kelly's office for Nancy's approval and signature. At which time, it will be sent to the court for Judge Decker's signature and court filing. It is not until we receive it back with a filing date that it actually becomes enforceable. Until then, you will continue to see Frank and Lilly on weekends according to the current stipulation."

"You've got to be kidding?" Vince bellowed incredulously. "That could take a month or longer."

"It usually only takes a couple weeks," Carol assured him. "In the meantime, you should start looking for a bigger apartment so your kids can each have a bedroom of their own."

"How the hell am I supposed to afford that?" Vince asked.

Carol sarcastically jibed, "You could try to get a full-time job."

"What about the child support? Can I start collecting that right away?"

"That's not enforceable until the stipulation is filed either," Carol said. "And I suggest you pay me as quickly as you can. I have no intention of typing up the stipulation and getting this ball rolling until you pay me. The sooner the stipulation is filed, the sooner you get your kids ... and the sooner you start seeing the child support."

"What if I fire you and hire another attorney?"

"You could try that, but it wouldn't do you any good," Carol smiled. "I won't release the files until you pay me."

"Shit, I thought we were going to get her to pay my attorney fees." Vince kicked the gravel on the ground. "I was counting on that."

"Sometimes, it works that way. Sometimes, it doesn't." Carol patted him on the shoulder condescendingly. "You got everything else you asked for. You should be happy."

"Oh, I'm happy. Believe me, I'm happy."

"Okay, I'll draft up the paperwork in the next day or two, but I need a payment from you before I can proceed on anything," she said. "Are we clear on that?"

"We're clear," he growled.

By the time he made it back to Vista Oaks, Vince had forgotten everything and everyone else. This day was all about him and his victory. His triumph was empowering. The reign of revenge had been victorious. All the years of sacrifice and sorrow had been justified now that he had dominated in the legal arena. His dominion was strong, and he intended to terminate Nancy and her family slowly and methodically. He didn't have any intention of allowing her anywhere near those kids. After all, she'd taken them away from him. Why should he let her have access? He hadn't had any. Driving back to Vista Oaks after court, he plotted new ways to torment his ex-wife.

Opening the door to his shoddy, one-bedroom apartment, he realized that things would need to change before he could move his children in. He scanned the torn couch and looked at the scattered, smashed beer cans tossed haphazardly around the room. For the first time, he actually noticed the piles of crumpled trash lying around, strewn next to heaps of filthy clothing. Traces of cocaine were on the coffee table, and the ashtray was overflowing with butts.

I've gotta make some changes ... tomorrow.

Hangovers never left Vince in a good mood. That August day was no exception. He had left several messages for Carol that hadn't been returned. His patience was waning. There was no chance he could provide for Frank and Lilly unless he had Nancy's money.

"May I please speak with Ms. Toranado? This is Vincent Cooper calling again."

"Mr. Cooper, I've written down your previous messages. I'll make sure to pass them on to Ms. Toranado as soon as she returns from court," the receptionist explained politely.

"And just when do you expect that to be?" Vince asked tartly.

"As I told you before, I never really know what time that will be, but she always checks in with me in the afternoon. I will make sure she knows you are trying to reach her."

"Thank you."

"Bitch," he muttered under his breath as he hung up the phone.

The enormity of what had occurred the previous day weighed upon him. He assessed his surroundings, lifestyle, and ability to provide for his children. He fell short in all three. He would need to get at least one more bed and figure out some way to keep those kids out from under his feet when he wanted to party.

How the hell am I going to do that in a studio apartment? Frank's not going to get in the way. He can sit down and watch TV anytime, but Lilly's always whining. I need to figure out how to get a bigger apartment so I can put her in a room by herself. I gotta find a school for them and a real job for me. Fuck! Maybe I should move back to Ohio and let my mom take care of them. She has a three-bedroom house that she's not even using.

Vince hadn't spoken to anyone in his family since his marriage to Nancy eleven years earlier. He had come from the small town of Wilton, Ohio, just outside of Columbus. His dysfunctional family of two older sisters, Marie and Darlene, and his chain-smoking mother had only met Nancy right before the actual wedding. They referred to her as his living Barbie doll. They had met the Christmas before they were married. Edith, Vince's mom, had been drunk for the entire visit.

The only member of his family with any redeeming

quality was his older sister, Darlene, but he hadn't spoken to her in years. He had gotten away from them as quickly as he could and moved to California. Now that he had the burden of raising two children, perhaps having older sisters would come in handy. Moving back to Ohio was the right thing to do.

"Hi, Ma. It's me, Vince," he said, taking a long swig of the beer he was holding.

"Vinny? Is that you? Vinny? Really? Is this really my Vinny?"

"Yeah, Ma. It's really me. How've you been?"

"How've I been?" she repeated. "I'll tell you how I've been, Vinny. Heartbroken. Downright heartbroken." She paused long enough to inhale and blow out the smoke from her cigarette. "You never so much as pick up the phone and call me. What? Are you 'shamed of your Ma?"

"No, Ma, I'm not ashamed of you. I'm calling you now, ain't I?" Vince replied, already exasperated.

"Are you in some sort of trouble?" she asked suspiciously.

"Er ... no ... not really," Vince answered, realizing she had figured him out that quickly.

"What's that 'posed to mean, Vinny? Either ya is or ya ain't. What happened? Did your sweet little Barbie doll run off with 'nother man?"

"Ma, how could you say something like that to me?" Vince bellowed.

"Vinny," she said in between puffs, "I ain't heard from ya in over ten years." She inhaled. "And ya just up and call me out of the blue." Exhale, cough, gasp, and wheeze. "What's a Ma s'posed ta think? Everything's dandy?" She took a deep drag of the cigarette. "I knows ya better'n that. What do ya want?"

"Nothin', Ma. I don't want nothin'. I was thinkin' about

you, and I wanted to talk to you. That's all," Vince said convincingly. His heart sank as he realized this plan wasn't going to work.

"Really? That's all?" she asked.

Sheer delight shone in her voice.

"Yup. I swear."

"Tell me, do I have any granchilluns?"

"Didn't you get the birth announcements Nancy sent out?" Vince asked, knowing full well she hadn't gotten them. He had specifically told Nancy not to send them to her.

"Uh, I don't think so. How long ago was that?"

"Well, Frank is eight. Lilly is six," he answered.

"Ya got two kids? An' I never even got a pitcher of 'em?"

"Ma, I'm sure Nancy's been sending you school pictures," he accused her. "Are you sure you're not just throwing 'em away?"

"Vinny, why would ya say somethin' like that ta me? I would never throw away pitchers of my own granchilluns. Now you make sure ta send me new pitchers today. Promise?"

"Okay, Ma, I promise," Vince answered, with no intention of doing any such thing.

"How is everything?" Edith inquired.

"Everything's good, Ma. Couldn't be better. Listen, I gotta run now. I'll call again real soon."

"Bye, Vinny. Call soon. Okay?"

Vince hung up the phone, shaking his head.

Strike that idea. I can't move to Ohio.

He reached for the phone again, preparing to make the call to arrange for the evening's drugs. It rang.

"Hello?" Vince said, wondering who would be calling him.

"Hi, Daddy!" Frank said exuberantly.

"Hey, buddy. How's it going?"

"How come you didn't call me yesterday?"

"Yeah, the news was pretty exciting, wasn't it?' Vince asked.

"What news, Daddy? You promised you'd call me every night to say good night, and you didn't. Why not?"

"I'm sorry, Frank. I totally forgot. I'll make it up to you this weekend. Our big news is that the judge told your mommy and me that you and your sister are going to come live with me."

"Really? When?" Frank asked excitedly.

"I'm not sure how soon. I still have to find that out. Right now, we are going to have to keep doing what we've been doing on the weekends. Pretty soon, you'll be staying here all the time. Won't that be great?"

"Yeah!"

"I love you, Frank!"

"I love you, too, Daddy! See you on Friday!"

"Mr. Cooper, this is Carol Toranado returning your call," Vince heard upon returning to his apartment. "As I told you after court, I will not be preparing any documentation regarding this new custody and support arrangement until I receive payment from you. Currently, the balance on your account is $14,743.65. That does not include yesterday's court appearance. Please contact my assistant, Sheila, and advise her when we can expect a payment."

"Fuck me!" Vince said out loud to no one. "Where the hell am I supposed to come up with fourteen grand?" He began to pace around his apartment like a caged animal.

Chapter Thirty Two

Nancy shut down. She heard the gavel hit the table, and she heard, "Mr. Cooper, your motion for full custody is granted." Then the haze moved in. A buzz swirled around her head as noises, lights, and people simultaneously moved in and out of focus. A gray fog surrounded her. Too dazed to cry and too mad to scream, she did the only thing she could. She collapsed.

Jackie and Olivia gently guided her out of the courtroom. Each woman had placed one hand under an elbow and delicately steered her.

"Nance, try to hold it together until we get out of the courtroom," Olivia whispered in her ear.

The walk felt like miles to Nancy. It was as if everyone was mocking her.

That's the woman who just lost her kids.

"Jackie, how could that have happened?" Olivia, shocked, questioned the attorney.

"Decker tends to side with fathers," Jackie tried to explain. "He obviously believed Vince's story more. Don't worry. It won't last long. We'll have it overturned before you know it."

"How soon does she have to turn over the kids?" Olivia asked.

"Legally, we don't have to do anything until the order has been prepared and both Nancy and Vince have signed it. The judge then has to sign it and file it with the court. That is when the order is actually legally binding."

Jackie explained the same thing to Olivia that Carol had just explained to Vince.

"I'm not sure that Carol Toranado is going to be satisfied with that, nor am I sure that Vince will be satisfied. However, that is what I am going to push for. We can probably drag that process out for two to three weeks."

"In the meantime, I'll start drafting an appeal to show that Vince has no means to support the kids and lives in a dump." She stood up, gathered her belongings, and turned toward Nancy. "I'll be in touch."

Nancy watched her walk away in dazed amazement.

"I thought she was supposed to be on my side? Why didn't she say anything in there? She just let that judge take Frank and Lilly away from me." Nancy buried her head into the crook of her sister's neck.

"Oli, what am I gonna do?"

"I don't know, Nance. I just don't know."

The two sisters huddled on the wooden bench outside the courtroom where Frank and Lilly Cooper had been legally given to their father. They held each other and cried. Neither felt like getting up and joining the outside world.

Nancy picked up her children from day care and went to her sister's house for the evening. She had called Trent after court and asked him to meet her there. As the five kids played in the backyard, a distraught Nancy filled Trent in about the details of the judge's decision.

"He'll never let me see them. I know he won't. And the

judge told him he didn't have to." Nancy could barely speak because she was crying so hard.

"Nance, you have to calm down," Trent said. His arm was around her shoulder while he comforted her on the couch. "The kids are gonna come in here and they're going to know something is wrong."

"They're gonna know something's wrong when they go to his house and never come back home either!"

"What did Jackie say?" he asked.

"Nothing! She's worthless," Nancy sputtered venomously. "I don't even know why she was there. She didn't do a thing at all for me. She let me do all the talking. She didn't stick up for me. She didn't tell the judge that he was lying. She was a waste of time and money as far as I'm concerned."

"Okay, okay, okay," he said calmly. "Let's do this one step at a time. Right now, you still have the order that only gives him visitation on the weekends, right?"

"Yeah, I guess," she replied halfheartedly.

He gently took her face in his hands and got her to look him in the eyes.

"And he doesn't get money from you right now with that order, so he's going to be in desperate need of money to fix up a new apartment," Trent continued.

"I don't see what that has to do with anything," she said dejectedly.

Trent explained as he let go of her face, "Until there's a legal order stating otherwise, that's the only order in effect." He stopped a minute to let that sink in. "He's gonna be itching for the new order to be filed. He wants your money. The new order can't be filed until you sign it, and the judge signs it."

Nancy asked, "How long will that take?"

"That, my dear, depends on the lawyers and the judge.

It could be weeks. It could be months."

"Really?" Nancy's eyes lit up.

"Uh-huh," he said, kissing the tip of her nose.

"Okay." She started to wipe her face. "Thanks." This new information gave her a glimmer of hope.

"Feel better?"

"I actually do. I think I can do something about this if I have time on my side."

"I really have to go," he said, starting to stand up. "It's a work night. I'm sorry."

"I know. You don't have to be sorry," Nancy said, standing up with him. "Trent?"

"Hmm?" he said, holding her close to him.

"Thanks."

"For what?" he asked curiously.

"Being you."

They stood together in their hug for a few minutes longer before he kissed her and went home.

After Nancy and her kids had gone home Olivia called their brother. Matt was livid when he heard what happened.

"That's crap, Olivia! We're not taking this lying down. We're going to fight this."

"Matt, she doesn't have any fight left in her," Olivia told her brother over the phone. "I've never seen her like this. Not even when she came back from Oregon after the rape."

When Nancy was away at school, she had been raped. She'd kept it a secret from everyone, including her family. When she came home at the holidays six weeks later, she'd broken down and told them. By then, she had become an emotionally fragile individual. It took almost two years for her to heal both mentally and emotionally from that encounter.

Olivia said, "I'm afraid she's given up. She's not going to let her kids out of her sight anymore. She knows she only has a little more time to spend with them, and she wants to get the most she can out of it."

"What does Jackie say?"

"I haven't spoken to her since she walked away after court. To be honest, I don't think she did Nancy any good. She sort of just stood there and let the judge take Frank and Lilly away. Vince spoke his piece. Jackie never objected. Judge Decker handed him the kids. That was pretty much the way the whole thing went down."

"That surprises me. It really does. I'd heard such good things about her."

"Well, she sure didn't impress me," Olivia said. "I'm afraid we might lose Nancy if we don't figure out a way to reverse this decision. I've never seen her like this before."

"Let me make a few calls and see what I can find out. I'll talk to you later."

Nancy wasn't too surprised when she received a phone call from Vince on Thursday night.

"Would you have lunch with me tomorrow?" Vince asked politely.

His tone caught her off guard. Just hearing his voice made her heart pound so wildly she could actually hear the beating in her eardrums. "You want to have lunch with me?" she asked, not trusting him.

"Yeah, I do," he said with sincerity.

"Why? To rub my face in your victory?"

"No, actually I want to discuss a different kind of settlement with you," Vince said. "Something I think you might like. Something that would let you keep your kids."

"Really?" Nancy said.

Her spirits were rising.

"Yes, really."

"Okay. When and where?"

Vince went on, "I was thinking that as long as I have to come to Greenbriar to pick up the kids tomorrow afternoon anyway, we could meet for lunch? You can pick a spot you are comfortable with. What time do you get a break?"

"Vince, are you being serious? You're not just saying these things so you can make me feel even worse?" Nancy asked skeptically.

"No, Nancy. I'm being serious. I want to bury the hatchet. Name the time and place," Vince responded sincerely.

They decided on a local café that was near Nancy's work and agreed to meet at one o'clock. Nancy hung up the phone with a sense of hope for the first time in days.

Nervously, Nancy waited for Vince to arrive.

Maybe this is his idea of a joke.

1:00 was now 1:15, and he still hadn't arrived. She kept looking out the window as cars entered the driveway. She was walking to her car when he screeched into the parking lot.

"I am so sorry! I got held up, and I didn't know how to reach you," he hurriedly explained. "I hope you didn't think I was going to stand you up."

He smiled at her with the crooked grin he'd disarmed her with so many years before.

"Well, the thought had crossed my mind," she said. "We haven't exactly been very nice to each other lately, and I wouldn't put anything past you."

"I could say the same thing right back to you, but that's not the reason we're having lunch," he said. "Can't we just start over and try to be nice … at least for lunch?"

"Sure," she said as they walked into the restaurant.

After they ordered, Vince broke the stilted silence.

"Nancy, I really don't think keeping the kids away from you is the best thing for them. I don't care what anyone says. I think kids need a mom and a dad. I would do anything to put this family back together, and I mean anything. I've quit doing drugs, I don't drink, and I don't smoke. I'll even move to Greenbriar, if that's what it takes. I just want a chance. One chance to prove to you that I've changed."

"Is this one of your tricks?" she asked dubiously.

"No, I swear this is the truth. I mean it. You can keep the kids. Just promise that you'll give me another chance. Just one chance is all I'm asking for."

"Can I think about it?"

"Hell yeah! Just as long as you don't say no!" He grinned. "As long as I know I still have a chance and that door isn't closed. That's all I'm asking. Just an opening."

"What about what the judge said?"

"I don't give a crap what the judge said ... well ... except for the support part. That would really help." He grinned sheepishly, "Could you start that right away?"

The light finally went on in her head.

"If I gave you money now, you wouldn't push to have the kids, too?"

"Yeah, something like that," Vince nodded. Thinking twice, he said, "What I mean ... I think it would be better if I got a two-bedroom apartment in Greenbriar anyway. That way, we're both closer to the kids. I'll find a job here, and we can start doing things together ... like a family again."

"I have to think about this, but I have to get back to work right now," she said, standing up after putting down money for her share of the lunch.

"Okay. Can you at least give me some of the support money right away?"

"I'll bring you a check when I pick up Frank and Lilly

Brenda Youngerman

on Sunday."

Chapter Thirty Three

"If you make this deal with him, none of it is legal!" Trent tried making her understand on Saturday after she told him about the previous day's conversation. "He can change his mind and take the kids away from you. Worse, he can say you have them against his wishes. All he has to do is show the signed legal stipulation from the court granting him full legal custody. You could go to jail."

"He'd never do that to me!" Nancy rebuked. "He wants to do what's best for the kids. He doesn't want to see me go to jail." She stopped and thought for a minute, wrung her hands together, and looked at Trent.

Hurt, she asked, "Why would you say something like that?"

Softly and tenderly, he asked, "Nance, are you forgetting who you're dealing with?"

"No, Trent, but these are my kids we're talking about," Nancy pleaded, begging for him to try to understand. "I can't just let them go without doing anything and everything I can to hold onto them."

"Okay," Trent countered quietly, "but I need to ask.

Would you seriously consider getting back together with him?"

"If that was the only way I could keep my kids, maybe…yes," Nancy answered.

Ashamedly, she looked downward. She couldn't look Trent straight in the face.

Stunned, he asked in disbelief, "You still have feelings for him after everything that has happened?"

The pain was apparent in his voice. Hurt could be seen in his brown eyes. He could not look directly at her.

"You have to understand that I would rather die than lose Frank and Lilly. If it means losing myself to Vince, then I guess that's a choice I am willing to make. It has nothing to do with my feelings toward him. Honestly, thinking about him makes my skin crawl. The thought of him ever touching me again makes me want to throw up. But those two children didn't ask to be put here. They certainly don't deserve to spend their life with him. If he's willing to include me in their lives, then I'm not going to shut that door."

"I can't say that I completely understand, but I'm trying. My biggest fear is that he's fooling you and he's setting you up. In the end, you're going to lose."

"I don't see where I have much choice anymore, do you?" she said, looking at him with tear-rimmed eyes.

"I don't know, but I'm going to back off and let you work this out. You know where to reach me."

On Sunday afternoon, true to her word, Nancy gave Vince $500. He immediately spent it in celebration of his new plan.

This is going to be the easiest money I've ever gotten. Now that I'm moving to Greenbriar, I won't be paying my rent in Vista Oaks. I won't pay back any of the money I owe

Public Lies

to Louie. After all, what's a drug dealer going to do about it? Call the police? I don't think so!

On Wednesday night, after speaking with Frank and Lilly, Vince asked to speak to Nancy.

"Hey, Nance, did you give any more thought to my suggestion from last week?"

"Some," she answered noncommittally.

"How 'bout if we all go to dinner this Friday? Be a real family again."

"Vince—"

"Come on, Nancy. I'm not gonna take no for an answer. I'll pick the kids up. Then we'll swing by and pick you up. We'll all go out and grab a pizza. Don't want to make it too late. After all, I gotta get the kids back to Vista Oaks at a decent hour! See ya on Friday."

He hung up before she even had a chance to say anything. She looked at the phone in dismay and shook her head.

How did he manage to pull that off? It's the same thing he did when we were dating so many years ago. He took complete control—and I let him!

Although she'd been dreading the evening for two days, when Vince came to pick her up with the Frank and Lilly already in tow, their excitement to see both parents in the same place at the same time calmed her down. They went to a small pizzeria with checkered tablecloths, melted candle wax on Chianti bottles, plastic grapes, and ivy leaves strewn across latticework on the ceiling. Frank and Lilly squished between their parents.

Civility was the course of action. Nancy found it easy to be pleasant as Vince's charm reminded her of why she had fallen in love with him a decade earlier. He was jovial, charismatic, and attentive to the children and her.

Maybe he really has changed.

They gathered themselves together to leave the restaurant.

"Hey, Nance, I'm a bit short. Would you mind pickin' up the tab?"

He winked and grinned over Lilly's bobbing head.

"No problem," she said, a little hurriedly. She didn't want to cause a scene in front of the kids.

I guess he hasn't really changed at all! This is exactly the same thing he used to do when we were dating.

"Mommy, can't we all stay here tonight? Daddy could come stay at our house. Wouldn't that be fun?" Lilly begged and pleaded with her long eyelashes rapidly batting. She was pulling on Nancy's hand to get her attention.

"Yeah, Mom! That's a great idea!" Frank agreed. "Dad hasn't ever been inside our apartment. I think he should come stay with us."

"Hang on. Not so fast, you two," Vince said. "I don't think your mom's ready for that just yet. Let's take this slow. If we're gonna work this out, we have to go slowly. We'll call it a night right now. Maybe we'll do something a little longer next time."

He took Lilly's hand out of Nancy's, brushing it lightly. He cajoled Lilly to come with him by saying, "I'm sure there will come a time when I get to see the inside of your apartment. Don't worry. I'm not going anywhere. I promise." Although he'd been talking to his children, he was directing his attention toward Nancy. When he said "promise," he winked at her. Shivers of fear ran up her spine.

"Go on. Give Mommy a hug and say good-bye. We have a long drive, and we have to get going."

Reluctantly, both kids hugged Nancy.

She whispered, "I love you," into their ears and watched

them leave. As she drove to her apartment, she wondered what Vince was up to. She knew him well enough to know he never gave anything without expecting something in return. She'd asked to have the kids call when they arrived in Vista Oaks, but she didn't expect him to comply.

She'd just gotten out of the bath and curled up with a book when the phone rang.

"Hi, Mommy!"

"Hi, lily flower! I'm so glad you called me! How was the ride to Daddy's house?"

"It was good. We talked all the way home." The word "home," raised red flags in Nancy's head.

How can Frank and Lilly already consider Vince's house their home?

She drew herself back to the present to hear Lilly continue the conversation.

"Daddy said you and him are gonna get married again and we're gonna be a happy family. Are we really?"

Nancy could hear the excitement in her daughter's voice.

"We'll talk about it when you get home, okay?" she answered, trying to keep her tone even for Lilly's sake, even though she was livid and her heart was beating.

"Okay, I love you."

"I love you, too. No matter what!" Nancy said.

"Here's Frank," Lilly said and got off the phone.

"Hi, Mom."

"Hi, Frank. Are you okay?"

"Yeah," he answered in a monotone.

But Nancy could tell that he was anything but okay.

"Did something happen?"

"Mom, I'm fine," he said, cutting her off over the phone.

"Okay, I'll see you on Sunday."

"Yeah … sure … whatever. Here, Dad wants to talk to you."

"Okay. Hey, Frank?"

"What?" he answered curtly.

"I love you."

"Whatever," Frank answered.

Nancy definitely knew something was wrong with her son.

He's never responded that way on the phone before. For that matter, he's never talked to me that way before, not even when he was mad at me in Castle City.

"Hey, Nance, how's it goin?" Vince broke into her thoughts.

"Fine, Vince. What's up?"

"I was just thinkin' maybe you'd want to come down a little early on Sunday. We could all do something together as a family. You know, maybe go to the park for a picnic, or the beach, or something like that." He was talking to her as if the past had never happened. Her heart was pounding. Her palms were sweating, and she was doing everything she could to keep her voice calm.

"Vince, are the kids hearing you right now?"

"Yeah. Why?" he asked, as if it was the dumbest question she could have asked.

"I don't think it's a good idea to tell Lilly that we're getting married again."

"I didn't tell her that," Vince spluttered.

"You might not have said it in those many words, but that's what she heard. Vince, she's seven. To a seven-year-old girl, having Mommy and Daddy back together is the best thing in the world."

"What's wrong with that?" he insisted.

"You asked if I would give you a chance to show me you've changed," Nancy tried to explain. She didn't want to cry, or back down, her usual tactic when it came to conversing with Vince. "I've only seen you for one lunch and one dinner. That doesn't change almost eight years of destructive behavior."

"Was it all bad?" he softly asked.

"Not all of it, but most of it," she said as her insides were lurching with fear.

Nancy knew deep inside that, if she screwed this up, he could very likely take the kids from her. She would never see them again.

"I'm not saying we can't do family things. I'm just saying ... not ... every ... time."

The phone went dead.

All efforts to reach Frank and Lilly for the rest of the weekend were fruitless. Messages went unanswered. She replayed the conversation in her mind numerous times and realized she would have to lose herself if she had any chance at all of keeping her children.

Chapter Thirty Four

Arriving Sunday at four o'clock in Vista Oaks, Nancy encountered one of her foremost fears face-to-face. Vince and her children were not there. She looked around the parking lot of the apartment complex.

Vince's truck wasn't there.

She knocked on the door to Vince's apartment. There was no answer.

She called on the telephone. There was no answer.

Vince didn't own a cell phone, and she didn't have any idea where they might be. She sat in her car and waited.

At 4:30, she called the Vista Oaks police department and spoke to the dispatcher. "My ex-husband is supposed to be at his apartment so I can pick up our children, but he isn't here," she spoke through the tears.

"What time was he supposed to be there, ma'am?"

"Four o'clock."

"If he doesn't arrive by six o'clock, call us again. We'll send someone out to take your report."

"Thank you."

She hung up and cried softly as she realized this was a game she didn't want to play.

What good does it do to have a court order stating that the time of exchange is four o'clock if there's no way of enforcing it? Vince has all the control. Maybe if I'd just agreed to do something as a family today, none of this would have happened. I would've been here earlier, and we'd be on our way back home. If Vince thinks he's won, he's going to find out that I have a lot more control than I used to have. If he wants money, he's going to have to earn it. When he shows up, I'll just act like nothing's wrong. He'll see.

Vince pulled into the apartment parking lot at 4:45. The kids were eating ice cream cones and ran over to Nancy's car.

"Hi, Mommy!" Lilly said. "We got ice cream!"

"I see that. Is it good?" Nancy asked, pretending not to notice that they were forty-five minutes late.

"Yup, wanna lick?" Lilly offered her cone.

"No, thanks. Are you ready to go?"

"Yeah, I'll get my stuff," she said, scurrying off toward Vince's apartment.

"Hey, Frank! How are you?" Nancy said, looking toward her sullen son.

"Good."

"Ready to go?"

"Yeah, I'll be right back." He headed toward Vince's apartment in a much different fashion than his sister had. His head was hanging, and he was dragging his feet. His mood reminded her of a beaten dog.

Vince looked up at Nancy and said, "What about next week?'

"What about next week?" Nancy retorted.

"Are we gonna do something?"

"I'll let you know."

"Okay. Oh, sorry about being so late. I didn't realize

what time it was."

"No problem, Vince."

Frank and Lilly came out to the car.

"Say good-bye to Daddy."

As far as Nancy was concerned, the next Friday afternoon came too quickly. She learned to hate weekends. On her way home from work, she stopped at the liquor store and bought herself a bottle of vodka. She needed anything to make the time pass faster.

Arriving home to an empty three-bedroom apartment, she filled a glass with ice and poured herself a drink.

One drink's not going to hurt me. The kids are with their dad ... I don't have to get up in the morning and go to work ...

She flipped through the television. By midnight, she was drunk.

Maybe I should go back to Vince. Then the kids wouldn't have to deal with this going back and forth. It isn't fair to them. I'll tell him Sunday that we can try again.

She vomited for two hours, and she stayed in bed all day on Saturday, nursing a hangover.

On another Friday afternoon, Vince was stuck in traffic.

I hate this damn traffic. I hate this damn drive. I hate Vista Oaks. I hate Greenbriar. I hate Nancy. I hate my life. I've had enough! It's time to get those bratty kids and get out of here. The judge said I could have them, and I should. Now I have to come up with a plan to get them. First, today, I have to get to that damn school!

Going twenty-five miles an hour on the freeway was beyond frustrating. It was maddening. Weaving and bobbing between trucks, cars, vans, and station wagons, Vince heard horns bleating at him. He didn't care. He was on a mission. Pulling up in front of the school, he smoked a cigarette to calm his nerves. Smoothing out his clothing, slicking back his hair, and primping as best he could in his rearview mirror, he entered the school to sign out his children.

Flirting with the receptionist, he said, "Hey, good-looking, did ya miss me?"

The busty young receptionist looked up from her desk and smiled as she recognized Vince. "Hi, Mr. Cooper! How are you today?"

"If I was any better, it would be illegal!" He smiled and chuckled, laughing at his own joke. "When are you going to say yes to me and put me out of my misery?"

"Yes to what?" she asked, dumbfounded.

"My marriage proposal," he said straight-faced as he winked.

"When did you ask me to marry you?" She looked puzzled.

"Just now. Don't you remember?"

His concerned tone caught her completely off guard.

"No, I must have missed it. But you know I have a boyfriend," she answered quite seriously.

"What does he have that I don't?" Vince asked, looking hurt.

"For one, he doesn't have any kids yet. I'd kind of like to start my own family," she said, looking thoughtful.

Vince winced, "Ouch! You really know how to hurt a guy!"

"I'm sorry."

"That's okay. I'll just lick my wounds and go find my kids," Vince said, shuffling his feet and looking toward the ground dejectedly. "I'll spend the rest of my days living alone because I already have kids." He sniffled. "Don't feel sorry for me. I'll be okay."

"Mr. Cooper?"

"What?"

He spun around with anticipation in his eyes.

"Are you all right?"

"I would be if you would go out with me!" he said, widely grinning.

"You know I can't do that."

"I know. I'm just having fun with you," Vince said.

He left the office to find his children. After getting them out of their classrooms and settled into his truck headed south for Vista Oaks. The drive normally took two hours. That afternoon, it took five. Vince's mood was foul. Every time Frank or Lilly said anything, he would tell them to shut up. As soon as they got close to his house, he bought them fast food for dinner. They went to the video store to rent movies. He rented two horror films, even though they both protested.

"Daddy, I don't like scary movies," Lilly said. "They give me nightmares."

Frank asked, "Can't we get a different kind of movie?"

"This is what we're getting," Vince said. "I don't want to hear another word about it!"

As soon as they got home, he put in the movies, sat in his recliner, and fell asleep. If the kids tried to turn it off, he woke up and yelled at them. They sat quietly in the corner of the ratty couch and watched the movie, afraid to move or speak.

On Saturday morning, Vince took Frank and Lilly to a miniature golf course. When they couldn't get the ball into the hole, he began to make fun of his children.

Frank took Lilly by the hand and said, "Lilly, it's okay. I'm sure he doesn't really mean it. He's just having fun."

"Frank, he's being really mean to you, and I don't like it," Lilly said as she started crying.

"Why the hell are you crying?" Vince yelled at Lilly.

"Do you always have to cry?"

"I'm sorry, Daddy. I'll try to stop, but you're yelling at me," Lilly whimpered.

"Frank, get your goddamn sister to stop crying!" Vince screamed.

"Dad, I think it might help if you stopped yelling," Frank said.

"What the hell? Do you think this is my fault?" Vince barked.

As a consolation to his kids, Vince took them to the toy store and let them buy anything they wanted. Upon returning to his apartment, he immediately locked himself in his bedroom while they played with their new toys. He told them he needed to take a nap. When he woke up, he would be in a better mood.

Frank and Lilly spent the rest of the afternoon watching television and playing together alone. Vince didn't reappear until almost six o'clock. Indeed, he was in a better mood.

Sunday was a much better day. They went out to breakfast and had pancakes and waffles. Afterwards, they went to a Sunday matinee of a new movie that was made for children. After the movie, Vince took his children out for ice cream before Nancy came to pick them up.

Nancy picked Frank and Lilly up on Sunday without saying a word to Vince. The ride back to Greenbriar was quiet.

Chapter Thirty Five

Bedtime in Nancy's house had always been special. After homework and television, Lilly took a bath. Then Frank took a shower. Nancy read a bedtime story, usually in Lilly's room. Frank and Lilly both squished together under the covers. As soon as the story was finished, Frank hopped out and ran to his room.

Nancy tucked in Lilly, kissed her on the forehead, and said, "I love you today." She kissed her on one cheek and said, "I love tomorrow." She kissed her on the other cheek and said, "I love you forever." Then she kissed her on the chin and said, "Always and all ways, good night."

Nancy then went to Frank's room and repeated the process. She had just gotten to Frank's chin when, without any warning, Frank flung his arms around her neck in a sudden hug. What happened next startled her the most. He started to cry. They weren't soft tears. They were gut-wrenching, hysterical sobs. She quietly lifted him up into her lap and held him there, letting him cry. His body was trembling. She tenderly rubbed his back and kissed the top of his head, never uttering a word. After several minutes, the crying subsided.

"Would you like to go to my room and talk?" she whispered in his ear.

He slowly nodded.

"Can you walk?" she asked.

"Mm-hm," he whimpered back.

Affectionately, she wrapped her arms around him as they walked down the short hallway to her room. They got under the covers of her bed. She ran her fingers through his blond hair and gave him a chance to settle down a little bit.

"What's going on?"

"I don't know." He sniffled.

"Okay, then tell me what you think is going on," she lovingly prodded.

"I'm really confused, and I think I'm mad."

"All right, let's start with what you're confused about. Then we'll move to why you think you're mad," she said, leaning on one elbow next to him while continuing to rifle through his hair.

"What are you confused about?"

"Daddy keeps calling you names and saying you did all sorts of bad things." He blurted it out so fast that she had a hard time understanding him. "But I've never seen you do anything bad, and I don't think you're any of those things he calls you. I've never heard those words before, but they sound really bad. I'm not sure what they mean. When I tell him you're not, he tells me to shut up. So I'm confused. I don't know who to believe."

Tears streamed again as he buried his head in her pillows. Nancy's heart felt like it had exploded, as she could feel her son's inner turmoil.

"Wow! I could see how that could be confusing." She tried to comfort him, even though she knew there wasn't much she could say that would ever comfort a child when one parent called the other parent those kinds of names.

She knew what Vince was capable of.

"Do you remember when I taught you that sticks and stones could break your bones?"

"And names could never hurt you!" he finished the old cliché for her.

"Yeah, that one." She delicately smiled at him.

"I remember that one." He beamed up at her.

"This is a good time to remember it even more. It doesn't matter what your daddy says about me. The only person you have to listen to is yourself." She spoke slowly and softly, trying hard to show her son that he knew the truth. "You know in your heart what is true and what isn't. You have known me all of your life. You know who I am and what I am. You know if I'm a good or a bad person. You know if I'm the kind of person he says I am. Just listen to your heart."

Frank looked at his mother with concern and confusion.

"But why would he say all those things about you if they aren't true?"

"I don't know," she said, shaking her head. Nancy looked straight at her son and earnestly said, "I do know that I decided a long time ago not to say anything bad about him, no matter what. I guess he didn't decide to do the same thing. At some point, you'll have to just say, 'Dad, she's my mom. I don't want you to talk that way about her.' But I don't think you should have to do that when you're nine."

"He's so much meaner than I thought he'd be. Sometimes, he's fun to be around. Other times ..."

He reburied his head in the pillow. She lightly rubbed his back as they lay in silence. She didn't want to pry, knowing he'd eventually share what was really bothering him. Snuggling, he rolled into her and wrapped his arms around her.

"Mommy?"

"Hmm?" she responded.

"I'm really sorry I made you find him for me," he said as the tears rolled down his cheeks.

"Frank," Nancy said, softly and gravely, "none of this is your fault. I should have dealt with your father a long time ago. I shouldn't have run away. Besides, if I didn't find him, he would have found us sooner or later."

"It's like he's two different people all wrapped into one. One minute, he's nice. The next, it's like he's someone else. He hits me and tells me I'm stupid." He stopped to breathe. "One time, he told me he could treat me like a dog because I wasn't any better than a dog. You've never said those things to me. Am I really not any better than a dog?"

Tears fell from his eyes and began streaming down his reddened cheeks.

"Sweetheart," she said, gathering him in her arms, "you're so much better than that. Your father has a way of saying things that he doesn't really mean. He doesn't know how much they hurt. He loves you, and he's trying to do the best he can to show it. I'm not sure why he would say those things. You can't really compare the way I treat you to the way he treats you. I've never really been a person who uses bad language and I don't believe in name-calling. If you'd like, I can talk to him about this."

"No," he said, visibly scared. "Don't tell him we even talked about it."

"Okay," she assured him, "we can keep this between us. I promise. Does he talk the same way to Lilly?"

"No, Lilly can't do anything wrong. She's his 'li'l darlin'. She gets everything she wants every time she asks."

"Is that why you won't talk to me on the phone when you're at his house?"

"Sort of," Frank said, looking down at the pillows.

"Mostly, it's because he listens to everything I say. He tells me how bad you are. I don't want him to get mad at me. When he's mad, he gets mean. If he thinks I like talking to you, then he thinks I don't agree that you're bad. And he gets mad." Frank looked at Nancy, pleading for her to understand his predicament.

"Mom, I don't think you're bad. But if I tell him that, he'll hate me. It's just easier not to talk to you when I'm at his house. Don't be mad, okay?"

"As long as I understand it now, it's okay," she said, hugging him again. "Maybe I should get you a cell phone. You can call me when he's in the bathroom or at the store or something. Would that work?"

"Yeah!" Frank said, delighted. "Or I could call you when he falls asleep on the couch when we're watching TV or when we're playing in the living room and he's in the bedroom with his friends."

"Okay, I'll look into that." Her mind was spinning with this new information. "Did that clear up some of the confusion?"

"Yeah," Frank said, visibly lighter now that his burden had been lifted. "Now do you want to know why I'm mad?"

"If you want to tell me."

"Well," he began slowly, "Last month after we went to pizza with you, Daddy told us that he's gonna move to Greenbriar and we hafta live with him." He paused, took a deep breath, and started to squirm in the bed. "If you don't move back in with him, he's never gonna let you see us ... ever. Not even if that's what we want."

Frank stopped to catch his breath and continued. But he talked faster ... as if he were trying to say it all in one breath.

"He doesn't even care what we want. He never cares

what we want. Most of the time, I don't think he listens to us. How come nobody asked Lilly and me what we want to do? Why do we have to live with him? I don't want to live with him and never see you again."

He'd worked himself back up into hysterics and sobbed into Nancy's chest. She held him tightly, allowing him a release.

Nancy's insides were screaming. Her instincts were telling her to pack up her children and run away again.

Instead, when the crying subsided and Frank was still, she softly said into Frank's ear, "Baby, I'm going to do everything in my power to make sure that you and Lilly get to tell a judge what you want. I'm also not giving up without a fight."

"You promise?"

"Yes, sir."

Long after Frank had been put to bed, Nancy lay awake, tossing and turning. She'd managed to put her children right into the lion's den.

What kind of a mother runs away and then comes back and puts her children in harm's way? You knew what kind of a man he is. You just stood by and handed them over. You should be ashamed of yourself. You really are worthless!

She continued the self-loathing for thirty minutes before resolving to concentrate every effort on regaining control of her children.

If I lose again, I'll move in with Vince. At least then I'll be close enough to protect Frank and Lilly.

Her final thoughts before drifting off were of reconciliation with the man she despised most in the world.

Chapter Thirty Six

"Matt, I need to find someone who's going to help me help my kids! Jackie didn't do it!" Nancy pleaded. "I don't care if it doesn't make sense to switch attorneys in the middle. Jackie did absolutely nothing for me! She stood by and let that vile judge take Frank and Lilly away. That's not in their best interest. I'm running out of time, and I need help fast."

"Hold up. What happened to the little sister that Olivia said was giving up?"

"She said that?" Nancy was taken aback. That only added more fuel to her fire. "I will die before I give up on my children. They are my life. Vince is not going to get his way. Tell me what to do."

"All right. Have you talked to Trent?"

"Not for a couple days. Why?"

Nancy didn't understand this sudden concern for her conversations with Trent.

"Does he know what you want to do?" Matt asked.

"I don't know. Why? What difference does it make if he knows or not?"

"How does he feel about it?"

"Why won't you answer my questions?" She was getting perturbed with her brother.

"I had a long conversation with Trent. He seems to think that you're willing to give up everything you've worked so hard for. He said you're going back to Vince."

Nancy's stomach lurched. The idea of going back to Vince was bad enough, but the thought that Trent had betrayed her was worse. It was as if she'd been slapped across the face. Beads of sweat formed across her brow and neck.

As she lifted her hair off the nape of her neck, she informed her brother softly but firmly, "I am not going back to Vince. Now are you going to help me or not? I don't have much time."

Nancy pounced at Trent on the phone later that night. She had pondered how to handle the situation with him, knowing she was a non-confrontational person. That was probably what had allowed Vince the ease of manipulation in the first place. But she had to let Trent know immediately that she felt betrayed and that it wasn't okay. Although it probably would have been better face-to-face, she didn't have the luxury of time on her side. Every nerve was alive as she allowed the anger to flow.

"How dare you tell Matt that I was going back to Vince!" she fumed. "I trusted you! I thought you were on my side! Why would you do that to me?"

"Whoa. Hold on a second. Catch your breath, and slow down. You want to let me know what's going on here before you chew my head off?" Trent said calmly.

"I called Matt today, asking him for help in finding me a new lawyer so I could get custody of the kids. He told me that you told him that I was going back to Vince. Did you or didn't you tell him that?" Nancy challenged.

"I might have mentioned that you might be thinking along those lines," he admitted.

"Why would you do that?" she asked, having calmed down a bit.

"Because I love you Nancy. I don't want to lose you," Trent said.

She was speechless. That was the furthest possible answer from what she had expected to hear.

After a silent moment, Trent asked, "Are you there?"

"Yes, I'm here," she softly replied, still taken aback by what she had just heard. "You've never told me you felt that way before."

"I know. I'm an oaf, and I never could quite figure out how to say it. Now I just sort of blurted it out. So, it's out there. I love you Nancy. I have for a long time. I don't want to lose you, and I certainly don't want to see you ruin your life and go back to that loser."

"I am not going back to Vince," Nancy assured him. "I have to play the game for a little while, even though I hate playing it. Right now, I don't have much of a choice. Wait a minute! Don't sidetrack me. Did you tell my brother how you felt?"

"Matt? Hell yeah. A long time ago."

"Oh, so he's checking up on me through you. You've been spying on me all this time?" she teased.

"I wouldn't exactly call what we've been doing spying," he chuckled. "Still mad at me?"

"I'll let you know the next time I see you."

She hung up the phone, giggling to herself. She realized she had a man who loved her for who she was, not what she could give him. It was a heartwarming feeling. She walked down the hall to check on her children, silently making them a promise.

I got us into this mess, and I'll get us out. I chose him, and I brought you into this world. I will find a way to get the truth told. The world has to find out what a monster he really is.

Vince thought he had Nancy right where he wanted her.

She has no choice but to come back to me. She'll never give up her kids. They mean the world to her. I could get money out of her, move to Greenbriar, fuck her anytime I want, and never have to work again. Hell, if I work it right, I might not even have to pay that lawyer any of the money I owe. Yeah, I've outfoxed Nancy this time.

He sat in his dilapidated recliner—drinking a beer, scratching his belly, and smoking a joint. He was reveling in his brilliance when the ringing phone startled him.

Fuck, who's calling me now? There's no one I want to talk to tonight. Just let it ring.

Paranoia was one of the many symptoms of too many days of not enough sleep and excessive drug use. Vince had discovered how to scam drugs out of more than one dealer.

After all, I'm leaving town. What do I care? This is going to be my last party.

"Vince, are you there? It's Friday, and you didn't pick up the kids from school." He heard Nancy's voice through the haze.

Am I imagining this?

"If you get this message, give me a call. I have Frank and Lilly with me."

"Wait! I'm here." Vince fumbled his way to the phone. "Nancy? Is that you?"

"Of course, it's me. Who else would it be?" she answered.

"I dunno. I must have the flu or something. I've been in bed for days. I musta lost track of the time. Is it Friday already?" he slurred, barely able to put a sentence together.

"Yes, Vince, it's Friday already." She could tell by his voice that he was drunk, high, or both.

Vince paused and asked, "Can you keep the kids this weekend?'

"Yes, Vince, I can keep the kids this weekend. That's never a problem," she answered, trying to keep the elation out of her tone.

"Tell them I'm sick and I'll make it up to them."

"Okay," she said, hanging up the phone.

She knew quite well that her ex-husband was anything but sick. But she didn't really care. She just got a weekend to spend with her kids.

"What do you guys want to do this weekend? Daddy's sick, and you're staying with me." She whirled around as soon as hung up the phone.

"He is? Really?" Frank asked.

"We do? Yippee!" Lilly hooted.

"You mean you're not upset about not getting to see your dad?" Nancy asked, pursing her lips and wrinkling her nose in mock confusion.

"No, not really," Lilly said. "I like it here a lot better," she answered matter-of-factly, as only a child can do. "I get my own bed, and you don't yell at us like he does."

"Where do you sleep when you're at his house?"

"In his bed."

"Where does he sleep?"

"In his bed."

"Where does Frank sleep?"

"In his bed."

"You all share one bed?" she asked with horror.

"Uh-huh."

"Oh, I guess that could be kinda fun," Nancy said, trying not to show how surprised she was.

"It would be fun if it was with you, but he snores. He

never cuts his toenails. His sheets are dirty, and they smell bad!" Lilly said, wrinkling up her nose.

"Oh!" Nancy said, wriggling up her nose back up at her daughter. "That doesn't sound like much fun at all. Maybe we should send him some new sheets and a toenail clipper."

"Mommy!"

Chapter Thirty Seven

Vince sobered up by Tuesday and called Nancy.

"Hey, I'm really sorry about the weekend. I hope the kids weren't too upset."

"They seemed to handle it all right. Are you feeling better?" Nancy asked sarcastically.

"Yeah, I was really sick there for a few days. Fever, chills. You name it, I had it."

"Well, it's a good thing you didn't pass it on to the kids," Nancy said.

"I was thinkin' the same thing. Um … er … Nancy?"

"What, Vince?"

"If I let the kids stay with you for a while, do you think you could front me a couple grand? That way, I could get set up Greenbriar before they move in with me." Vince was pleading and trying not to sound needy at the same time. "Maybe I'll just come get 'em for dinner a couple times a week until I settle in. I don't really know how long that'll take. I figure I should be settled in by Christmas."

"What?" She asked, stunned he'd just extended her time with the kids another four months.

"Are you even listening to me?"

"I'm trying, but you're not really making much sense."

She sat back on the couch, trying to keep the room from spinning out of control around her. On one hand, he was telling her to keep the kids. On the other, he was preparing to take them away.

"What doesn't make sense?" he asked, getting incensed at being questioned.

"I don't know. Maybe I'm just tired. Can you start over, please? What is it that you'd like to do?"

Now I'm getting pissed. She's mocking me. But I need the money!

"O … kay Nancy," he said, drawing out each syllable slowly to show his disgust with her stupidity. "I'll try again, slower this time, so I don't lose you. I was thinking that, seeing as how the school year just started, it might be better if we let the kids stay with you until I get settled into Greenbriar. But I need a little loan. I was wondering if you would front me some money in exchange for my letting you keep the kids. Now do you get it?"

At that precise moment, Nancy realized her ex-husband only understood one language, and it had absolutely nothing to do with her children.

"Yeah, I get it. How much?"

"Why do you have to sound so hateful?" Vince asked. "I'm trying here. I really am. I know I haven't been the nicest person, but I want to make everything right. I'm moving to Greenbriar so we can all be together. If we can't figure out some way for me to do that, I don't think I can keep living like this anymore. I might do something stupid. I'm just asking for a little help here. Do you really hate me that much?"

Once again, Vince managed to push the right button.

"I'm sure we can work something out," Nancy sighed, not even realizing she'd fallen right into his trap.

Nancy was excited at the prospect of being able to keep her kids for a while longer. When she tried to share her excitement with her sister she was immediately shot down. "Nance, you're a fool if you give him one cent!" Olivia said after hearing of the discussion. "There is nothing legally binding. He could take the money and still take the kids!"

"He'd never do that to me," Nancy insisted.

"Why not?" Olivia said, furrowing her brow in amazement that her sister was still allowing her ex-husband to make a fool out of her.

"Because he just wouldn't."

"Did you even suggest that you get something in writing from him?"

"Er ... no. But I could. Why? Do you think I need that?" Nancy asked naïvely. "I still haven't seen any paperwork from Jackie or his attorney with anything from that fiasco at the end of August. He doesn't even have legal custody of the kids yet, and he said he would let me keep them until the end of the Christmas break. Why do you think he would lie to me about something like that?"

"Maybe because everything out of his mouth is a lie," Olivia answered. "Nance, have you forgotten everything he's done? How badly he scared you? Doesn't that mean anything to you?"

"Of course, I haven't forgotten! Oli, I would sell my soul if it meant keeping my kids!" Nancy whined.

Olivia solicitously talked to Nancy, "Don't you think he knows that? I'm only saying that I think there might be a better way."

"Yeah? What?" Nancy said, drawing her knees to her chest.

She sat on her sister's kitchen countertop, watching her make sandwiches for the kids.

"I don't want to run the risk of losing Frank and Lilly. Money seems to be a language that Vince understands. Sex and money. I'm not giving him sex, and I'm willing to part with money. Maybe this will buy me enough time to come up with another idea or way to get rid of him."

"Get rid of him?" Olivia sniggered. "Who are you kidding? He's not going anywhere! If you give him money now, his hand will be out for the next twenty years. Are you willing to pay him that long?"

"What other choice do I have?" Nancy whispered.

"Why not fight him in court?"

"We saw how well that went the first time," Nancy countered. "Why would I want to do that again? As far as the court is concerned, I have no legal rights to my own kids. Vince is their legal guardian."

Olivia gently pounced.

"That's right! And he can pull that card on you anytime he wants. Don't you realize that, if you give him money now, he'll get pissed off sometime down the road, throw something in your face, and claim his legal right?"

"I guess I never thought about it that way."

"Maybe you should!" Olivia looked Nancy sternly in the face. "What is it about Vince that makes you lose all perspective? Nance, you're not dumb, but you sure do dumb things when it comes to him."

"I don't know. Maybe I know what kind of a man he could be," Nancy replied sadly.

"He isn't that kind of a man! So stop wishing on the stars and get a grip! Do not give him any money!"

After putting Frank and Lilly to bed, Nancy toyed with the conversation she'd had with Olivia. She wandered through her apartment, picking up toys and clothes as she walked. She was figuring out how to phrase the topic simply enough to manipulate Vince to sign a legal document waiving his rights to custody.

If he wants money that badly, he'll have to give up something in exchange.

The ringing of the phone startled her out of her reverie.

"Hello?"

"Hi, Nancy! Did you give any thought to my offer?"

Vince was upbeat at the other end of the phone. She was sure he was stoned. She heard loud music playing in the background. That was always a good indication of his indulgence.

"Hello, Vince. Frank was wondering why you hadn't called him tonight. He waited until 9:30, but you never called."

"Yeah, I got hung up at work. Tell him that I'll make it up to him this weekend."

"I'll do that," she barbed back.

"Did you think about it?"

"Uh ... yes ... and ..." She hesitated, took a deep breath, and said, "I think we need to put it in writing."

"What?"

"Well, I just want to make sure that, whatever we decide to do, you don't change your mind and take the kids back." She knew she was taking a huge risk. He could easily change his mind, but she had to take that chance.

"I'd never do that to you."

"I just want to make sure."

There was a stilted silence. To Nancy, it seemed to last a long time. It was actually only forty seconds.

Vince said, "Okay, do whatever you have to do. I'll sign anything."

"Really?"

Without realizing it, she'd been holding her breath waiting for his response. His answer was both a surprise and a relief.

"Yeah, really," he said with resignation in his voice.

"Okay, I'll call my attorney tomorrow and have her draw up the papers," Nancy said. "She can call your attorney if you want …"

"Wait. Don't get my attorney involved," he interrupted.

"Why not?"

"Can't we do this without attorneys?" He was adamant. "All they do is suck us dry. We end up paying them money that we could use for other things."

"Well, I guess I could ask Matt if he could do it. He wouldn't charge me anything," she hesitantly suggested. Thinking out loud, she said, "It's too late for me to call him tonight. I'll call him tomorrow and let you know."

"In the meantime, can I have a little money?"

He sounded almost desperate.

"How much?"

Chapter Thirty Eight

"Nance, I can draw up the papers for both of you to sign, but you have to understand that they're not legally binding in any court," Matt tried explaining over the phone the following morning.

"But if Vince and I agree, why can't we just ignore the other order and use this one instead?" Nancy asked.

"You can," Matt said. "But Vince hasn't been a very honest human being, and I use that term quite loosely." He chuckled. "What makes you think he's changed now?"

"I have to believe him now … for my kids," Nancy pleaded. "Can you please draw it up? I told him I'd give him $1,000 a month per child or $2,000 in exchange for his waiving his rights to legal custody."

"You what?" Matt exclaimed.

"I figured, if I gave him more than the judge did, he wouldn't be as likely to want the kids. You know how money drives Vince."

"All right, I'll draw up the paperwork. Just so we're perfectly clear, Vince can change his mind and enforce the stipulation the judge ordered at any time. If you want to change that order, you'll have to go before a judge to have it legally changed. I can only write up a contract," Matt explained.

Nancy Suzanne Lewiston Cooper will pay $500 per week from September 15 through January 15 to Vincent Cooper. In exchange, Vincent Cooper waives all custodial rights to his children, Franklin Vincent Cooper and Lillian Rose Cooper. Vincent Cooper will relocate to Greenbriar, California, and will be granted visitation to his children every other weekend, commencing October 1. This contract is entered into by both parties and is considered legally binding.

Vince was anxious to sign the contract. He was really anxious to receive $2,000 a month for doing absolutely nothing. As far as he was concerned, he'd just hit the mother lode. His first check went directly to Louie, which made a dent in his debt. It enabled him to get more stuff. He immediately went further into debt and a foggy haze for four days.

When he reemerged into the real world, his four-day stubble, wrinkled clothes, dry mouth, disheveled hair, and foul odor revolted him. He vowed this was the end of his partying ways. It was time to say good-bye to Vista Oaks and drugs for good. He stumbled into the bathroom to take a much-needed shower. The pounding of the hot water on his skin felt good. A full fifteen minutes later, he emerged with welts of reddened skin protruding from his widened middle. A wave of dizziness overcame him. He sat on the toilet.

Now to put the plan into action. I move to Greenbriar and clean up my act. Woo Nancy. Get back into her good graces and totally crush her. And I'm using her money to do it!

He actually laughed out loud.

By the end of September, Carol Toranado still hadn't

received a payment from Vince. True to her word, she hadn't drawn up any paperwork from his August court appearance. She wasn't worried that he'd report her to the California Bar Association. The courts were so backed up that they wouldn't notice the missing paperwork for months. Jackie Kelly wasn't calling requesting the paperwork either. As far as Carol was concerned, Nancy could keep her children until Vince paid his legal fees.

Jackie Kelly hadn't heard from Nancy since the day they parted company in August, but she hadn't really expected to. The outcome of that custody hearing was much different than she'd expected. She was in the process of drawing up paperwork for an appeal. Appeals rarely worked in family court. Nothing short of a miracle would change the court's mind.

Chapter Thirty Nine

Vince moved out of Vista Oaks on October 15 and moved to Greenbriar. He'd collected enough money from Nancy to put down a deposit on a new apartment, move, and make a small payment to Carol, wherein she released the stipulation for signatures. On Monday, October 20, he signed the stipulation that was drawn up confirming his custodial rights, per Judge Decker's order from August.

It never crossed his mind that he was betraying Nancy's trust. He was simply claiming what was rightfully his.

The stipulation giving Vincent Cooper full legal custody of Frank and Lilly Cooper was sent to Jackie Kelly's office on October 23. When Nancy received the paperwork in the mail, it was as if a knife had been driven through her heart. She was in shock. Vince had betrayed her!

How could he?

She didn't know whether to scream or cry or be sad or mad.

Goose bumps ran up and down her body as her stomach churned, and her body shook uncontrollably. She reached for the phone with shaky hands and dialed Jackie Kelly's office.

Trying to remain calm, yet firm, she said, "I have no intention of signing this paperwork. I'm requesting a court-appointed attorney for my children."

"You what?" Jackie asked in disbelief.

"You heard me," Nancy replied, gaining confidence as she spoke. "I don't think anyone in that courtroom was thinking about what was best for Frank and Lilly. I think the court needs to appoint an attorney who will keep their best interests first. With that in mind, I will not sign this stipulation. I want to find a psychologist who is willing to speak on their behalf and then find an attorney who is willing to do the same thing."

Nancy was shaking as she spoke, but she said this to Jackie just as she'd rehearsed. She and Trent had spoken about this several times, just in case this day ever came. This was her only hope of ever keeping her children out of Vince's grasp.

"Are you going to draw up the paperwork requesting that, or do I need to find a different attorney?"

"No ... er ... I mean ... uh ... yes ... I'll draw it up," Jackie replied, bewildered into agreement.

"Thank you. How soon can I come by your office and sign it? I'd like it filed with the court immediately."

"I should have it ready for filing by the end of the week."

Nancy hung up the phone dazed, still in shock over Vince's betrayal. She really thought he'd changed.

Or was it just wishful thinking?

The difference between Vince and Nancy's homes was vast. Frank and Lilly shuttled between the two without complaint, but it was apparent to anyone close to them that it was difficult. They each had their own room at Nancy's house. In Vince's new apartment, they were still forced to share a room. Where Nancy tried to give them space and individual rights, Vince seemed to consider them as one person. He never thought that Frank might not want to do what Lilly wanted or vice versa. Nancy's home was neat, clean, and orderly. Vince's house was disorganized, dirty, and often void of food. The children felt they were in the way when they were with him, even though he bought them toys and junk food whenever they asked.

With Nancy's permission, he would pick them up from school and take them to the park in the afternoon until she would get off work. Invariably, he would then try to get himself an invitation to dinner at Nancy's house. Sometimes, it actually worked. The kids were never aware of what their father was trying to do, but Nancy was. He was slowly trying to wheedle his way into their lives and conjoin them again.

The betrayal of the legal papers made Nancy realize she could never trust him. She never let on that she had received them. Vince never said a word either.

It quickly became routine on Thursdays before Lilly was going to spend the weekend at Vince's house for her to get a stomachache. She would complain that she didn't feel well and was afraid of the dark. Frank would begin to act differently as well. He became moody and sensitive. Nothing was right, and the slightest events would set him off.

Lilly was lying down on her bed one Thursday when Nancy went into her room and asked, "Is there something going on at Daddy's house that you haven't told me about?"

"No," she whispered, not looking at her mother. "Not really."

"Not really," Nancy prodded. "Or no?"

"Maybe there's something," Lilly confessed, rolling over to look at her mother.

"Can you tell me about it?" Nancy quietly asked.

"Promise you won't get mad?" Lilly asked, looking at her stuffed animals.

"I promise," Nancy said.

Her stomach lurched. She hoped for the best, but she feared the worst.

"Daddy keeps telling us that he's going to take us far away if you don't move in with him, or if he can't move in here with us."

Lilly's hands started fumbling with her pillow as Nancy drew her near to her.

"That's okay, lily flower. Go on."

"I'm afraid I'll never see you again." Lilly's tears started flowing.

"Oh, baby girl," Nancy said, scooping up her daughter. "Don't you know I would find you, even if it meant going to the very ends of the earth?"

"Really?"

"Really!" Nancy said, holding Lilly very close to her. "But I think I have an even better idea."

"You do?" Lilly said, looking up with wonder at her mother.

"Uh-huh. Do you know how to dial 9-1-1?"

"Yes," she answered as if it were the silliest question her mother could have asked.

"Do you know my name?"

"Of course, silly. It's Mommy!"

"No." Nancy laughed. "I mean my other name."

"You mean Nancy Cooper?" she asked with delight.

"Yeah, that one," Nancy said. "Do you know our phone number?"

"No, I don't think so."

"We'll take care of that. I think the school is selling those identification bracelets," Nancy commented. "We'll have to get you one with our phone number on it. How does that sound?"

"Good. Mommy, how does that help?" Lilly asked, perplexed.

"If Daddy does what he says, which I don't think he'd ever do …" She kissed Lilly on the tip of her nose. "You just find a phone, call 9-1-1, and tell them who you are, who I am, and how to find me."

"That's all?" she asked, amazed.

"That's all. And I'll be there."

Chapter Forty

Jackie Kelly's office processed the paperwork appointing Frank and Lilly Cooper an attorney of their own. Nancy signed it on October 28. The request that an attorney for Frank Cooper and Lilly Cooper, both minor children, be appointed was sent to Judge Arnold. The request further stipulated that Michael Fenton be the attorney in question. A second request to set aside the initial ruling for custody was also sent to Judge Arnold, pending the outcome of the findings for a new attorney petition. Copies of all requests were forwarded to both Vincent and Nancy Cooper.

When Vince received his copies from the court advising him that his children had been appointed their own attorney and his custody was being questioned, his attitude altered dramatically. No longer was the joviality present. In its place came blatant hostility. Although Nancy was prepared for this on the surface, she wasn't emotionally prepared for the damage it would cause her children.

"You piece of shit! After all I've done for you! I've let you keep your kids. And this is how you repay me? What makes you think you're going to win? I'm going to bury you. You bitch! Just wait and see! You'll be lucky if you ever see your kids again."

His threats so shook Nancy that she took Frank and Lilly to the police station and had their fingerprints taken just in case he took them away. She wanted something to have ... just in case.

The horror stories of their time spent with Vince continued as Frank and Lilly would come home on Sundays and unload their grief. Nancy could only listen and comfort her children. The guilt of getting her children into this mess was overwhelming. The only consolation she had was the knowledge that he would eventually get his due and the hope that the new attorney would get them some justice.

The entire time they were with Vince, Nancy was miserable. Her stomach would be tied up in knots wondering what horrific situation they were in. The kids would tell her stories, but she would never know whether they were true or not. Vince would deny everything. She would often drink on Friday nights just to make the time pass faster.

Both Frank and Lilly had been coached numerous times on how to handle the situation if Vince took them somewhere dangerous or away from Nancy. Lilly had been equipped with an identification bracelet. Frank knew the phone number by heart. Nancy could only pray that no harm would come to her children.

Nancy met with Michael Fenton and explained why she felt it was necessary for Frank and Lilly to have representation of their own. She was completely honest with him, including everything from the past. She was certain that, in his meeting with Vince, the truth would be skewed. She could only hope that her sincerity would come through.

Vince met with Michael Fenton and told him that he thought an attorney for the kids was a waste of money. He only hoped he wasn't getting the bill.

"The judge granted full custody to me because she stole those kids from me. She didn't have any right to do it. Now she's trying any stall tactic she can come up with to get them back. You're just her last chance."

"So you feel that it's in the children's best interest to be taken away from their mother?" Michael asked.

"If that's what the judge thought, who am I to argue?" Vince answered.

"Well, you must have an opinion, Mr. Cooper."

"You can call me Vince."

"Okay, Vince, do you have an opinion of your own?"

Vince answered, "I think the kids do just fine with me. Going back and forth is really not that good for them. It's just too confusing."

Michael Fenton was scheduled to meet with Frank and Lilly Cooper on Monday afternoon. Vince left Michael Fenton's office, feeling sure he'd made a favorable impression on that attorney.

I got nothin' to worry about. This one's in the bag. They're mine! All mine. You lost this one, babe! Just you watch! You think you outfoxed me, but you didn't!

Running in to the school to pick up Frank and Lilly, Vince flirted with the receptionist again, like he did every week.

"Hey, good-looking, did you miss me?"

"Hi, Mr. Cooper!"

"When are you going to start calling me Vince?"

"Okay. Hi, Vince!"

"That's better. Sorry, no time to chat this week. I'm running late. Have a good weekend," Vince said, searching for Frank and Lilly. When he found them in their classrooms he hurriedly rushed them out.

"Daddy, why are we in such a hurry?" Lilly asked as she was scurrying and trying to keep up with Vince's long stride.

"Lilly, why are you always whining?"

"I'm not whining," she said as she started crying.

"It's okay, Lilly. C'mon. Just run to keep up with him," Frank said.

"I have to meet someone. Is that okay with you?" Vince asked sarcastically.

"I'm sorry, Daddy. I didn't mean to make you mad," Lilly said.

"Just hurry up!" Vince yelled as he opened the door to the restaurant they'd stopped at. "Go sit at the first booth you find."

Frank and Lilly ran past him and sat at the first booth. Vince didn't follow them in. Ten minutes later, he found them and sat down.

"Okay, now we can relax."

Frank and Lilly just stared at him.

"What? You have nothing to say to me?"

"No."

"Not really," Frank said.

"Well, I have something to ask you," Vince began. "Today I met with a man who wants to be your lawyer."

"What's a lawyer?" Lilly asked.

"Well, that answers my question," Vince said. "Never mind. Let's get something to eat."

After dinner, Vince told Frank to take Lilly to the bathroom. He said he would meet them in the truck.

On that same Friday night, as Nancy was preparing for bed, the telephone rang.

If this is Vince calling to cuss me out again, I don't want to talk to him. But it might be the kids, so I better answer it.

"Hello?"

"Mrs. Cooper?"

"Yes." She hesitated. She didn't recognize the voice.

"Is this Mrs. Nancy Cooper?"

"Yes, it is. Who's calling, please?"

Nancy didn't recognize the voice, and she wasn't in the mood for any practical jokes.

"This is the California Highway Patrol."

A cold shiver ran through her body, like nothing she'd ever felt before. Every hair on her body was standing straight up, as her fingers became cold as ice. She tried to focus on the voice at the other end of the phone.

"Are you Mrs. Nancy Cooper?"

"Yes. I am. What's this about?"

"I'm sorry, but there's been an accident. We have a squad car en route to your house to pick you up. They should be there any minute." The monotone voice droned on. No emotion … no feelings … nothing.

"What? Why? What are you talking about?" Nancy heard herself asking.

She was shocked and confused. At the same time, she was mad that someone had called her out of the blue.

Is this one of Vince's twisted jokes?

"Who are you?"

"As I said, ma'am, I'm with the highway patrol. There should be someone there any minute to pick you up."

Just as he said that, the doorbell rang. Nancy walked over to her door in a fuzzy haze.

"Mrs. Cooper?"

She heard a man's voice through the door.

"Yes?"

She was having a hard time talking.

"I'm here to take you to Greenbriar Community Medical Center. You're needed right away, ma'am."

No, this isn't a joke. There is a man in a uniform at my front door.

"What happened? Who's hurt? What's going on?"

She demanded answers as she opened the door to this stranger in a uniform.

"Honestly, ma'am, I really don't know. I was just told to come pick you up and get you to the hospital as quickly as I could."

Nancy quickly threw on some clothes. They drove to the hospital in silence. Nancy's mind was whirling. She didn't have any idea what was going on.

Is it Trent? Is it Olivia? Is it Vince? Who's hurt?

She was driven directly to the emergency room entrance without another word being spoken. Her mind was racing as her heart beat wildly. Puddles of sweat were forming in her armpits, and her palms were clammy. She was having a hard time catching her breath, and nothing seemed to be in focus. The lights began to meld together. Nancy felt like she was in the middle of a nightmare. She was sure everyone was staring at her as she entered the double doors of the emergency room.

Upon entering the hospital, the smell of antiseptic in the air overwhelmed her.

The sights and sounds of the emergency room haunted her as she passed through it—anguish in the eyes of the ill, despair and desolation in the air. She tried to glance at no one as she followed a nurse down a long corridor, but that was a difficult task. Wringing her hands, she wondered what she would see as she turned each corner. Nothing in her life could have prepared her for the shock.

Chapter Forty One

The curtains were pulled aside. All Nancy saw was her beautiful daughter lying in a bed. Her brown hair was fanned out across the pillow. She heard the beeping of the machines and saw a myriad of tubes running into her thin arms. Nancy's knees buckled as she gasped.

"Oh my God! What happened? Is she all right? How'd she get here? Where's my son?"

"Your son is right here, Mrs. Cooper," the emergency room nurse said.

She pulled the curtain aside to show Nancy that Frank was lying in the bed right next to Lilly. Frank was also plugged into monitors and machines. Frank had cuts running all over his body.

"What happened?"

"I'm not really sure. They were in a car accident, and they came in about thirty minutes ago. An officer will be by to give you the details after the doctor fills you in on their condition."

"Mrs. Cooper ..." A man in his early forties wearing surgeon scrubs with a full head of brown hair, gentle blue eyes, and a soft smile approached Nancy. "I'm Dr.

Silverton. Let me tell you what we know right now."

Nancy listened as the doctor explained that Lilly's wounds appeared to be superficial. She was banged and bruised. She would be sore for a few days. Right now, the best thing she could do was rest. They wanted to keep her overnight for observation just to make sure there wasn't anything they had overlooked.

Frank, on the other hand, was more seriously injured. There was definitely internal bleeding, and they would need to go in and repair it. There was no way to know what else they would find. Her signature was required on the consent forms. Time was of the essence. He was fairly confident that the injuries were not life-threatening and Frank would make a full recovery. He had already scheduled an operating room.

Nancy was listening, but she wasn't really hearing anything.

"Is there someone I can call for you Mrs. Cooper? Mrs. Cooper?"

"Huh? What?"

She emerged from the haze.

"I asked if there was someone I could call for you?" the doctor repeated.

"Yes, I think I'd like to have my sister here."

Nancy gave Olivia's number to the nurse.

Olivia made it to the hospital and found Nancy sitting by Lilly's bed.

"Nance, what happened?"

"I don't really know. I got a call from the highway patrol. They came and got me. They brought me here. Frank's in surgery. I signed a form. Lilly's sleeping. I don't know what's going on. I don't even know how they got here." Tears were streaming down Nancy's face. "I never even said good-bye to them today when they went to school. I never told them I loved them. I didn't get to say good night to them. What if Lilly never wakes up? What if Frank dies on the operating table? Oli, what am I going to do?"

"What did the doctor say?" Olivia asked, stepping right into her role as the practical older sister.

Nancy didn't answer her as she silently stroked Lilly's hair.

"What did the doctor say?" Olivia repeated.

"Huh? He said their chances are good, but you never know," Nancy dejectedly answered.

"Nancy, snap out of it!" Olivia reprimanded her sister. "If the doctor said their chances are good, you need to be positive. They're going to need you to stay positive. We need to find out what happened. How did they get here? Where's Vince?"

"I don't know." Nancy stopped herself and thought for a minute. "I really don't know. I didn't even think about him. I was so worried about the kids."

"Who's supposed to tell you what's going on?" Olivia insisted.

"An officer was supposed to find me after the doctor told me about Frank and Lilly, but he hasn't come by yet."

Frank was in surgery for four hours. He had two broken ribs, a punctured lung, and a broken nose.

When he was quietly resting in the recovery room, Dr. Silverton walked over to Nancy and said, "He is one very lucky little boy. If he had landed any differently, he might very well have broken his neck. He is going to be quite sore for a few days, but the beauty of being young is they heal fast. He'll be out raising hell before you know it. He should sleep for at least eight hours, but you can talk to him after that. I'd like to keep him here for a few days so we can keep an eye on him. After that, he can go home, but he will need to have quiet bed rest for at least seven days."

Nancy sat by Lilly's bed, lovingly looking at her precious daughter.

I'd die if anything happened to you. You are more important to me than life itself.

She watched as the blankets rose with each breath, surveying the contours of her face ... the upturned nose, the freckle-speckled cheeks, the perfectly curved, extra-long eyelashes, the tiny dimple on her chin, and her porcelain fine skin.

What happened to you, lily flower? How did you get here?

Nancy did something she hadn't done in a very long time. She got down on her knees next to the bed, closed her eyes, and prayed.

Dear God, I know I haven't done this in a while, and you probably don't even remember me, but I've kind of had a rough time. I thought that, after living through hell on earth, there really couldn't be a God. But right now, I have to believe you're there. Frank and Lilly don't deserve to die because of a decision I made twelve years ago. This is all my fault! Please, God. Please give me back my children. I've been trying so hard to do what's right by them, and I know I sometimes get lost, but I have to believe that your angels are watching over us. I guess that's all. Amen.

As she was praying, tears began steadily streaming down her cheeks. She didn't bother to wipe them away.

Nancy slowly resumed her vigil at Lilly's bedside, lovingly stroking her hair. Lilly's eyelids began to flutter, and she slowly opened her eyes. Gradually, she focused on her mother, and her face lit up as her smile spread.

"Hi, Mommy!"

"Hi, Lilly! I'm so glad you woke up!"

Nancy tried so hard not to cry, but she couldn't hold back her tears.

"Mommy, why are you crying? Did I do something wrong? I called 9-1-1 like you taught me. You found me, right?" Lilly asked with a look of consternation across her face.

"Sweetheart, I'm crying because I've been so worried about you. Do you remember anything about what happened?"

Lilly scrunched her brow up, trying to think, and said, "I remember Daddy yelling at Frank. He was really mad. We were driving somewhere. I don't remember where."

She stopped for a minute and looked off to the side to remember.

"Where was Frank sitting?" Nancy quietly asked.

"Frank was in the backseat of the truck, and I was in the front seat."

"Okay. Then what happened?" Nancy gently nudged.

"I sorta remember Frank yelling at Daddy that he hated him. That made him even madder. Then Daddy turned around to hit Frank, and Frank scooted away from him."

"How did he do that?" Nancy softly asked.

"I'm not sure. I think he took off his seat belt, but Daddy wasn't watching where he was going because he was looking back at Frank. Then I remember a lot of bumping and noises. When all the shaking stopped, we were in a bunch of bushes. I used Frank's cell phone and called 9-1-1 like we practiced. Then I must've fallen asleep because I don't remember anything else."

"How did you get Frank's cell phone, baby?" Nancy asked.

"He let me hold it because I was in the front seat." Lilly answered her mother, as if it should have been obvious. "Mommy, I'm really tired. Can I go back to sleep?"

"Yes, sweetheart, you can," Nancy said, stroking her daughter's hair. "I'll be right here when you wake up. I promise."

But Lilly hadn't heard. She was already asleep.

Chapter Forty Two

By the next morning, an officer had come by and explained to Nancy that Vince had driven off the side of the road and flipped his truck. Lilly, who had been sitting in the front seat and was wearing a seat belt, had minor injuries. Frank had been tossed around in the backseat because he wasn't wearing a seatbelt. Vince had suffered major head trauma in the accident and had died at the scene. What they could not explain was why he was facing backwards. Vince's blood alcohol level was 0.24. He had tested positive for cocaine.

Lilly had used her brother's cell phone to call 9-1-1. They had found the truck using GPS. Before she fell asleep in the ambulance, she told the policeman how to call her mom … just like they had rehearsed so many times.

Two weeks after the accident, Frank's visible bruises had almost disappeared. He explained to Nancy exactly what happened on the night of the accident. Vince had told Frank and Lilly that they were going away and there was no way he was going to let them have their own attorney. He wasn't going to let them meet Michael Fenton on Monday. He wasn't going to let them see their mother ever again. When Frank stood up for them, Vince had become enraged and reached into the backseat of the truck to hit his son. Frank scooted out of his reach, which only made Vince madder. When Frank told Vince that he hated him, Vince turned his body completely around and lost control of the truck. It went off the road.

"Mommy, did I kill Daddy?" Frank asked through his tears.

"No, sweetheart, you didn't," Nancy said, holding her son. They sat that way for a long time until she finally said, "I guess it's time for me to let you in on something that my mother used to say."

"What?"

"A tiger never changes its' stripes."

"What does that mean?" Frank asked, puzzled.

"Well," Nancy began, "I think it means that people are who they are, no matter what you want them to be. What you don't know about the night of the accident is that your dad had three times as much alcohol in his body as he was supposed to have to drive. And he had drugs in his system. So, no, Frank, you didn't kill your daddy. Your daddy killed your daddy."

She added, "Sometimes we just have to accept things and say, 'It is what it is.' And move on."

"But is it okay to miss him?"

"I wouldn't expect anything less from you," she said, hugging her son. "That is why I love you so much! You need to learn from the good and remember the bad so you won't repeat it. Every relationship in your life is going to be a learning experience. I hope you will take something out of each and every one of them."

"I love you, Mommy."

"I love you more."

For more information go to www.brendayoungerman.com

Turn the page for a preview of <u>Hidden Truths</u> the new novel by Brenda Youngerman, coming out in early 2008.

For more information go to www.brendayoungerman.com

Hidden Truths

Pancakes dripping with melted butter and syrup, scrambled eggs, bacon, coffee and orange juice; the aroma in the air made his mouth water. Drool slid out the side of his mouth and onto his pillowcase. His mother floated around the table, humming softly to herself as she set out the breakfast. The scent of jasmine drifted over the wafting odors of the fresh baked griddlecakes. He reached for her and fell...hard.

Wayne Foster picked himself up off the floor, looked in the mirror and said, "What're you looking at?" and disgustedly turned away. At sixteen he was five foot eleven with lifeless gray eyes, straggly blonde hair, a misshaped nose, crooked teeth and a fairly clear complexion. Wayne was slightly overweight; he never exercised, ate junk food and had a passion for beer. He shuffled down the hallway to the bathroom, scratching himself as he walked. The rest of the house was dark.

Wayne left his house at the same time every morning; passing the huddled figure of his father, who was down for the count on the couch, or the bed, depending on where he'd landed the night before. Sometimes he never made it to the furniture at all, he just dropped to the floor. Just shove everything out of the way and plop himself down where he was; that was Dad...good old Dad. The only reason Wayne left the house anymore was so he wouldn't have to deal with his dad. It hadn't always been this way.

Wayne Robert Foster was born into the loving arms of Patricia and Stanley Foster, of Crest Haven, California, an upper class neighborhood with beautifully manicured lawns, expensive security systems, three car garages, and a daily service staff of chefs, nannies and gardeners. Wayne was the eldest of two sons born to the Fosters, his younger brother, William, or Billy, coming along four years behind him. Patricia was a stay-at-home mom who was involved with her sons' daily activities. As soon as the day was over, Patricia's attention turned to Stanley.

Stan and Pat, as they were known in their social circle, entertained frequently. When not entertaining in their lavish home, they would be out with friends. The Fosters did not sit down and have family dinners; the boys ate before Stan came home from work, and Pat ate with Stan. Never was there a 'family fun night,' that wasn't Stan's thing.

"Mommy, can't you stay home with us tonight?" Billy cried one rainy Friday night. "I'm scared the lightning monster's gonna get me."

"Honey, no monster's going to get you," Patricia reassured her son.

"Pat, stop mollycoddling the boy," Stan reprimanded her. "Do you want him to grow up and be a pansy?" Stan was firm about raising his sons to be men, there was not going to be any backing down on boys being boys.

Even though he didn't really understand what his father was saying, (he was only five years old,) Billy began crying harder when he heard the harsh words. "I'm not no pansy!"

"Then toughen up, boy!" Stan yelled at him. "We're going out and that's that!"

"Mrs. Church will be right here with you and she'll make sure you're safe." Pat tried to calm her hysterical son. "Wayne's here, too. If you want, you can sleep with him until I come home. I'll carry you into your own bed after you fall asleep."

"You'll do no such thing, Patricia!" Stan scolded, "He'll go to sleep in his own bed, and he'll be just fine. It's time he knew that there's no such thing as monsters, and that he needs to be a big boy." Turning his attention to his youngest son, he said, "Will, you do know that there's no such thing as monsters, don't you?"

"Yes, Daddy."

"Then you also know that the lightning can't hurt you, right?"

"Right..." he answered, not too convinced.

"Then tell your mother you'll be just fine while we're out, or she'll be worried and won't have a good time."

"Mommy, I'll be fine while you're out. Don't be worried, and have a good time." Billy said, as if he'd rehearsed it many times before.

Patricia leaned over and hugged him, "Okay, Silly Billy, I love you, I'll see you in the morning; sleep good." Turning towards Wayne she hugged him and told him she loved him too.

That was the last time William and Wayne Nelson ever saw their mother alive. The next morning walking into the kitchen, Wayne was shocked to find Mrs. Church sitting at his table, "Where's Mommy?" he asked.

"There's been an accident," she replied, not looking at Wayne as she spoke. She continued speaking...more into her coffee cup than to the child, "Your dad's coming home soon."

Wayne and Billy met their father at the door. "Daddy, where's Mommy?" Billy asked.

"When's she coming home?" Wayne inquired. Stan walked right past both boys as if he hadn't heard a word they'd said. His hair was ruffled and he had bloodstains on his collar; there were stitches across his cheek and forearm, but the boys didn't notice any of that. They wanted their mother.

Bewildered, Billy asked again: "Daddy, where's Mommy?" his teary eyes followed his father's movements across the room.

Stan stopped. Slowly he turned around and looked at his youngest son. Mockingly he repeated, "Daddy, where's Mommy?" Stan continued with anger and disgust, "Maybe if you weren't such a Mommy's boy she'd be here right now instead of hooked up to every machine imaginable! That's where Mommy is…fighting for her life in a hospital bed because you're such a cry baby!" He turned around and left the room as Billy began to wail.

Wayne, who had been standing next to Billy during their father's tirade, took his little brother's hand and they went to their room. Wayne said, "Whatever happened, it wasn't your fault. Mommy'll be home soon and she'll make him stop yelling at you; she always does."

Neither Pat nor Stan had any living relatives so Mrs. Church stayed with the boys for three days as they saw their father come and go, but he never talked to them…it was like they didn't even exist. Time had no meaning to the boys. Mrs. Church did the best she could to keep them to a schedule; but she kept them home from school on Monday, and told the chef and nanny to take the day off.

Billy missed his mother and Wayne wasn't enough of a comfort. The television made the time pass, but even their favorite shows could not ease the ache of not knowing where she was.

Finally, on Monday afternoon, Stan came home. Dragging himself into the living room, which was usually a 'forbidden' room, he slumped on the couch with tear-brimmed eyes. He informed his sons that their mother was dead.

"What do you mean she's dead?" Wayne asked. The only thing he'd ever seen that was dead was their pet gold fish. When he had died they'd flushed it down the toilet. Was that going to happen to his mother? Wayne's mind started wandering to what it would like to flush his mother down the toilet. His father's voice brought him back.

"I mean she's never coming back," Stan answered.

"Daddy, we're never going to see Mommy again?" Billy's lip quivered and his eyes brimmed over with tears.

"What happened?" Wayne whispered as he reached for Billy to sit next to him on the couch. He had forgotten that they were in the living room; the room where little boys were never allowed to play, or sit, or touch anything. He and Billy sat down next to each other on the far end of the couch and stared at their father for answers. Wayne's head was filled with questions.

"What happened? What happened?" Stan started screaming, "You want to know what happened? I'll tell you what happened."

Wayne and Billy cowered away from their father as he started his tirade. They were accustomed to his anger, but now their mother wasn't there to run interference. They sat quietly as he continued: "Your mother was so upset at the party that your precious little brother was afraid of the lightning that she kept yelling at me." He had a glazed look in his eyes as he recalled the party from three nights earlier. "She was yelling and yelling. Finally I agreed to come back home. I didn't see the truck coming and we were hit. Your mother's injuries were too much for her to handle and she died." Stan started crying, slowly at first and then in loud gut wrenching sobs.

Wayne and Billy were shocked. They'd never seen their father cry before. Never! Just as they were about to comfort him, he stopped and said, "That's what happened! Thanks to your little brother and his lightning monster," Stan looked directly at Wayne, "your mother is dead!"

Billy slowly crept off the couch and slunk over to his father. "Daddy, I'm sorry." He quietly sobbed, "I didn't mean to kill Mommy." Then he turned and walked out of the room crying.

Stan just sat on the couch weeping, as if he had not even heard his youngest son. Wayne was at a loss; should he comfort his father or not? He sat on the end of the couch, looking around this room he'd only been allowed to peer into before. The furniture was overstuffed and off-white. It was not very comfortable. The walls were painted a slightly darker shade than the couch and loveseat, and the carpet was the same shade. There were family portraits hanging on one wall. Wayne was staring at how beautiful his mother was.

Suddenly it hit him: he'd just lost his mother, and his father was sitting in the same room with him, crying. What was going to happen to him? He curled up on the end of the couch and started to cry…not only for him, but for all of them.

When Wayne woke up, in the same spot, on the end of the couch, the room was dark. Stan was no longer in the living room; Wayne had no idea how long he'd been asleep. He went to find Billy.

Wayne left the living room in a dazed stupor. Losing a parent is not easy, at any age, and Wayne was two months short of his tenth birthday. Wayne Nelson was extremely intelligent. He was at the top of his fifth grade class and was reading at a seventh grade level. His math skills were highly advanced as well, but Wayne was extremely shy. His light blonde hair fell to his shoulders and he rarely looked at a person when he spoke to them. He lacked self-confidence and would prefer to read a book, than play outside. Often he would overhear conversations between his parents; his mother would stick up for him; "Stan, he's shy, he'll outgrow it. Don't be so hard on him."

Walking down the hallway towards the bedroom he shared with Billy he thought about those conversations and wondered, "Who's going to stick up for me now?" Wayne was not very fond of his father. He was a hard man to like. Stan left in the morning before the boys went to school and came home after the boys ate dinner. As soon as he came home from work, Pat's attentions were focused on Stan. Wayne could not really remember anytime when there was a family event when the four of them did anything fun. He could remember lots of time when Billy and Wayne did things with their Mom, but never with their Dad.

He turned the corner into their bedroom, and turned on the light; the first thing he noticed was how messy it was. "Mommy would be mad." And then it hit him again; she wasn't coming back anymore. Tears began to flow as his stomach lurched. Wayne started to pick up the toys as he worked his way towards Billy's bed, thinking maybe Billy was in it, when he realized that it was empty. He threw the toys in the toy box and looked under the beds, assuming his little brother was hiding from their dad. Again, no Billy. Wayne searched the closets, behind the doors and everywhere he could think of that his brother would hide before he went to find his father.

Hesitantly creeping into the master bedroom, Wayne heard his father's snoring before he actually saw him; and smelt the familiar odor before seeing the outline of his father on the bed. "Daddy?" he shyly questioned into the darkened room.

"Mmmmm."

"Daddy?" he queried a bit louder, with more urgency.

"Whhhaaa"

"Daddy!" Wayne spoke louder and had garnered more courage as he blurted out: "Billy's gone!"

"What?" Stan asked, half asleep.

"I can't find Billy," Wayne said, through tears.

"Whatcha mean ya can't findim?" Stan slurred as he rolled back over and fell back into a drunken slumber.

As Wayne stood staring at his father's back, wringing his hands together, he debated what to do. Should I try to wake him up again and get him mad? Or should I call the police? Should I wait until tomorrow and see if I can find Billy? I wish Mommy were here, she'd know what to do. This was the turning point in Wayne Foster's short life: "Daddy! Wake up! Billy's not here!" Wayne was willing to suffer the consequences of his father's wrath. His little brother needed him.

October is National Domestic Violence Awareness Month
Every Day should be Domestic Awareness Day

For a complete list of Resources, by state, please go to www.brendayoungerman.com

Printed in the United States
87284LV00002B/1-99/A